KT-147-383

The Mimosa Tree Mystery

Ovidia Yu

CONSTABLE

CONSTABLE

First published in Great Britain in 2020 by Constable

1 3 5 7 9 10 8 6 4 2

Copyright © Ovidia Yu, 2020

Illustration on page xii © Shutterstock
Illustration on page 305 © Liane Payne

The moral right of the author has been asserted.

A CIP catalogue record for this book is available from the British Library.

ISBN: 978-1-47213-202-4

Typeset in Contenu by SX Composing DTP, Rayleigh, Essex
Printed and bound in Great Britain by Clays Ltd, Elcograf S.p.A.

Papers used by Constable are from well-managed forests
and other responsible sources.

MIX
Paper from
responsible sources
FSC® C104740

Constable
An imprint of
Little, Brown Book Group
Carmelite House
50 Victoria Embankment
London EC4Y 0DZ

An Hachette UK Company
www.hachette.co.uk

www.littlebrown.co.uk

Dedicated with respect to the memory of real-life hero
Lieutenant Adnan Saidi,

piar putih tulang, jangan putih mata – death before dishonour

Author's Note

The Mimosa Tree is also known as the sweet silk tree since the stamens of its sweet-smelling flowers are much longer than their petals and look like strands of silk.

The Mimosa is a common tree, which can grow to at least thirty feet tall. It's a popular tree because its bark can be used to soothe bruises and skin irritations or boiled for an infusion to treat worms and its seeds feed chickens, pigs and goats. But the most interesting thing about the mimosa tree is that the leaflets of its bipinnate leaves closely slowly at night and during rainstorms, as though hiding themselves. That's why locals also call it the 'rain tree' and Japanese refer to it as the *'nenenoki'* or 'sleeping tree'.

Field Screening

———◆———

'Do you see the Mirzas?'

'Mind your own business!' my grandmother hissed at me.

Japanese soldiers had banged on the doors of Chen Mansion before dawn, ordering our entire household to report immediately to the Gakuen school field. Now, with our neighbours, we were shivering in rows in pre-dawn dark, surrounded by soldiers armed with bayonets.

'There were soldiers outside the Mirza gate when we went past. And I don't see them now.'

'Keep quiet!' Shen Shen, my uncle Chen's wife, hissed. Uncle Chen, his arms around Little Ling, their daughter, said nothing.

The Chinese way is to keep quiet and try to stay unnoticed and out of trouble. It doesn't always work. After the Fall of Singapore, ethnic Chinese like us were picked out and massacred during the Sook Ching, or 'purging through purification'.

I had dared hope the worst was over. Colonel Fujiwara had announced that Singapore, now Syonan, was an important part of the great Japanese Empire. He said that all who co-operated

1

would be rewarded. Under his administration, factories, businesses and schools had reopened. Trams and buses were running again. There were even taxis on the roads. I had been thinking of taking a job in a Japanese factory. The work would be tough, but my family was less likely to be marked as anti-Japanese.

'They're coming!'

'Ssh! Don't look!'

The informer was walking towards our part of the field. That he could walk meant he had not been tortured so he was probably collaborating for profit. The Japanese paid well for information, and if you turned in enough people, you were less likely to be executed yourself.

'Who is it?'

'Can't see.'

The informer wore a loose dark blue shirt and khaki trousers, rough workman's clothes, and a hood with an eye-slit cut into it to keep his identity secret. People were known to take revenge on informers.

'Su Lin, don't stare!' My grandmother's grip was painful on my arm. At some level, she probably believed that if she hurt me enough the gods would leave me alone. On her other side, Shen Shen's face was pressed against her daughter in her husband's arms. Over her head I met my uncle's eyes. I was most afraid for him. The Japanese targeted Chinese men. But here in the east of Singapore, we had got off relatively lightly. So far.

What was this about?

The informer moved closer to us, pointing at people without

speaking. When the kempeitai pulled them out of line and dragged them away, the sound rose of desperate protests and begging. But quietly: no one dared protest too loudly. A woman on her knees begging to be spared was hit on the head with a rifle butt and dragged off. All those selected were Chinese.

I wondered again why I hadn't seen Mr Mirza and his daughters. Theirs was the next house but one to ours.

Was it black-marketeers who were being picked up this time? Or people who had been overheard speaking out against the Japanese at a private gathering?

My brain automatically looks for patterns in things. It's why I learn languages and solve puzzles so fast. But at times like this it was a pointless distraction. Who cares if someone is walking funny when that someone holds the power of life or death over you?

I stared at my toes, showing through the holes in long-worn-out shoes, and tried to calm my breathing. The best way to survive was not to draw attention to yourself. I was small and skinny, with a polio limp, so it was easy for me not to look threatening.

But something about the informer drew my eyes back to him. Something about the way he moved was wrong – or, rather, familiar in an unexpected way.

Ah Ma was muttering prayers to my dead grandfather, my father and assorted gods, interspersed with curses on the Japanese. She might look like a feeble old woman, but she had managed the family businesses after the deaths of her husband and eldest son, my father. She had also kept me alive and in the family, despite the fortune-tellers who warned that I was a bad-luck girl. Everything I was I owed to Ah Ma. In the old days, she was a force in the local black market. Those who knew her feared her, and those who underestimated her didn't last long.

Everything had changed after the British surrender.

The soldiers walked past us, but the hooded figure paused. The eyes behind the slit slid over us. Then the hooded informer pointed at Uncle Chen.

One of the soldiers gestured for him to put Little Ling down. This was generous of him. In the early days they would have taken the child too. Shen Shen threw her arms around Uncle Chen and Little Ling, wailing. 'You mustn't take him! He hasn't done anything!'

'Don't be a fool!' Ah Ma grabbed Shen Shen and held her back.

'Take Little Ling!' she hissed to me.

But I had just realised why the hooded figure was so familiar.

I stepped out of line and bowed low to the soldiers.

'Respected sirs. I must humbly inform you that the informer, Madam Koh, is married to my uncle's former charcoal supplier,' I said, in my best formal Japanese. 'My uncle stopped buying from him because he soaked his charcoal in seawater to make it weigh more. My uncle has done nothing wrong. Madam Koh is calling him out from spite.'

The soldiers glanced at each other uncertainly. I don't know whether my low bow or their surprise saved me from being bayoneted to death. If I hadn't been speaking Japanese they would probably have knocked me down at least, to teach me a lesson.

The hooded figure looked between me and the military

police, clearly not understanding me. It jabbed a finger at Uncle Chen saying, 'Him! Him! Him!' in Teochew, in Madam Koh's voice.

'No business of yours!' a soldier told me. 'Get back in line! You,' this to Uncle Chen, 'hurry up!'

'Well done, Miss Chen.'

The small, thin Japanese man who came out from behind the military truck was dressed in Western-style civilian clothes. Immediately all of the others snapped to attention. He was someone important.

I was short-sighted and had to squint to make him out. The man wore round sunglasses clipped over his spectacles and what the British called a 'coolie hat' and the Japanese called jingasa, a light waterproof straw hat.

'Your Japanese has improved,' Hideki Tagawa said, in fluent Oxford-accented English.

Years ago, when war was still considered a distant domestic issue in Poland and China, I had met Hideki Tagawa in the Singapore home of his cousin Mrs Maki, my first Japanese teacher.

'Hideki Tagawa is a Japanese spy and one of the most dangerous men in Japan's military secret service,' Chief Inspector Le Froy, my boss and mentor had said.

Later I had learned that Hideki Tagawa was part of the Blood Brotherhood that had assassinated Japanese prime minister Hamaguchi, finance minister Junnosuke Inoue, Baron Takuma Dan, and others who had spoken out against Japanese military aggression.

The Home Office in London had always mocked Le Froy's

'obsession' with Japanese spies. I guessed they weren't laughing now.

'Miss Chen, it is a pleasant surprise to see you again. You are looking well,' Hideki Tagawa said.

So he was still a liar. I knew I looked terrible.

'Ohayō gozaimasu,' I responded, bowing even lower in his direction with my hands clasped. 'Hajimemashite.'

These were the most formal greetings I knew, and I needed time to think.

I had heard Hideki Tagawa was back in Singapore as a 'special adviser' to the Japanese Military Administration. But what was he doing in a death-selection field far from the city centre so early in the day? Had he set this up? Had he ordered Uncle Chen's arrest?

And why?

'I am impressed. Your accent has very much improved. You speak very good traditional Japanese,' he said. 'My cousin will be very proud of you.' Hideki Tagawa also switched to Japanese.

I guessed this was for the benefit of the soldiers, who watched us with open curiosity. Though not in uniform, he clearly outranked them. If only I could get him to give the order, they might let Uncle Chen go.

Hideki Tagawa studied me. I could almost see him updating the file in his head. I remembered him keeping detailed notes in the black book that was always in his pocket. He was calm, like a tiger: eyes fixed on its prey – me – but picking up everything going on around it at the tiniest movement of air.

'My uncle has done nothing wrong. Please let him go.'

'Your boss, Thomas Le Froy, have you heard from him? How is he?'

'You should know better than I!' He had caught me off guard. I had worried so much about Le Froy that just hearing his name from this man had triggered an unfortunate response. I had no idea what had happened to Le Froy since he was taken away after the official surrender. There were rumours of beatings and questionings under torture. One good thing: I had not heard that he was dead. Now my brusque words hung in the air between us but Hideki Tagawa seemed not to have taken offence. A soldier grinned, then quickly hid it.

'He is in prison.'

Just be nice to him, I told myself. 'Thank you, sir, for your interest,' I bowed low. Don't give him an excuse to burn down Chen Mansion with all of us in it.

'Sir, we must proceed. May we take the suspects?' a soldier asked.

'Please, sir,' I said, using konsei, the formal Japanese term for entreaty and appeal. 'Please, help us, I beg you. Onegai shimasu, I humbly request your honourable lordship to help us.'

I had memorised those phrases from books he had once lent me – perhaps that helped. Or maybe it was the refined Tokyo accent I had picked up from his cousin, especially when his soldiers were speaking a crude army patois.

Hideki Tagawa turned from me and barked orders in Japanese, too fast for me to follow. One of the military policemen pulled the hood off the informer to reveal Madam Koh, as I had predicted.

She looked taken aback but smug. After all, the Japanese were paying and protecting her.

'Her also.' Madam Koh pointed to me. She had nothing to lose now that her identity was revealed. 'She is also involved with the Chinese triads. That whole family is involved. You should take the whole family. For years they have been cheating us. That girl works for the British. You should shoot them all!' Madam Koh spoke in Teochew to one of the kempeitai, clearly the translator.

But instead of translating her words, the man looked to Hideki Tagawa for instructions.

'You worked for the British?' Hideki Tagawa said to me, in Japanese.

He knew very well I had, and that was dangerous: most local civil servants had been rounded up and shot for their assumed loyalty to the British. 'Play the game,' he added in English.

It was for the soldiers' benefit, then.

'Many years ago,' I said. Somehow my voice sounded calm, though my heart was thumping so hard that it hurt. 'Just before the war, I was an apprentice hairdresser, working for Oshima Yukimoto.'

My grandmother had found me the job. Working for a Japanese business had probably saved my life.

'Ah, yes. Oshima Yukimoto. He was not eager to return to Japan so Japan came to him.'

'Take the whole family! They are all anti-Japanese!' Madam Koh shouted, in a shaky voice. Clearly she was sensing that things were not going her way.

The kempeitai holding Uncle Chen looked between her and Hideki Tagawa, waiting for directions.

Hideki Tagawa waved at Madam Koh, without looking at her. 'Take her in with the others and deal with them,' he said. 'Except this man.' He pointed an elegantly manicured finger at Uncle Chen. 'Take him to the detention centre. Under my charge. No one is to question him till I come.'

Madam Koh struggled and shouted as they dragged her away to the trucks with the people she had picked out. 'I'm doing what you told me to do! Tell them!' She was appealing to someone among the Japanese officers, but no one responded.

Hideki Tagawa lifted Little Ling from Uncle Chen's grasp and looked at her. Shen Shen, sobbing on the ground, clutching at Uncle Chen's legs as his wrists were chained behind him, seemed not to notice.

'Your cousin?'

I couldn't breathe. All the stories of soldiers slashing children came back to me. Little Ling looked terrified but didn't cry. 'Please,' I said again. 'Please don't hurt her.'

Hideki Tagawa handed Little Ling to me. She buried her face in my shoulder. She was trembling violently.

'Come with me.' Hideki Tagawa's soft voice was more threatening than a shouted threat.

I squeezed Little Ling, then passed her to Ah Ma.

'Don't go with him. Don't go,' Ah Ma said.

'Go home. Uncle Chen and I will be back later,' I told her.

As I followed Hideki Tagawa, I hoped I would keep that promise.

Hideki Tagawa

◆

'You were always good at learning languages, also at solving crimes,' Hideki Tagawa said. 'I should have known you would come out of this all right.'

His car, a battered Ford Eifel, stood on the mud track at the edge of the field. He opened the front passenger door and indicated that I should sit. He stood by the back door so we were looking out at the field. It had been the football pitch shared by the Telok Kurau English and Malay Schools: we had come here for festivals and kite-flying before the Japanese turned it into a killing field.

The sun was coming up. The military police were herding prisoners into the back of trucks. Everyone else stood around, trying not to attract attention, daring to hope they would be allowed to go.

'Do you know what this is all about?'

'Someone robbed the Mirza house last night,' I guessed.

'What makes you say so?'

'I saw military police outside the gates when we walked here. The Mirza house is two lots down from ours.'

'Mirza Ali Hasnain was killed last night,' Hideki Tagawa said.

'Oh!' I was taken aback, not by the death but by the fuss the Japanese were making about it. After all, so many locals were killed daily.

'Mirza was murdered in his garden. It happened very near to your home. Didn't you hear about it?'

I shook my head. 'We were asleep when the military police arrived at our house and made us come here. They didn't tell us anything.'

My thoughts sped on: their interest suggested that the dead man had been a collaborator and the Japanese hadn't been responsible for his death – or they had, and were looking for someone else to blame.

'He had two daughters. Their mother is dead. Now they are orphans. Don't you want to help them?'

I didn't see how I could. 'I didn't kill him and I don't know who did.'

'So, how do you think Chief Inspector Le Froy would solve this murder?'

'Why don't you ask him?'

Speaking in English, I had dropped the formalities but, even so, that was rude.

To my surprise, Hideki Tagawa laughed. 'We all have choice in any situation. We can do our best or do nothing.'

I had no choice in this situation. Except to do what I could to stay alive. I nodded.

'Did you know that Chief Inspector Le Froy accused me of being a spy and tried to get me deported?'

11

Why did he keep bringing up Le Froy? I wondered if he meant to torture me to make Le Froy talk.

I decided that if he took me to Le Froy, I would shout that he was not to say anything on my account, regardless of what I might admit later. I was strong for a small, thin girl with a polio limp, but I was under no illusion that I could hold up under Japanese torture. Just thinking of the stories of what they did to their victims made my bladder twist and suddenly I needed the WC. I was also desperately thirsty, but I knew better than to say so. I had heard terrible things about Japanese water torture …

'He hunted me, like a shiba inu, following me through all the twists and turns. I knew what he was doing, of course.' Hideki Tagawa chuckled. His train of thought had run far from mine. 'I tried to make it interesting for him. Do you know what a shiba inu is?'

'A kind of dog?'

'A very tough, very small Japanese hunting dog. It is not aware it is a small dog so it tackles enemies much larger than itself. And it generally scores low marks for obedience.'

He might have been describing Le Froy as his superiors in London saw him. I pushed away the thought.

'He was doing his job, of course. If he was here, he would expect you to do your job and help to solve this murder. Don't you agree?'

'What?'

'Mirza's killer must be caught and publicly punished or people will think it is all right to kill informers. Or those they suspect of being informers. Or they will just kill anyone they don't like and accuse them of being an informer. There will be

12

chaos. Everything we have done up to now to establish peace and order will have been for nothing.'

'My uncle had nothing to do with it,' I risked saying. 'He did not leave the house last night. Besides, why would he?'

'Mirza feared local Chinese triads would attack him. Your uncle has connections with them, does he not?'

'There's no triad activity here. There hasn't been in years!'

That was not quite true. Yes, fewer gang-related clashes had been recorded. Largely because – and Le Froy had been aware of this – a working peace had been enforced by the Chen family triad. My family.

'Some believe Mirza was the informer who blamed Operation Jaywick on local triads. They were angry with him.'

'The Japanese no longer believe local triads responsible?'

'We now have sources confirming that the Australian marines were behind Operation Jaywick. They sent soldiers over by boat, in the night, to plant explosives on our ships.'

'That doesn't seem likely.' Australia was far away. But I felt a spark of hope deep inside me. Though distant, Australia was much closer than Britain. If the Australians had not given up on us, maybe there was hope after all.

'It would not do to make it public,' he said.

Of course not. It would make the Japanese look stupid.

I was angry about that raid too. The sabotage of seven Japanese warships and one cargo ship in Singapore harbour had resulted in the worst reprisal killing of locals since the invasion.

'But if Mirza gave the Japanese the wrong information, maybe the Japanese killed him for making you look bad.'

'Sir.'

It was one of the military policemen.

'What do you want?'

'Sir, Colonel Fujiwara wants the investigation completed as soon as possible. Heicho Han wishes to know if he can proceed with the executions.'

'Tell Heicho Han I am taking over this investigation.'

'Sir,' the kempeitai looked scared, 'he must make the report. Colonel Fujiwara is waiting.'

'I will make the report myself,' Hideki Tagawa said. And to me, 'Get into the car.'

Car Ride

———◆———

Hideki Tagawa drove us to a huge mansion in Shori Estate. It was a long time since I had been in a car. The fact that Hideki Tagawa had one and petrol to put into it showed he was Somebody in the Japanese hierarchy. The way he drove – recklessly fast, hardly slowing to wave a pass and shout at security checkpoints – showed he probably hadn't got where he was by slavishly following the rules. He probably hadn't been given a dented car, which would have been a sign of disrespect, but had caused the dents himself: a clear sign of his impatience.

And it was possible that, having survived war and a year of occupation, I was about to die in a car accident. I braced myself against the dashboard and dared ask, 'Where are you taking me?'

'Centre of Operations. Victoria Avenue.'

He had used the old British name for the smart residential area. The Japanese had commandeered rows of big colonial houses in Victoria and Albert Estate, which had formerly been occupied by high-ranking British administrators and

15

Westernised Christian converts, who had been rich enough for the British to accept them as civilised. In the old days there had been glittering parties here. Now that the Japanese had requisitioned the houses and grounds, there were guards outside the gates.

'Why?'

'I have an idea.'

The way he drove, maybe his idea was suicide by car accident.

I swore to myself that if, by some miracle, I ended the journey alive, I'd get us all – Ah Ma, Uncle Chen, Shen Shen, Little Ling and myself – out of Singapore. Never mind where we ended up or how we'd survive, nothing could be worse than clinging to life as we were, like crabs in a bucket waiting to be picked out and lowered into boiling oil.

After such a narrow escape, even Ah Ma couldn't insist on us waiting till the British came to rescue us. She believed the way to survive was to stay unnoticed. After all, that was how she had kept the Chen family and its black-market businesses safe under the British. As an added precaution against the Japanese, she had cut off the women's plaits and rubbed our faces with hairy weed to give us spots.

Of course I had to get Uncle Chen out, too. Ah Ma and Shen Shen would never leave without him. I cursed myself for not making him go into hiding. The Japanese had informers everywhere and someone must have heard him ranting against them. We should all have gone. There were isolated farms in the Malayan jungles and highlands where we could have waited out the war.

Though if we had gone, I might now be cursing myself for not making us stay in Singapore.

I'd heard that the Japanese soldiers held shooting parties up-country, wiping out entire villages that had not shown enough respect or had presented them with food and women they didn't like. Maybe those were just stories. Maybe not.

Maybe there was no guaranteed safe decision. But I was alive. If I was still alive tonight, I would consider that a small victory.

The roads were more crowded when we got into town, and it was morning by the time the car stopped and Hideki Tagawa sounded the horn at a gate, which was opened by two armed soldiers.

'This is now the Shori headquarters, Colonel Fujiwara's office and residence.' Hideki Tagawa left his small car alongside two grand official vehicles and led the way to the front door, where guards stood at attention. They did not salute but didn't stop Hideki Tagawa letting us in and rapping on a door.

To my amazement, a white woman opened it. 'Mr Tagawa! But you haven't an appointment.'

'We are here to see the colonel,' Hideki Tagawa said, in English. He inclined his head to her. A Japanese bowing to a white woman? I felt sure she was the colonel's mistress.

And I knew who she was, too: Miss Emily Bennington-Smith.

Colonel Fujiwara

———◆———

'He is in his office,' Miss Emily said. 'He's busy.' She gave Hideki Tagawa an awkward jerking nod, not quite a bow, then looked at me and gaped. 'I know you, don't I? What do you want? What are you doing here?'

Emily Bennington-Smith was the cousin of Miss Margaret Smith, one of the teachers at the Mission School, where I had been a pupil. Miss Margaret had taught us music, penmanship and Living by the Bible.

Miss Bennington-Smith had come out east in search of adventure and a white rajah in Borneo or a white colonel in India but, sadly, they were all taken. She couldn't teach at the Mission School with her cousin because the Mission Centre didn't have funds for another teacher but, in any case, Emily Bennington-Smith had said, she 'wouldn't be caught dead doing good works in a mission'.

Emily Bennington-Smith was a modern career woman: I had hero-worshipped her for her independence, and because she reminded me of the lady journalists I so admired and dreamed of emulating. But later, when I started submitting my own writing and even got a few articles published in weekly journals, she had made fun of my attempts and called me 'a monkey with a typewriter'.

Now she was also the writer-editor of the Syonan-To, the English-language weekly propaganda mouthpiece of the Japanese government in Singapore. It had been launched in 1942, boasting that Japan's position was 'impregnable', following the capture of Singapore by the Greater Japanese Empire. From what I had seen of the paper, it was mostly translations into English of orders to army and navy officers to live up to imperial instructions, and to local citizens to appreciate the honour of being occupied.

'Hello, Miss Emily,' I said quietly. She closed her mouth, but continued to stare at me. We hadn't been friends but we'd met before there were any real enemies.

A voice was shouting furious Japanese somewhere deeper inside the house. A muffled crash followed.

Hideki Tagawa walked across the hall and stopped outside a door. He turned and flicked a finger in my direction, like a rat-catcher summoning his dog. I hurried over to him, passing Miss Emily without another word. I am very good at obeying orders, especially when my life is on the line.

Hideki Tagawa banged on the door. The furious Japanese shouting stopped. Then the same voice yelled, 'Enter!'

A thin, hunched servant, who had been standing just inside, slipped out of the room without a word. Shards of porcelain and a brass ashtray lay at our feet, which I guessed had been thrown at him.

Colonel Fujiwara faced us across a broad desk. Of course I had seen photographs of him – he was Singapore's highest-ranking Japanese military administrator and we had to bow to his ceremonial photograph, hung in the place of honour next to that of the Japanese Emperor – but this was the first time I had seen the man in the flesh. And there was a lot of it.

Colonel Fujiwara looked older and fatter than he did in the official pictures, but somehow smaller all over. He might once have been muscular, but now his belly was bigger than his chest. His face was round and red and sweaty, despite an electric fan standing in the corner.

'Tagawa! What do you want? You have been disrupting interrogations!' he said. 'What are you doing here? Why have you brought this girl? Who is she? Your local mistress?'

'This is Miss Chen Su Lin. She was trained in criminal detection by Chief Inspector Le Froy. She will be a useful local ally in the Mirza case.'

After bowing deeply and respectfully to the colonel, I kept my eyes on my feet.

Hideki Tagawa left me by the door and crossed to the colonel's desk.

The two men started arguing. Continued arguing, I should say. Even though it was too low and too rapid for my basic Japanese to follow, it was clearly the continuation of a heated discussion that had been going on for some time.

They seemed to have forgotten me and I took the opportunity to look around. When you're already in the lion's den, it's too late to keep your eyes closed and hope to wake out of the nightmare.

Colonel Fujiwara's office was a pleasant, airy room with polished wood floors and teak shelving. Five enormous grey metal safes along one wall clashed with the rest of the décor and were recent additions. But the heavy dark-wood desk at which he sat clearly belonged with the house.

On the desk a framed photograph faced away from him. In it, a younger, thinner version of him stood in full uniform with a long sword; a kimono-clad woman sat next to him, a toddler of about the same age as Little Ling in her lap, and two older children – a boy and a girl – posed at either side of them.

For the first time I saw the colonel – or any Japanese officer – as a man who had had a life and a family before the war. Where was the toddler now? She and her siblings were clearly not in Singapore with their father. Despite the luxury of his surroundings, their father was in a war zone, responsible for keeping down civilian enemies in Japan's occupied territories. I wondered if his wife, watching over their children, knew that her husband had condemned tens of thousands to death since taking office.

'So, why bring her here?' Colonel Fujiwara snarled. 'If she knows something, find out what it is. Don't bother me. Why are you running around picking up women instead of working on Le Froy?'

They were speaking in Japanese, but my ears pricked at Le Froy's name. Hideki Tagawa was supposed to be working on Le Froy? This was the first confirmation I had had that he was alive. But I was in greater danger than I'd realised. If they thought I knew something (which I didn't), I might not be alive tomorrow. Or even tonight.

I listened with all my attention now, forgetting myself enough to look directly at them.

The man still had the eyes of a soldier. My attention alerted him, and now his eyes darted around and behind me as though he was checking for snipers.

'You understand Japanese?'

'Forgive me, sir, I don't know anything,' I said, in my most respectful formal Japanese.

'Miss Chen is also fluent in Chinese dialects, English and Malay,' Hideki Tagawa said. 'She knows local ways and has studied codes and ciphers. Also, her family has connections with the local triads. Her grandfather was a very powerful man. Even the British considered him a threat.'

This interested Colonel Fujiwara. I didn't point out that my grandfather had been dead for more than forty years. I've always found it easy to pick up different languages. I believe it came from growing up exposed to the Chinese dialects, Malay and English that form Singlish. 'I know nothing of that, sir,' I said.

'With her position and connections, Miss Chen was able to help Le Froy. She may be able to help us.'

Colonel Fujiwara studied me, then laughed. 'This is your local woman, I can tell. Trust you to pick up such a skinny bitch. Can't handle a larger woman, eh? At least you picked one smart enough to speak good Japanese. You were always fussy. Look at my gaijin pillow – lots of good meat on her, but hopeless at learning anything useful.'

He gestured towards Emily Bennington-Smith, who had followed us and was standing in the open doorway. She hadn't understood the colonel's words, but his meaning was clear. Still, she was smart enough not to look angry with him. She stared resentfully at me instead. I didn't mind.

'Girl! Which district are you in? Who is your district commander?'

'East 221, sir. We report to Heicho Han.'

Colonel Fujiwara looked questioningly at Hideki Tagawa. 'Heicho Han was complaining about you interfering. What kind of name is Han?'

'He's one of the Korean conscripts. He signed on two years ago.' Hideki Tagawa sounded like a talking reference book. With a jolt of surprise, I realised he had my kind of memory. 'He took over District Command after the former officer in charge was killed in an accident. Heicho Han is in charge of investigating Mirza's murder last night.'

'Korean boy.' Colonel Fujiwara snorted. 'I know Han. He's always barging in here shouting, "I eat kyabechu on Pujisan!"' His bad mood seemed to have disappeared now that he was mocking Heicho Han's Japanese pronunciation.

Many Koreans said 'kyabechu' for the Japanese 'kyabetsu', meaning cabbage, and would probably have called Mount Fuji 'Pujisan' instead of 'Fujisan'. The Japanese 'tsu' might not exist in Korean.

I was very lucky that my first Japanese teacher, Mrs Maki, Hideki Kagawa's cousin, had been particular about pronunciation. In fact, thanks to her, I could even tell that my second teacher, the hairdresser, spoke Japanese with a non-standard accent.

'Do what you want with the girl – I won't interfere. But you must investigate Mirza's murder. Han is eager but so stupid. He wants to kill one prisoner a day until the murderer is caught.

Says that, sooner or later, we'll get him, even if he doesn't confess. He'll waste a lot of bullets if I let him do what he wants.'

They were going to kill a prisoner a day? It sounded so horrible that I believed it.

The kempeitai had been relatively easy on us in the East Coast district, maybe because they saw us as workers and farmers far from the city centre. But I knew in Bukit Timah, where we now were and the resistance had been fierce, Colonel Fujiwara had ordered that all Chinese – men, women and children – within a five-mile radius were to be shot.

'You mustn't disrupt the boy's interrogations if you can't come up with the murderer yourself!'

'I want to confess. I killed Mirza,' I heard my shaking voice say.

I guessed they meant to kill me anyway, after using me to make Le Froy talk. This way, if my death stopped the reprisal killings for Mirza, I would have done one small thing.

'Don't be a fool!' Hideki Tagawa said. 'Shut your mouth!'

But Colonel Fujiwara leaned forward across his desk and asked, 'How?'

I thought fast. 'Mirza Ali Hasnain's house is not far from my grandmother's. I climbed over the wall and went into his house where I killed him.'

'And what did you kill him with?'

Oh, why on earth hadn't I paid more attention to Hideki Tagawa when he was telling me about Mirza's murder? Why hadn't I asked more questions?

'I'm not sure. It was dark. I just grabbed something. Something sharp. And heavy.'

Colonel Fujiwara sat back. He was grinning, which I found more frightening than his glare. 'Girl, you are not the first to make false confession. Do you see us all as fools? The last man who made a false confession was executed for lying. And his wife, whom he was lying to protect, was executed also. Are you married? No? Ah. Since you are not married, shall I I execute Hideki Tagawa for your crime of lying to me?'

'No, no, you can't! Please, sir, don't!' I didn't know why I was worried about the fate of that one-time Japanese spy.

'Ha!' Colonel Fujiwara was laughing loudly with his mouth open, thumping Hideki Tagawa, then his desk when Tagawa moved out of range. Hideki Tagawa's expression was a mixture of wry amusement and exasperation: a surprising echo of the look I had often seen on Le Froy's face. He closed his eyes briefly but said nothing.

'I knew it! I knew it! I knew it! You finally found yourself a little cat for your pillow! A loyal little cat too. Did you see her face when she thought you were at risk? After facing talk of her own death so calmly? So, that's why you want to employ her to work on your investigations with you.'

What?

'Sir, Miss Chen has investigation skills learned from Chief Inspector Le Froy. I have stated in my reports—'

'Hideki Tagawa! You have an obsession with your gaijin Chief Inspector Le Froy!' Colonel Fujiwara was still laughing. He winked at me.

There was a certain justice in the description: for years Le Froy's superiors had thought him obsessed with Japanese spies – Hideki Tagawa among them.

'The gaijin Le Froy has nothing to do with this case. Mirza was killed by locals!'

'Sir. Le Froy was Miss Chen's sensei. A man very skilled in detection. He taught her the art of detection. It is Le Froy's methods that Mirza was studying to solve the stone codes.'

Colonel Fujiwara silenced him with a fist to the table. Hideki Tagawa had gone too far.

But Hideki Tagawa was not done yet. 'Give us some privacy,' he said to Miss Emily, in English. 'Take Miss Chen to the kitchen and stay there until I send for you.'

I saw indignation flash on Emily Bennington-Smith's face. 'Sir?' She looked to Colonel Fujiwara, but he waved dismissively at her.

'Go! Go away! Get lost. Bring me some beer in fifteen minutes.' His English was strongly accented but understandable.

'Come, Su Lin,' Emily Bennington-Smith said sourly.

Emily Bennington-Smith's Kitchen

◆

'That man is so rude, ordering me around like a servant! I have my own office here. I am an employee, like anyone else. What does he mean, go to the kitchen?'

But we had indeed ended up in the kitchen, rather than her office.

'How did you get involved with him? Is he running your district? Which district are you in anyway? Who is in charge of the area? Why are you getting involved in this? Don't you know how dangerous it is? This is typical of locals like you, pushing your way in. You don't know how much trouble you may be getting yourself into.'

I had already answered most of her questions for Colonel Fujiwara, but she hadn't been able to follow the exchange in Japanese, though she understood Hideki Tagawa's dismissal.

'What's wrong with you? Why are you standing there like that?'

'Please may I use the WC?' I asked. 'And I'm really, really thirsty, if you can spare some water.'

When I got back to the kitchen, her temper had cooled, as had the cup of boiled water she had ready for me.

'Thank you.'

'How come you speak such good Japanese? You learned English very fast too, right? Were you a Japanese spy even back then?' Emily Bennington-Smith lowered her voice to a whisper, because speaking English, or any language other than Japanese, was forbidden. 'You can tell me. You were working for the British police, weren't you? Were you spying on them?'

'Of course not! And I lost my job there. I was apprenticed to a Japanese hairdresser.'

I had been against the idea, but Ah Ma had insisted. Just as she had insisted on sending me to learn English at the school set up by the Mission Centre.

As I had already learned basic Japanese from Mrs Maki, it was easy for me to pick up enough to make myself useful in translating orders and questions. And, of course, the more I spoke it the more fluent I became.

Even before Hideki Tagawa had found me, soldiers in our district had been coming to ask me to translate their orders and instructions. Most of the time they wanted me to explain to the locals in Malay and various Chinese dialects that they were looking for pro-Britain and pro-China traitors. Anyone who handed over any such traitors would be rewarded. Most people understood this without translation.

'You always were a little Goody Two Shoes, weren't you? Working hard to be a teacher's pet. Do you know what's going on? Which district are you living in?'

'East District, Division 221.'

'So, you live near to the man who was murdered last night?'

Apparently Mirza's death was such a big issue that even Emily Bennington-Smith, with her limited Japanese, knew about it.

'What happened? What are the officers running your district doing about it? Who is in charge of your district?'

'The officer in charge is called Heicho Han.'

'I know him, tall, fair chap. A captain. Much better-looking than most of the Japs, don't you think?'

'His name is on all the proclamations but his men take care of the patrols and inspections. Not much happens in our district, it's so far from town.'

Until the murder.

Word had it that Korean-born Heicho Han of the Japanese Territorial Army was even more savagely ruthless than the Japanese soldiers. Was he good-looking? I honestly couldn't have said.

'I've seen him here a few times. They all have to come here, you know, to report. Most have better manners than that Hideki Tagawa who brought you here.' Emily Bennington-Smith changed the subject abruptly. 'He can't be trusted. He's a snake. A rat. Don't let him talk you into doing anything.'

'What do you mean?' Already I intended to be wary of Hideki Tagawa, but I never turn down a free tip.

And Emily Bennington-Smith was so clearly bursting with information that it was a kindness to take some off her. 'I came out east as a reporter and, as the writer-editor of Syonan-To, I could tell you a lot about these people. A lot of the British are in favour of Hitler, especially the big names, because he's the only one willing to stand up against the spread of Communism. Besides, much of British high society is German all the way to the top. The Royal Family were Saxe-Coburg-Gotha until they changed their name to Windsor during the last war. They're making speeches in the House of Lords saying Hitler's a sound chap.

'I'm not rich. I was sent to Germany as company for my wealthy cousin and I saw how wonderful it was there. If I'd stayed in England, I'd be working in an aircraft or munitions factory. Germany is thriving, no unemployment. And look at England! Totally dreary and depressing.'

'What did you do in Germany?'

'Balls and art and music! Everything you could want!'

I found her point of view interesting. Some British soldiers had supported Hitler and the Nazis, but only up to the invasion of Czechoslovakia. After that, Germany was the enemy. And since we were part of the British Empire, it was our enemy, too.

Emily Bennington-Smith lowered her voice still further, 'Hideki Tagawa is working for Colonel Fujiwara, but the colonel doesn't like or trust him. He'd get rid of him if he could find a way, but Tagawa has connections in Japan. I'm only telling you this for your own good. Sometimes when he comes here Colonel Fujiwara shouts at him for hours. I'm always so terrified he's going to shoot him right there in the office and I don't know how I'll ever get his blood out of the floor. They can just replace the boards in his room but if it happened in the hall or the lobby on the marble ... It's so absorbent and impossible to match here. It was imported from Italy, supposedly for somebody's palace or memorial in Java, but whoever it was fell out of favour before they had time to use it. And the transport ship was redirected to Singapore because they were all fighting over there as to who was going to take over and these locals must have got it cheap. But, given how difficult it is to look after marble in the tropics, I don't know that it was such a bargain.'

Before the war, elegance and class had been defined by Western standards because Westerners were in power. Now they were defined by Japanese standards. This didn't make much difference to me, since I had no claim to either. But, close up, I saw that Emily Bennington-Smith's eyebrows were plucked almost freakishly thin and she was wearing a thick layer of very white powder, like a mask of rice paper, over her face.

She had always been pale – the British, like the Japanese, valued fair skin as a sign of beauty – but now there was a clear line between that white face and her flesh-coloured neck.

I told myself not to judge. We were all doing our best to hang on to what was left of our lives before the war. And she wasn't doing badly. Most other Europeans had been rounded up and gaoled as prisoners of war. It didn't make a difference to the Japanese whether they had been sent out to expand the British Empire or had come out east to get away from the British weather.

'Would you like something to eat?'

'No, thank you.' I lied politely. I was hungry, but wasn't everybody hungry all the time? No matter how much tapioca and sweet potato leaves we ate, our bodies craved protein.

'You might as well have something while we wait. After all, Hideki Tagawa sent us to the kitchen.'

Emily Bennington-Smith produced a small bowl of white rice

topped with dried seaweed and put it on the table in front of me. 'You look like you could do with it. And there's plenty of food here. That's one good thing about this place.'

I thought I would be too tense to swallow, but surprised myself. I couldn't remember the last time I had tasted white rice. I longed to take some home for Ah Ma and Little Ling, but she seemed to read my thought: 'When a servant girl was caught sneaking leftovers to take home, the colonel had her fingers cut off.'

'Thank you for the warning,' I said, not sure if she was joking. 'I hope you won't get into trouble for feeding me.'

Emily Bennington-Smith snorted. 'I work here. I'm running their paper practically single-handed. What can they do to me?'

She was living with access to clean water and plenty of food in the kitchen, but I didn't want to think about the price she paid for it. It wasn't the hours she spent on translation work I was thinking about.

Her thoughts were running in a different direction. 'You really should try to make a bit more of yourself, you know,' she said. 'As I said, you mustn't trust Hideki Tagawa. But there's no reason why you shouldn't make him like you. And you're not even trying, are you? Look at you. The least you can do is make sure you're clean and presentable!'

I looked at my feet and the hems of my sam foo trousers, which she was staring pointedly at. They were muddy from my pre-dawn trek along the road to the inspection field.

I had thought I might die in those clothes, shot or bayoneted. I might still be tortured and killed, and she wanted me to look presentable?

A rude retort was swelling in me, but before I could tell her what I thought of her, we heard footsteps approaching down the corridor. 'Thank you,' I said quickly. 'Please take care of yourself too.' I meant it. As things were, either of us could be dead before tomorrow.

'Here.' She snatched up something wrapped in kitchen cotton and pressed it, soft and warm, into my hand. 'Sticky rice cake with peanuts. Take it with you. Don't let anyone see.'

Perhaps she hadn't been joking about the colonel cutting off someone's fingers for stealing leftovers. I tried to refuse. 'No need.'

But she pushed it at me, hissing, 'Take it! Food is food! These damned Nips won't get away with treating us like this for ever.'

With the kitchen door already opening, I pushed the warm damp package into my pocket under my handkerchief and hoped it would not cost me too many fingers.

'What's that about food?' Hideki Tagawa asked, with his usual oily smile. He spoke in English.

'Oh, I was just telling Miss Emily we grow tapioca, sweet potatoes, kangkong and peanuts at home.'

'And bananas,' Hideki Tagawa said, 'and rambutans and mangoes. You have some very valuable trees on your property.'

He'd said that just to show how much he knew about me and where I was living.

Colonel Fujiwara's Office

◆

'What's wrong with you?' the colonel demanded. 'Why are you so crooked?'

When we returned to his office, he studied me with more interest than he had shown before. What had Hideki Tagawa told him about me?

'Sir?'

Colonel Fujiwara was looking at me in the way my grandmother poked at a haunch taken off a diseased old wild boar. You could see she didn't think much of it. But with no other fresh meat available, wild boar, rats and alligators were better than nothing and she was already figuring out what spices and seasonings she could use.

I waited. I was used to being looked at and talked about. People tended to think that because I walked with a limp I was deaf, too.

'Your leg? Why do you walk crooked like that?'

'Polio, sir. When I was a baby.'

'Ah, yes.' Colonel Fujiwara nodded. I sensed Hideki Tagawa

had already told him that. If I had been crippled by a Japanese soldier's beating he wouldn't have wanted me anywhere near him.

'Sit down. How long did you work for the gaijin Le Froy? We were warned about him. I said sit down!'

I perched on the edge of the chair in front of his desk. It was forbidden for locals to sit in the presence of even minor Japanese officials, not to mention one as high up as Colonel Fujiwara. But it was even more forbidden to disobey a direct order.

Hideki Tagawa had ignored Emily Bennington-Smith, but she followed us down the corridor and into the office. She sat down when I did, on one of the chairs against the wall, so that Tagawa was the only one left standing. I was shocked by her daring. Hideki Tagawa continued to ignore her. But Colonel Fujiwara gestured at her and said, in strongly accented English, 'Your Japanese is very good. Not like my stupid woman!'

Miss Emily looked sullen. I hoped she wouldn't say anything to provoke him. I was very conscious of the rice cake in my pocket, squashed between my thigh and the wooden chair frame. It felt warm and damp.

Colonel Fujiwara switched back to Japanese. 'I will call you Ebisu-Chan. You are like Ebisu, the Japanese god of fishermen. He also walks like that.'

He stood up from his chair – it was a bit of a struggle, with him being a large man and the leather seat soft – and exaggeratedly limped around the side of his desk, mimicking my gait and roaring with laughter.

He reminded me of a large, drunken crab. I was sure I didn't look anything like that. Then it struck me that my expression was probably as resentful as Emily's. Not a good idea.

I laughed. I even clapped my hands. It was easy for me to act the part after years of playing the cripple in Jesus-miracle plays at the Mission Centre. After He had healed me, I was hidden behind a convenient stage prop and replaced by another girl, who had sound legs. I learned that fake miracles have hidden costs, but also that if you go along with the act, you get cake after the show.

Colonel Fujiwara grinned. 'Ebisu was born a cripple. But he became a god to bring people good luck. You must bring me good luck.'

I bowed and thanked him. I wondered what Hideki Tagawa had told him about the events at the field inspection that morning.

'Ebisu-Chan, you come highly recommended.' He returned to his seat. 'You can help us. The murder of Mirza Ali Hasnain was carried out by local gangs. It must concern you that he was murdered in his own home, close to your family's. You must fear for their safety. Unless, of course, you know who was responsible.'

'No, sir.'

'You withdraw your confession?'

'Yes, sir.'

Another roar of laughter.

'It is our responsibility to make sure that all of you are safe in your homes. You know that we are here only to improve the living conditions, for your own good. But you must help us.'

Thanks to the Syonan-To, I knew that, under Colonel Fujiwara, the Japanese attitude to locals had switched from 'All you have to do is die: whether quickly or slowly is up to us' to

36

'Be grateful that we, your fellow [but superior] Asians, have freed you from Western imperialism.' As though being ruled by other Asians was less onerous than being ruled by Westerners.

But I had seen enough of Japanese methods to fear that, if Mirza's murder wasn't solved quickly, Japanese soldiers would return to the mass killings of the early days to 'cleanse' our neighbourhood. Hadn't Heicho Han already mentioned killing a prisoner every day?

'You honour me too much, sir,' I said, from the depths of another bow. 'I don't know what I can do to help you. I'm only an ignorant girl.'

'You understand local ways and local people. And this man says that you are intelligent. He tells me that you are from a good family.' He gave Hideki Tagawa a meaningful look I didn't understand. 'He says you can speak English and local dialects as well as you speak Japanese, and you are good at solving the kind of puzzles the British like.'

'Puzzles!' Miss Emily laughed. She spoke in English but had clearly understood enough Japanese to follow what was being said. 'If you wanted someone to teach you to play cards or do crossword puzzles you should have asked me.'

'Why, after all the effort I have taken with you, can you still not talk Japanese as well as this Chinese dog girl?' Colonel Fujiwara demanded.

I prayed that God, or whichever gods might be watching, would stop Miss Emily criticising the colonel's English in return. She had a sharp tongue.

'Some people are just better at languages,' Emily Bennington-Smith said, in English. 'If Su Lin finds out who murdered the

Muslim, won't that show she's better at solving murders than Japanese police?' She looked slyly at me.

We might have shared a moment of friendship in the kitchen, but now she was using me as provocation.

'Also,' Hideki Tagawa ignored her, 'Miss Chen can demonstrate for us the British methods of detective investigation. And she can interview Mirza's daughters for us.'

'You don't seem to have had much luck there.'

'As they are Muslims, they don't talk to men,' Hideki Tagawa said. 'But Miss Chen is a neighbour and female.'

'What do you know of Mirza and his daughters?' Colonel Fujiwara asked me.

When Mirza's wife died a few years ago, Ah Ma and Shen Shen had said she had poisoned herself because Mirza wanted to take a second wife. But that is the kind of thing people always say when a married woman dies, and no second wife had appeared in the years since.

'Nothing.'

'What can you tell us of your father and mother?' Colonel Fujiwara had exhausted his English conversation and switched back to Japanese.

For a moment I thought I misunderstood him.

'Do you look like your mother? You have the eyes of a Hokkaido beauty. Was your mother very beautiful?'

Hokkaido beauties had small, slanted eyes? 'I don't remember, sir. Both my parents died long ago.'

'You have no photographs of your dead mother? No photographs of your mother and father? No photographs of your family at all? That is very strange. Isn't your family quite well off?'

'My parents died of cholera when I was a child.'

'You remember nothing at all of them? Of your mother? Children always remember their mothers, don't they?'

'No, sir.' I didn't know what he was trying to get at, but elaborated because I didn't want him to think I was being rude. 'My family has superstitions. My parents died of illness, and it was believed it was bad luck to speak of them. So they were not spoken of at home. At least, not in front of me.'

'And you saw no pictures?'

There was a photograph of my father in his ancestral altar, but only a line drawing of a woman in my mother's. This was not unusual: few families had the money to take a photograph. Especially not of a female.

'Why aren't you married yet?' Colonel Fujiwara asked next. 'Your people marry girls off early, don't they? As soon as girls are ready to have babies, you send them to be fed by somebody else's family. Are you secretly married? To one of the jungle rebels?'

I sensed a dark edge to his banter. I had heard stories of the jungle rebels. I even had my suspicions that some of my closest friends had gone to join them. What if he asked me about them? What if …

'Look at her,' Hideki Tagawa said, 'with her crooked leg. You don't know how superstitious these people can be. They think she will bring bad luck to their families and all her children will be born with crooked legs.' His words sounded cruel, but I could tell he was trying to protect me.

'Ebisu-Chan is a bringer of good luck. The girl is not bad-looking. She is young and fertile, too.' Col Fujiwara turned to

Miss Emily and spoke in English. He was enjoying himself. 'You must see that she is younger than you. And she is smarter than you. Shouldn't you be jealous of her? Shouldn't you be afraid of losing your privileged place to her?'

Her face twisted. It was as though there were words inside her that wanted to gush out, like a flood of vomit, and she was using all her strength to keep them inside. Her eyes bulged as she stared at me. But she managed to hold it all in.

The colonel looked highly amused. 'All women are jealous of all other women,' he observed. 'That is the reason why they are not fit to govern and will always remain weak. You don't want to run things, do you?'

This last was directed to me.

'No, sir.'

'Good. You have a respectful attitude. Well, if Tagawa-san thinks you can be useful, he can pay you out of his department.'

Colonel Fujiwara wanted me on the job, even though he had made fun of Hideki Tagawa for bringing me in. But payment? That changed things.

I like money as much as any other Singaporean. Our respect for it is the only thing that keeps our enjoyment of food in check. But payment isn't only about earning money: it's a signal that you are providing value to the one who is paying you. Official pay from whatever department Hideki Tagawa belonged to would do more to keep my family safe than patching tyres in a Japanese factory or informing on neighbours. But if I failed the consequences would be dire.

A kernel of panic twisted painfully in my gut. I had helped to solve several mysterious deaths but that had been under Le

Froy's guidance and direction. It is easy to solve a puzzle when all the parts are laid in front of you and nothing is at stake except the challenge. Now I wouldn't know where to start.

I looked at Hideki Tagawa.

'So, I take it we have a deal,' he said in English.

Before I could answer, Colonel Fujiwara leaned forward. 'Be careful, Ebisu-Chan.'

The Offer

———◆———

'Beware of this man, young woman!'

Colonel Fujiwara was still in a very good mood. Later, I came to see he was, if anything, even more dangerous at such times. Then I was just glad he wasn't sending me – or Emily Bennington-Smith – for immediate execution by firing squad.

'You must watch out, Ebisu-Chan. Do you know there are already rumours that you are his illegitimate daughter from his old days in Singapore? That you are a Tagawa. If not by birth, then alliance. They say that is why you speak Japanese so well.'

He roared with laughter, thumping the table. When he saw Hideki Tagawa looking as stunned as I was, he laughed even louder.

I was sure there had been no such rumours. How could there be? Hideki Tagawa must have been about Le Froy's age – eighteen to twenty years older than I was. There was no way he could have been my father because I had already been in my late teens by the time he came to Singapore.

But if there had been no such gossip up to now, there would be once Colonel Fujiwara spread his stories abroad.

Of course he was teasing me. It reminded me of how British soldiers had yelled comments on my friend Parshanti's long hair or budding figure. It was his way of showing he liked me. I made a show of trying unsuccessfully to stop a giggle.

Colonel Fujiwara beamed. 'I believe I see a resemblance in your face. Either that or the man is hoping to make you his mistress. Not a bad choice, eh? He has no wife, no children. He is from an old line, but most of the family has died out without reproducing. We have been trying to make him settle down for years. What a joke if he ends up starting a new line in Syonan. What would your ancestors say to that, Tagawa?'

Hideki Tagawa bowed, his face frozen. 'Miss Chen, you will help us translate English, Malay and Chinese dialects into Japanese. As a female, you will also be able to talk to Mirza Ali Hasnain's daughters.'

'Thank you for trusting me with the honour.' I bowed in my chair. 'I will do my best.'

But he didn't notice. Hideki Tagawa had gone to the colonel's desk and the two men were engrossed in a muttered conversation.

While they talked, I put on a politely respectful mask and tried to scramble my thoughts into some kind of order. Colonel Fujiwara had mentioned a salary. I would be employed by the Japanese. They had reopened local food and equipment factories, hiring locals under Japanese supervisors. The wages were in Japanese banknotes, the work was hard, and the supervisors harsh – you could lose a hand or your head if they got angry with you. Not many people wanted to be factory workers, so it

43

was announced that in every household with two or more adults someone had to work in a Japanese-run factory or risk being denounced as anti-Japanese. So far we had been lucky in our district: the only two such businesses – an abattoir and the soap factory that had processed fats from the butchered animals – had remained closed.

If I received a salary, Chen Mansion would not be raided as anti-Japanese. And I would be working for them, much as I had for the British, not selling my body or information on our neighbours. At least, I hoped it would stay that way. Working for Japanese occupying forces was not so different from working for the British occupying forces, right? Especially when the point was to stay alive.

I suspected Uncle Chen and Ah Ma were paying protection money to the Japanese kempeitai in our area. It was almost laughable: our family had been collecting tributes over the past thirty to forty years for keeping our area safe. But anything that kept us safe was worth doing. I would do my best to help. At least, I would go through the motions. I didn't have to pass on information that would damage anyone.

'You will be our local liaison,' Hideki Tagawa said. I saw his relief. He had been tense too. For me or himself? I wondered if he would be punished if it turned out I was wasting his and the colonel's time. Strangely, I found myself hoping not.

'I will do my best,' I said.

'Do you still write letters for the people in your district? You can tell us what we're missing.'

For years I had read and written letters for less-educated neighbours. 'No, sir,' I lied, 'people are too scared to write letters now.'

44

And I would explain to any who asked me why they should be too scared to ask me to write their letters for them.

'Mirza was helping Tagawa decode stone code messages sent between PoWs and Australians.' Colonel Fujiwara clearly did not like being left out of the briefing. 'Tagawa thinks Le Froy was behind the murder. Mirza was getting close to cracking their code. That's why they sent someone to kill him.'

Le Froy was involved with these coded messages?

'Sir, you can leave her briefing to me. We must not take up any more of your time.'

'Hah! Now he wants to keep you to himself!' The colonel was unabashed.

'Did Le Froy or the police have anything on record about Mirza?' I asked.

'What are you talking about?'

'Under the British, the police kept records on some local people.' Local people they thought might be troublemakers. 'They probably had something on Mirza.'

'Hah? Tagawa?'

I guessed Hideki Tagawa, with his fluent English, had gone through the police records. He had probably enjoyed reading what they had compiled on him.

'Minor infractions only,' Hideki Tagawa said. 'Mirza considered Le Froy an intellectual rival, and Le Froy knew it so he was very careful to record all his encounters with him. Mirza tried to provoke him into responding. He considered baiting the authorities as entertainment. But Le Froy concluded that Mirza wouldn't do anything to upset the balance of things. He was a philosopher in his way. He felt he had no right to do anything other than observe the course of events. It amused him to watch people doing stupid things. And it amused him even more if he had warned them and been ignored.'

I had helped to type some of those observations.

'So. When was the last time you heard from Le Froy?' Hideki Tagawa asked, as though following where my mind had gone.

'Not since the surrender,' I said honestly.

'Apart from the politics that made us enemies, he and I might have been good friends.'

Might they? Though I couldn't imagine Le Froy with friends. What did men do with other men? Drink beer and talk about women? Le Froy had never been interested in such pursuits. Come to think of it, I couldn't imagine Hideki Tagawa being interested in bonding over beer and women either. Maybe the two could have solved jigsaw puzzles or murders together. They had more in common with each other than they did with either Colonel Fujiwara or the politicians in London.

'I would like to help with deciphering the stone codes, if I may,' I said. 'These are patterns made of stones? Where were they found?'

'We believe the resistance is communicating with PoWs through arrangements of stones,' Hideki Tagawa said. 'Several were found in the vicinity of the PoW camp.'

'Children playing put them there?' I said. 'Like five stones? Or stone offerings?'

'These were not created by children. The stones were carefully arranged, sometimes with a tree branch to indicate direction. It is some kind of message. We had the area watched for some time but have not seen who left them. When previous messages were picked up, the branch was removed to signal they had been seen. But recently there have been no messages. They know we are watching. The day before Mirza died, he sent word to Colonel Fujiwara that he had important information for us. We know he was close to a breakthrough. We believe that is why he was murdered.'

'He was bluffing!' the colonel bellowed. 'He wanted to bargain for more rations. Just the day before that he was asking what kind of branch was found around the stones. They were discovered in the middle of the jungle, surrounded by all kinds of trees and branches!' It was clearly an old argument. 'That man was clueless, just trying to buy time and coming up with more lies to cover his stupid mistake about the bombing!'

'Why don't you ask Chief Inspector Le Froy about the code?' I asked Hideki Tagawa quietly.

Le Froy had taught me all I knew about codes and ciphers. 'If he is your prisoner, you can make the same deal you are making with me, and he is much better than I am at seeing code patterns.'

'We have already presented the matter to Le Froy.' His words seemed to pain Hideki Tagawa. 'We offered him the chance to use his expertise for the common good. But he refused to co-operate. He said he didn't think himself capable.'

I didn't believe you could present Le Froy with a code that he would not at least attempt to decipher. If he refused it must be because—

'You think Le Froy came up with a code.' And they thought that, as someone who had studied under Le Froy, I would be able to reverse-engineer his way of thinking. 'I'm sorry. I can't help you,' I said, recklessly daring. Betraying Le Froy by breaking his encryption codes for the Japanese was entirely different from trying to figure out which of Mirza's daughters' lovers, for example, had quarrelled with Mirza and hit him on the head with a rock.

I could not betray Le Froy.

'This probably has something to do with him. It smells of him!' Hideki Tagawa's excitement and frustration were clear. 'But even if Le Froy came up with the basis for the code, it is unlikely he is involved. I know he is not. I stake my family name on it.'

'Why do you say that?'

'Because of you, Miss Chen.'

'Because of me?'

'We have been watching you, Miss Chen. If the messages had had anything to do with Le Froy, he would have attempted to send word to you or get news of you.'

It was true. Even if it had nothing to do with me, I was sure I would have heard if Le Froy had managed to send word out of prison.

Against my better judgement, I was curious. 'Can I see the coded messages?'

'You will see copies. So, we are to be partners? Help us solve this murder and see what you make of the stone codes.'

'Well, it's good that you have enough sense.' Colonel Fujiwara was clearly preparing to dismiss us. 'We have a deal. I will leave it to Tagawa to brief you further. Your salary will also be paid through him. After you have found Mirza's killer, your uncle will be released.'

'Wait!' I cried, without thinking. 'I can't do that!'

'Do you agree it's wrong that a man can be murdered in his own garden?'

'Yes. Of course.'

'Do you agree that the local people are not going to trust Tagawa with his rat's face? Or any other of my men?'

I looked at Hideki Tagawa.

'So. Find Mirza's killer,' Colonel Fujiwara said. His face was still genial, but I saw cruelty beneath it. 'Or watch your family suffer for your failure.'

'The colonel is joking,' Hideki Tagawa said. 'If he executed people for failing to solve problems, he would have no staff left.'

'I see that if I execute you, I will have to execute Tagawa also,' Colonel Fujiwara said. 'Two problems out of my life. It might be worth it.'

Hideki Tagawa's Car

———◆———

'If he takes you to see the Mirza girls, don't eat anything they offer you,' Emily Bennington-Smith warned me, as we left. 'Those Arabs are all dangerous. They know how to poison people so that it looks natural.'

On the earlier ride, I had felt Hideki Tagawa's car was carrying me to my doom. Now the battered old car rattling us away from Colonel Fujiwara's residence felt like a haven of safety. I hadn't imagined I'd get back into that car but Hideki Tagawa opened the door for me so naturally that I got in automatically. My traitorous body heaved a huge sigh of relief, releasing some of the tension that had built in me while I was in the colonel's office. After all, my animal side reasoned, I had survived my first ride in that vehicle. It was hard to believe that that had been just over an hour ago.

'It went better than I'd expected.' Hideki Tagawa switched to English once we were back on the road. I don't know whether it was to put me at ease or because he wanted to stay in practice. 'Now you have a job it will be easier for you to move around.

Mirza Ali Hasnain was a neighbour of yours. What did you know about him? What stories have you heard?'

'He was a very rich man. He worked with the British. He had many connections and business dealings in Singapore, in the region and beyond, and he was working with the Japanese too.'

I thought about what I knew of Mirza. Even Ah Ma had stayed clear of him. Of course she sent gifts to the Mirza house at Chinese New Year and Hari Raya, the celebration at the end of the Muslim fasting month, and Mirza, or someone in his household, always reciprocated. That was what neighbours did. But it showed my grandmother wanted to stay on good terms with him, or that Mirza had something on her. Had that been the case? It didn't mean the man had been a blackmailer. My grandmother had many businesses, which existed on both sides of the law.

Le Froy had called Mirza Ali Hasnain a very intelligent man.

Once, Mirza had come into the Detective Shack to complain of police harassment. He had caught a foot patrol chatting to one of his daughters and wanted them flogged. He had stayed talking to Le Froy for over an hour. I had heard bits of their conversation, which had to do with how the Arabs had unified Greek and Indian learning to create algebra.

After that, Le Froy had issued a decree banning flirting in uniform. He also ordered some books on algebra, which he lent to me after he had finished with them. My hunger for books was well known. Algebra had not been taught at the Mission Centre School, where the toughest calculations had to do with pounds, shillings, pennies, halfpennies, threepenny bits, florins, crowns, half-crowns and so on. Le Froy claimed a grounding in basic algebra was vital to any real-life problem-solving. Was that just another coincidence or was I imagining connections with Le Froy everywhere I turned?

Hideki Tagawa drove on at a steady pace. I assumed he wanted to be out of sight of the guards outside Colonel Fujiwara's house before he dropped me off. But he didn't stop.

'Sir? Why is Colonel Fujiwara so interested in finding out who killed Mirza?'

'His job is to bring peace and stability to the whole region. It will be good for all because fighting wars is expensive. Finding and punishing murderers is part of that.'

'But why Mr Mirza?' So many people had been murdered in recent months. 'And why does he think the local triads are responsible?'

'Remember the sabotage of Japanese battleships that led to the Double Tenth Investigation?'

The Double 10th Massacre was what we locals called it. 'Of course.' The day after the seven Japanese warships had been sabotaged in the harbour, on the tenth day of the tenth month, the Japanese kempeitai had launched mass arrests and killings in retribution.

'It was Mirza who concluded that local Chinese triads were responsible for the attack on the ships. According to his analysis, there was no way the Australian navy could get close enough to infiltrate the port. Therefore it had to have been the local Chinese triads who had sabotaged the ships, hoping to loot supplies to sell on the black market. We questioned more than five hundred men. But there was no solid evidence. No leads. We had to conclude that Mirza had sold us false information and that local triads had ordered his death in revenge for the Double Tenth Investigation because, thanks to Mirza, it had focused on local triad members.'

'Colonel Fujiwara would like to believe that,' I said.

Hideki Tagawa swore and honked at a slow-walking line of prisoners. Their guards saluted and whacked them out of the road. I didn't let myself look away, though I wanted to.

'But you don't agree,' I guessed. 'Why not?'

'What makes you think I don't agree with him?'

'If you did, you'd be hunting down the local triads . . .' My brain was stirring and stretching. It was tired of feeling scared and was eager to get back to work. '. . . not saving the life of someone from a family involved, allegedly, with them. Do you think Mirza made it up? Are you worried about what other information he might have made up?'

'Thank you for creating more scenarios for me to worry about.'

I wasn't sure if he was joking.

'Heicho Han, the district commander, confirmed no outsiders entered or left the district the night Mirza was murdered. It is unlikely triad members came in, killed the man as a warning, then left without claiming responsibility. Even if they blamed him for the last round of killings.'

I wasn't sure about that. If Mirza had still been alive, I might have been tempted to kill him myself. And I wouldn't have left a note saying I'd done it.

'Besides, if the Chinese triads were involved they would have burned the house down, with Mirza and his family inside. Don't you agree?'

I wasn't going to speak on behalf of Chinese triads. 'What other information did you get from Mirza? Who else might have wanted to silence him?'

His hesitation was only momentary. 'He told us there was a group of ex-police and ex-army rebels from Singapore hiding in the jungles around the coast nearest the southern islands. Mirza claimed he had paid a lot for the information. That didn't pan out either. But we found signs that someone had been there. It is possible that Mirza warned them – for money – after selling us the information. But that was what led us to the stone codes. The men discovered them when searching the area.'

It would have been just like Mirza, a canny businessman, to take money from both sides. And that only made it more likely that the Japanese, to save face, had got rid of him themselves. Blaming it on the local Chinese triads was the icing on the cake.

'So everyone knows he sold you false information.' Everyone also knew the Japanese hated being made to look foolish. A couple of Japanese soldiers might have decided to take revenge on him. But I wasn't going to open myself to a charge of treason by saying so.

'Can I see the stone codes?'

'I believe they were concocted by tricksters solely to waste our time.'

'But you're still working on them, aren't you? Were directional branches always found? Could whoever found the code have changed the direction of the branch to show the message had been received?'

'Mirza asked the same thing.'

The car slowed as we approached the checkpoint – the Japanese had set them up on most of the city's roads.

'Here. Hold onto this,' Hideki Tagawa handed me a piece of paper with an official chop, signed by Colonel Fujiwara and himself. 'It is an official pass.'

I hesitated. This, more than anything else, would mark me as the jau kow, or running dog, who worked against her own people for the Japanese occupiers. But such a pass also meant protection for my family as well as myself. And was it really so different from what I had been doing for the British?

Besides, when the Japanese offered gifts, you didn't survive for long if you said no. Then again, this man didn't behave like most Japanese.

'I still don't understand what you want from me,' I said carefully.

'You still don't trust me,' Hideki Tagawa said.

'Why are you being good to me?'

'Maybe because I am a good person.'

I couldn't tell if he was joking so I stared, with all my attention, at our island's new flag, the Hinomaru, with its red circle on a white background, raised over the Cathay cinema building, the grandest, largest commercial edifice in Singapore. Things had changed so much for us since it was built. But if you were a bird in the skies above or an ant on the street below, would you see any difference at all?

Hideki Tagawa eased the clutch and the car inched forward as vehicles in front of us cleared the checkpoint.

'Le Froy was responsible for keeping the triads in order when he was police chief in Singapore,' he said. 'If the triads had murdered Mirza on his watch, he would have done what we're doing now. He would have hunted down the killer. And you, if you were still working with him, would have helped him. This is really no different.'

'And if I help you, if I try to help you, you will free my uncle and leave us alone?'

'I will keep your uncle safe if you help us with this problem,' Hideki Tagawa said. 'Right now, he is safer in detention than out on the streets. All I am asking of you is to do what you would have done to help Le Froy if he were working on this case. Help us for his sake as well as your own.'

'What if I fail to find anything?' I asked.

It was easier talking to him while he was driving. He kept his eyes on the road and the people walking along it so I didn't have to watch him watching me.

Hideki Tagawa gave a little laugh. 'As your Le Froy always said, failure just means you haven't finished the job yet.'

How much time had this man put into studying Le Froy? I know that should have made me even more wary of him. But it was good to hear Le Froy's name spoken after I'd pretended for so long that I didn't know him or anyone from the former British administration, while hoping against hope that he was still alive.

Murder Garden

———◆———

'This is not the turning. We're not at my grandmother's house yet – it's another half-mile down the road.' Caught up in my thoughts, I hadn't paid attention to where we were driving, until the car slowed down and Hideki Tagawa put out the indicator to turn left.

'Wouldn't Le Froy want to see the crime scene if he was investigating a murder?'

Of course he would. But I wasn't Le Froy. I didn't like murder scenes and I was tired of being compared to Le Froy, who didn't have to contend with being Chinese, female and walking with a polio limp.

Given the choice, I would have preferred to study facts on paper rather than poking around in bloodied surroundings. For a start, there were fewer mosquitoes indoors. But Hideki Tagawa wouldn't care about that any more than Le Froy had.

'Why are you so interested in Chief Inspector Le Froy?'

'Don't you think he's someone you can learn from?'

In recent years, I had learned that Le Froy and the British

Empire he represented were not infallible. But, then, Le Froy had never claimed to be. That was only part of why I still believed in him.

When I did not answer, Hideki Tagawa continued, 'I have studied Thomas Le Froy. I studied him for many years as an antagonist. And in that time I came to respect him. We're alike in some ways. We both work for the good of our people, and we struggle in defining who our people are.'

'I don't think Le Froy had any problem there.'

'Oh, no? And his superiors in London had no problem with his definition of loyalty either?'

'You probably know more about that than I do.'

'Yes,' Hideki Tagawa said. There's no shame in being a spy as long as you're spying for the winning side. 'And I know that he was a good deal more concerned about the people here, on the ground, than on making profits out of them. So am I.'

I must admit I was curious. Until now, I had seen Mirza's residence only from outside. I must have walked past those high, white-painted brick walls a few hundred times, with the tops of trees within showing over the multicoloured glass shards cemented to the top to deter animal or human visitors. Privacy had been important to the dead man.

The Japanese soldier guarding the gate saluted Hideki Tagawa's car and waved us through without checking identification. There was a covered car port with room for three cars, but Hideki Tagawa left his vehicle in the driveway.

Another guard saluted and opened the front door for us. I was surprised. 'I thought you said he was killed in the garden.'

'Good. You know how to pay attention. That is a valuable skill too few cultivate, these days. Yes, in the side garden. The shortest way there is to cut through the house.'

Hideki Tagawa walked as though he had been inside it many times. I followed. The interior was richly decorated and it did not look like a house in wartime. Indeed, it did not even look like a house of this century, or our part of the world. There were carpets and wall tapestries and richly framed mirrors.

Hideki Tagawa headed for double doors that opened onto a veranda at the right side of the hall. I followed. Even the grand furniture in that house seemed able to tell I had no idea what I was doing there.

The garden was intricately laid out. In pre-war days it had probably been cared for by an army of gardeners. Even now, untended, I could see how beautiful it had once been. It was laid out in the European style, with a strip of grass lawn we walked across, a small pond surrounded by a path of granite paving stones, and trees, which provided privacy from the house. The lawn was overgrown with string bush – I saw the spiky tips crowded with tiny white star-shaped flowers and yellow berries swelling and ripening. There was aring-aring, too, its blooms shaped like tiny sunflowers: we used to pick them from the roadside to present to our homesick teacher at the Mission School just to hear her say, 'They look like daisies!'

It was not the kind of garden I was used to. Chen Mansion had large grounds, but even when there wasn't a war on, everything we grew was strictly practical, for either human or animal consumption. The trees produced fruit or were cut down.

A tree that provided only shade or beauty was a luxury we could not afford.

What surprised me most about Mirza's garden was how much I liked it. I had never realised such a garden was possible, let alone at a private residence – the stone bench, for instance, where someone could sit with a book by the pond, gazing at blooming water-lilies and Koi carp. This, along with the library, made me wonder anew what Mirza had been like. Had he designed the garden for himself? Had he paid someone to do it?

There would be mosquitoes in the evening, I reminded myself. And likely wasps as well, since the low-growing yellow flowers were attracting bees even now in the warm afternoon sun. I couldn't talk myself into disliking the place or calling its designer impractical.

'This way,' Hideki Tagawa said.

I followed him along a winding paving-stone pathway landscaped with bamboo and bougainvillaea, which had grown tall enough to block out any view. Eventually we found ourselves in a small circular area with a hook from which an oil lamp could be hung.

'This is where Mirza was killed.'

'Here?'

As a garden, it was beautiful. As a crime scene? I didn't know where to start.

'He was hit on the back of the head with one of the ornamental rocks.' Hideki Tagawa nodded to a gap in the row of decorative bricks. 'There was blood on it. When he was down, he was stabbed in the back with the blade from that thing.'

I looked at the tree trimmer on the ground: its blade had

been removed. It was the best tool to use for harvesting fruit from large trees, if you had no small boys or a trained monkey. One blade was fixed to the long bamboo pole propped nearby, and the other was held in place with a hinged spring: it was like a huge pair of scissors, operated by the rope that ran the length of the ten-foot pole. I was surprised the pole hadn't been taken as evidence.

'It was all very convenient for the killer. There are lots of bricks and stones around here. You pick up a brick and hit him. He falls, and you stab him with a blade on a stick that just happens to be there.'

I looked around the paved space we were standing in. It was surrounded by trees, including rambutan and mango, which might explain what the tree trimmer had been doing there. But rambutans were not in season and I didn't see any ripening mangoes. Besides, anyone who grows their own mangoes knows they taste better if you leave them to ripen on the tree until they fall. So why was the tree trimmer there? I saw a scattering of withered branches on the ground.

'I don't see any blood.'

'Over there – on the grass.'

It was actually hard-packed earth and weeds, under the dense shade of a tree.

'Was there a gardener working here the day Mirza was killed?'

'They don't have one. Not since— No, no gardener,' Hideki Tagawa said.

'But the tree trimmer belonged to the house?'

He didn't bother to answer. Where a garden tool had come from was of no interest to him. Le Froy would have wondered.

When he was starting an investigation, Le Froy was interested in everything. But I didn't tell Hideki Tagawa that.

'This is where Mirza held private meetings,' Hideki Tagawa said. 'People could come and go unseen. At least, from anyone watching the front of the house.'

'You had someone guarding it even before he died?'

'Mirza had his own guards. The man on duty doubled as his driver. He had two Gurkhas, on shift.'

That had been smart of him. Malay sentries might have been reluctant to shoot Malay robbers, and Chinese sentries might have closed an eye to Chinese housebreakers, given that everyone was related to almost everyone else in the community. We all accepted that Gurkhas, from Nepal, on the job, would shoot anyone their duties required them to shoot. Their presence and reputation would have been enough to keep the place safe.

'Where was the tree trimmer kept when it wasn't in use?'

'There is a shed for garden tools on the other side of the property. Most likely there.'

'Who would have known it was there?'

'I doubt it's a great secret.'

'That the security guard doubled as Mirza's driver shows he was Mirza's personal bodyguard rather than hired to protect the house or family. And yet Mirza was careful to arrange a meeting place hidden from the house and his own security. Why?'

'You can ask, but I cannot answer you,' Hideki Tagawa said. 'That is why you are here. To find answers. What do you make of this place?'

I turned in a slow circle. It was just a space: a small paved area with two stone benches and the hook from which an oil lamp could be hung. Everything relevant to the murder had long been taken away. There were trees, bushes, various birds above and bugs below. It was private and—

'There must be another entrance.' I looked around but couldn't see it. 'Otherwise his visitors would still have to come in by the front gate, no matter how private this place is. And they would be seen. If he didn't want his security to see who was coming in, there must be another gate.'

Hideki Tagawa seemed pleased. He pointed to a stone statue against the base of the wall, half hidden by the bougainvillaea cascading around it.

I went over to it and pushed aside the heavy branches. The greenish-grey rock depicted a child holding a fish in one hand and a dish in the other where a candle might be set. On it lay two keys.

'One for the door, the other for the padlock.'

'Door? Padlock?'

You wouldn't have seen the door unless you knew where to look for it. It was set into a section of the wall thickly overgrown with brilliantly flowering maiden's jealousy. The padlock was attached to a thick link chain that looped around the door handle and the metal rings set into the stone wall.

'Apart from the front gate, it's the only way into the property.'

An inconspicuous back entrance that could be locked only from inside: it was not covered by the guard stationed in front of the house.

'What's on the other side of the wall?' As it ran at a right angle to the main road, I expected neighbours' gardens to be on the other side.

'A storm drain.'

Storm drains – often little more than open trenches barricaded with planks – were dug between buildings to reduce flash floods during the monsoon season.

'If you were coming here to see Mirza, he expected you to come through the drain and climb up the side to the door. He unlocked it when he was ready to see you. And he locked it again after you left.'

Hideki Tagawa sounded as though he was speaking from experience, and that Mirza had been the kind of man who enjoyed humiliating people. Storm drains might be fun for children hunting guppies and tadpoles, but they were also hunting grounds for rats, cockroaches and an occasional crocodile.

I used one of the keys on the padlock, then pulled the chain links through the handles fixed to the door and wall. It was a laborious business and my fingers were bruised by the time I'd finished. Then I unlocked the door and pulled it open with an effort. No one could have sneaked in unless someone on the inside had unlocked the door and removed the chain.

On the other side, as Hideki Tagawa had said, a deep three-foot-wide drain ran along the outside of the wall. The water level was low, but it didn't look welcoming. It was bordered on the other side by the back walls and fences of other properties and patches of wild grass.

'Was the door bolted when the body was found? Locked and padlocked?'

'It was not.'

'So anyone could have come and gone.'

'It was padlocked but not locked.'

'Could he have overlooked it?' The chain and padlock were obvious but it would be easy to miss an unlocked door.

'Mirza was particular about locking it. He always locked it, even after someone had come in. The chain and padlock were an added precaution. He only put on the chain at the end of the day. As you saw, it's a much more effortful process.'

I might have been able to get fingerprints from the padlock, but what would have been the point? Le Froy had made many attempts to set up an official fingerprint register in the region, but the higher-ups called fingerprinting 'new-fangled nonsense'. And even if I had had access to them, the few hundred fingerprints filed at the Detective Unit would be useless, given the influx of Japanese.

'If Mirza always locked the door, whoever killed him had to unlock it in order to go out.'

I still missed the beautifully worked-out filing system I had created for the Detective Unit but ordered myself to move on. Systems are only functional if they work for you.

'If the guard at the front of the house didn't see anyone leave, whoever killed Mirza left by this door, then someone else put on the chain and padlock without locking it, and either went into the house or left another way. Was anyone else in the house other than Mirza's daughters?'

I thought it very likely that at least one of Mirza's daughters had been involved.

'Unfortunately it's not that simple. Earlier in the day, Mirza sent a message to Colonel Fujiwara saying he had discovered something and needed an immediate appointment.'

'What was it about?'

Hideki Tagawa ignored my question. 'Mirza sent the house guard with the message. He'd done so before, even though he'd been reminded that he had no right to use soldiers as errand boys. Most of the time his errands were trivial and pointless. It was clear that sometimes it was purely a distraction, so that one of his daughters could go out to collect black-market beef for him.'

'Black-market beef?'

'Mirza had thousands of connections and hundreds of people he could put pressure on. When the Officers' Club served beef, somehow the best cuts found their way to Mirza's table. Colonel Fujiwara assumed the message was another such distraction and told the house guard to take the rest of his shift off.'

'So no one was watching the gate.'

Hideki Tagawa nodded.

But that didn't clear the Mirza girls, because only someone in the house would know that Mirza had sent the guard away. Unless someone had already been in the garden with him when he sent the message.

'So someone could have walked through the front gate after the guard left. What time was this? And do you know what time Mirza's daughters last saw him alive?'

The timing made a difference because of the curfew. Civilians were supposed to stay off the streets at night, though 'night' was measured by Japan time, which was in the middle of our afternoon. If someone had visited Mirza in the dark, it was more likely to be one of the Japanese personnel, who could move about freely unchallenged.

'Maybe you should ask them,' he said. His tone told me he thought the Mirza girls were lying about something.

And the way he started back towards the house in a straight line, trampling on overgrown flowerbeds and pushing through artfully landscaped bushes, told me I would have to work it out for myself.

Something else he and Le Froy had in common.

The Mimosa Tree

Though familiar with the house, Hideki Tagawa was clearly uncomfortable in the overgrown garden. I started to follow him, then stopped and made my way to the base of the wall. Just in case we were missing something.

It wasn't easy. The undergrowth was thickest there, with thorny creepers coming down from the trees above. My every step into the dead leaves and decaying mulch stirred up plant dust, beetles and worms.

'What are you doing?'

'I just want to look around.'

'The men have been over this. No one came over the wall. What are you looking for?'

'If I knew, I wouldn't have to look.'

It had come out automatically, another of Le Froy's favourite sayings. I'd even said it with his inflections.

I don't know if Hideki Tagawa realised this, but he didn't get angry. Instead he made his way back and watched me.

The wall around the Mirza property was more than six feet

tall with broken glass shards cemented into the top. Anyone trying to climb over it would be savagely slashed and would leave a trace: I saw no dried blood or ripped cloth.

The level of security was very different from that of the other houses in the area. Most private residences there didn't even have fencing. Those that did had wire netting designed to keep young children and chickens in, and wild dogs out. I turned back towards the path we had walked along. 'All this — the wall, the secret door, the security — was constructed some time ago, long before the war. It's almost as though he was already afraid of someone or something.' Had a long-term enemy finally seized the opportunity to settle an old score?

'As a wealthy man, he might have been worried about kidnappers,' Hideki Tagawa suggested.

'Do you think so? His daughters would know. He would have warned them. His death might not have had any connection with the work he was doing for you.'

'We can ask his killer when you find him.' Hideki Tagawa shrugged, but I saw my questions had pleased him. They had already occurred to him, then.

If Mirza had put his security precautions in place long before the occupation, it was not the Japanese he had feared but the local Chinese triads ... Was it possible that Mirza had antagonised someone so seriously? Had he been threatened and put on his guard? Had someone with a grudge against him passed by outside, seen the guard gone and taken the opportunity to settle an old score?

But if this hypothetical someone had entered and left through the front gate, why had he bothered to chain and padlock the secret door?

'There's nothing more to see here.' Hideki Tagawa turned away again, this time to the path.

I started to follow him. Back at the circular clearing, I looked again at the scattered branches that had been cut, not torn, down and were withering on the paving. 'Did your men cut down these branches?'

'Of course not. Why would they?'

'Maybe something was caught in them.'

We squinted up at the young mimosa from which most of the branches seemed to have come. It was broad daylight so the leaflets were open and dancing in the warm breeze.

Mimosa flowers are fluffy globular clusters of pink and cream, which become flat pods covered with bristly hairs. But there was no sign that someone had been cutting flowers or fruit, just branches. Why would Mirza – or his killer – have been cutting mimosa with the tree trimmer that had killed him?

If you are unfamiliar with the mimosa tree, one of the first things you'll be told about it is that its leaflets open during the day and close at night. Like the creeping mimosa, or 'touch me not', but much more slowly. The leaflets of the mimosa branches on the ground were folded inwards, as though they were hiding. I felt like that: I wanted to close in on myself to hide and stay safe from the world. But when you have already been cut off, hiding won't save you.

Hideki Tagawa headed towards the side of the house, away from the double doors we had come through earlier. Behind a row of miniature palms, a set of sliding doors opened directly from the garden path into Mirza's office. I glanced up at the house before following him through. I saw the dark outline of a head and shoulders, a face watching us from an upstairs window, quickly pulled back. The movement had caught my eye.

Even if the external entry to Mirza's garden meeting place was concealed from the house, someone inside could easily have monitored his comings and goings.

It was clear at first glance that someone, whether the kempeitai or his daughters, had searched Mirza's home office. Compared to the glimpse I'd had of the rest of the house, it was chaos. Books had been pulled off the shelves and tossed onto the floor, drawers had been emptied, and the heavy safe in one corner stood open and empty. What looked like a metal flower lay on its side in front of it. I thought at first it was made of gold, but its weight told me it was brass, beautifully ornamented like an old key. Its three petals were tipped with tiny beads.

This would have made more sense if Mirza had been killed in his office, but I had just seen the spot in the garden where the murder had taken place.

'What were your men looking for in here?'

This time there was exasperation as well as amusement in Hideki Tagawa's look.

'They were instructed to take back our property – copies of the stone code diagrams he was working on for us. I'll have to get official permission before you can see them. But that shouldn't be a problem.'

Of course it wouldn't. I was not a security risk: they could always shoot me to keep me quiet.

There was something very sad about the disorder in the room. It had been beautifully arranged, with the bookshelves, good chairs and a reading corner. The mess made me think of a classically beautiful woman falling down drunk, her hair awry, her make-up smudged.

'You won't find anything more here,' Hideki Tagawa said. 'Would you like to question Mirza's daughters now?' Clearly he liked to get things done fast. 'They're upstairs. I'll have them brought down to us.'

'Actually,' I said, 'I don't want to talk to them until I've seen the autopsy report, everything to do with the stone codes and anything else Mirza was working on for you.'

That was another Le Froy principle. Don't question anyone until you know the answers you want from them. I would also ask Ah Ma and Shen Shen to tell me all they knew about the Mirza girls before I met them. Though I had seen them about, we moved in very different circles.

I also wanted to let Ah Ma and Shen Shen know that Uncle Chen and I were alive and well – for now. Had it only been that morning that we had been dragged out of the house? I felt as though what had happened at the inspection field had been a lifetime ago.

'I told you,' Safia Mirza said, 'that my sister won't talk to men without a chaperone. If you let me know when you want to speak to us, I will arrange for someone to be here.'

She must have come down the stairs when she heard us in the house. I wondered if it had been she who was watching us from upstairs.

Mirza's House and Daughters

———◆———

Safia Mirza was a pretty, plump girl, with a mouth and cheeks that looked like they were used to smiling. She was not smiling today. I remembered seeing photographs of Safia wearing sequins and feathers at flapper parties before the war. She looked very different now. She was wearing a Western frock, a dull grey one that reached to mid-calf.

'That's why we have a female assistant,' Hideki Tagawa said. He gestured at me. 'And you will be with her. You can chaperone each other. Call her down.'

'A female sibling does not count as a *mehram*.' She meant a male relative or guardian. I hadn't realised the Mirzas were such a conservative family.

And they weren't: Safia was standing there glaring at us and seemed to have no problem talking to Hideki Tagawa with her hair uncovered.

'I want to look at the autopsy results and the stone codes

your father was working on before I ask you any questions,'
I said. 'Right now, I only want to know if you and your sister are
all right. My family lives up the road.'

'How can we be all right? Didn't you hear? Our father is dead!'

I took her hands. 'I know. And I'm very sorry. Is there
anything we can do to help? Even if you don't feel like eating
you must keep your strength up. I can bring you some tapioca
buns and fish soup later.'

Instead of answering, Safia Mirza burst into tears.

'I can walk home from here.'

It was barely ten minutes from the Mirza house to Chen
Mansion. And I would spend most of that time walking down
the long driveway from their house to the main road and up the
equally long driveway from the main road to our house.

'Why? Are you afraid of being seen with me?' Hideki Tagawa
held open the car door and I got in.

He had been taken aback when Safia started crying, and
surprised that I had refused to question her with more pressure
when her guard was down.

'I don't know what I want to ask her yet,' I pointed out. And
I tried to turn his Le Froy obsession back on him. 'Le Froy
always said you should know the answers you're looking for
before you ask any questions.'

It had seemed to work.

'So, you're friends with Mirza's daughters? You did not tell
me that.'

'We're not friends. But our families have been neighbours a
long time.' Living with servants meant you heard all the gossip

74

about the other even if you'd never met. Now I had met Safia, I wished I'd had a chance to get to know her before I'd met her as a murder suspect. Because that was how I saw her now.

'You Chinese consider people like them outsiders, don't you?'

'What do you mean "people like them"? The Arabs used to own more than half of Singapore. And if you mean Muslims, they were in Singapore long before the Chinese.' Most Straits-born locals had a lot more in common with each other than with the British and the Japanese.

The British had never been able to understand that either, not even the Mission Centre ladies. Being Singaporean had little to do with what you looked like or where you came from, and everything to do with how you treated others.

'Calm down.' Hideki Tagawa sounded amused. 'You saw something in the room. You believe there is something to be found in it. I saw your eyes going round and round. Tell me what you saw.'

I was disconcerted. I had studied the garden, the office and Safia Mirza without a thought that he might be studying me. Le Froy might have trained me to be an investigator, but he hadn't taught me to be a spy. 'I don't know,' I said. 'I think there is something to be found there, but I don't know what it is. It was the mess I was looking at. I couldn't tell what might be missing. Your men took his ring binders?'

'How do you know he had ring binders?'

'There was a half-used notepad with holes punched for a two-ring binder. And there was a two-ring punch and unused paper folders, also with two holes for a ring binder. He must have had ring binders somewhere.'

He nodded.

I was telling the truth – part of it, anyway.

'I want to go back there and put the room in order. I can't find anything in such a mess. Maybe if we tidy it, the girls will be more willing to talk. Or when things are put in place we'll be able to see if Mirza had been working on anything else that might have upset somebody.'

'You shouldn't trust the girls. They weren't so upset when their father was found dead. And one of them was seen sneaking out yesterday evening. We don't know which one, because she was wearing the full religious head-covering. It was more likely the elder because the younger one, as you saw, does not wear the head-covering.'

'Unless it was a deliberate disguise.'

'Neither of them admits to it. You should know that one of the sisters, possibly both, is lying to us. I suspect one, perhaps both, is working with the triads or the local resistance.'

'But you suspect everybody of that, don't you?'

Hideki Tagawa laughed. He had certainly relaxed since Colonel Fujiwara had approved of his hiring me. 'You're not seeing the best of us. There is much more to Japan. But the West treats us like dogs underfoot, and that is how they taught you to think of us.'

I couldn't argue. The West didn't think much of us either. And I doubted that anything would ever change. There was always someone talking about self-rule, but that seemed an impossible dream. After all, things were even worse in China, from what I had heard, the rival warlords fighting each other for dominance when they weren't fighting the Japanese.

———

The gates at Chen Mansion stood open and Hideki Tagawa drove me right up to the house. My back and legs were grateful. I had been on my feet since the military police had roused us before dawn, and when I climbed out of the car I found that every part of me hurt.

'Thanks.' I meant it.

'I'll bring you copies of the stone codes soon,'

'Are you still sure that a local killed him?'

'Who else is there to blame?'

'If the Japanese ordered Mr Mirza killed, you would still have a trial and convict and execute locals, wouldn't you?'

'You don't believe he was killed by a local? You think that if you prove he was murdered by a Japanese kempeitai we would cover it up?'

I thought about it, stretching one leg and then the other as I held on to the car.

'I don't think you would,' I said, 'but you don't run the Japanese military here.'

'I'm not even in the Japanese military,' Hideki Tagawa said. 'But I don't believe the kempeitai killed this man.'

I matched his honesty with my own: 'It was probably a local who killed him. If the Japanese wanted him dead, they wouldn't have had to sneak around. They could just have shot him. Like you're going to shoot my uncle if I don't come up with someone else to take the blame. But that someone may be someone else's uncle or father or husband. It doesn't feel right.'

'Miss Chen, I'm not asking you to pick out a scapegoat. I'm asking you to help me find a murderer.'

Shen Shen, carrying Little Ling, came round the side of the house from the kitchen and peered past me at the car. When she saw the back seat was empty and I had come home without Uncle Chen, she glared at me and disappeared without greeting me.

'Your uncle's daughter is very small for her age.'

I knew it was true. Little Ling was too small and thin. Too often she felt cold, even in the heat of Singapore. 'We are all small, all the girls in my family.'

He nodded and shifted the car into reverse gear. 'Remember, no matter what you do, somebody will get angry with you. You might as well do what you believe is right.'

Chen Mansion

———◆———

Chen Mansion was probably as large as Mirza's house, but while the Mirza house felt like a cross between a museum and a palace, Chen Mansion housed half a village crammed under one roof.

The house I had grown up in was a local *rumah panggong*-style building with many long windows for ventilation. The trees around the house – rambutan, jackfruit, starfruit, banana, papaya and mango – meant there was plenty of shade and ants all year round. And behind the outside kitchen there was a deep well, or *perigi*, that provided us with fresh water even at the highest of high tides. This was a blessing because we didn't have to carry water from the official pumps, which made us as self-sufficient as it was possible to be in occupied Singapore.

Ah Ma had made over the front hall and dining room to two of her tenant families who had lost their homes and businesses when their shophouses were bombed. Three distant cousins – sisters with their children but without husbands, who were missing – occupied what had previously been the servants' quarters.

I spent most of my time in Ah Ma's bedroom, where I was sleeping once more on the roll-up mattress I had grown up with, and in the kitchen, where Ah Ma maintained absolute control. Others were free to cook on the three charcoal stoves in the courtyard, but she ruled the food stores in the kitchen.

Ah Ma also had chickens, ducks, goats and a couple of pigs hidden behind the communal latrines where the Japanese would not find them. Even inside the WC or my grandmother's bedroom you heard animals and people calling, talking, crying, arguing non-stop. I wasn't ready to face all those people inside yet, not to mention my grandmother and her questions. She would be in the kitchen where Shen Shen would have told her I was back without Uncle Chen.

Of course they would ask me where he was, but I didn't have any answers for them. And I wanted to think over all that had happened and what I had agreed to do.

I couldn't go on standing out there with a damp rice cake in my pocket. My pass permitted me to leave my residence by the colonel's authority, but there was nowhere outside for me to go.

I detoured to use the WC behind what had once been the driver-gardener's shack before joining Ah Ma in the kitchen. That meant I came up on the side path used to carry night soil to the vegetable gardens, a trek I usually avoided because of the stink. This was where the kitchen herbs and vegetables grew – lemongrass, yellow ginger, and a variety of chillies as well as corn, tapioca, ladies' fingers and sugar cane.

Shen Shen wasn't in the kitchen. She didn't see me because she was deep in discussion with Formosa Boy, who was large, slow and perpetually hungry. He was one of Heicho Han's men so I was sure he was spying on us, no matter how friendly he tried to appear.

The first time Formosa Boy came to Chen Mansion, he had stopped outside the back door to take off his shoes, unlike any other Japanese soldier. Ah Ma went on bowing and saying she couldn't understand Japanese until, with a shock, she realised the Japanese soldier was speaking to her in Hokkien: 'Aunty, please may I take some of the kangkong growing just outside your fence? I am very hungry.'

Our vegetable plot had spread wild, and the soldiers' rations were not much better than ours.

'How come you, soldier-Jepun, can talk Hokkien?'

'I'm from Formosa – you know, Taiwan.'

Formosa had been a province of the Japanese Empire since before the Great War. But old-timers, like my grandmother and Formosa Boy's parents, still called it Taiwan. Like Choson, or Korea, Formosa had supplied many conscripts for the Japanese war in Asia.

'Do you know how to cook kangkong?'

'No, Aunty.'

Ah Ma had cooked a huge quantity of kangkong for Formosa Boy, with a bit of salt fish. Now he often dropped in. He would help carry water buckets or dig sweet potatoes every chance he got. He would bring food he scavenged – he was not allowed to cook for himself at camp – and sometimes made himself sick by eating fruit and weeds he found. And occasionally he brought fish or birds that Ah Ma would cook for all of us.

It was hard for Formosa Boy because locals hated the Taiwanese even more than the Japanese soldiers, largely because when soldiers were looking for women to have sex with, they almost always had a Taiwanese with them to make themselves understood. The Japanese officers didn't treat the Taiwanese conscripts very well either.

Formosa Boy had been useful in other ways.

Ah Ma insisted on going to shop for food at the Joo Chiat market despite frequent Japanese raids on hawkers operating without licences. There, she could barter with our sweet potatoes and homemade achar. One day I was surprised to find her at home with Formosa Boy less than ten minutes after she had left in search of supplies and gossip.

'What happened? Are you all right? Why are you back so fast?' I might have given Formosa Boy a dirty look. Even if I didn't like Ah Ma risking herself at illegal stalls, I didn't want her staying at home to cook just because this enemy oaf was hungry again.

'Hi yah, girl. You tell me, don't go to Joo Chiat. Then when I don't go, you ask me what is wrong.'

But I knew that my grandmother didn't change her mind easily. 'Did something happen? What happened?'

'Something is going to happen,' Formosa Boy slurred, in his usual deep, slow voice. 'The soldiers are going to raid Joo Chiat market today. I told Aunty better stay at home.'

Ah Ma had laughed at my surprise. That day, I had helped her to prepare steamed clams for Formosa Boy.

Even though he had become a semi-regular fixture at the house, I didn't like seeing him and Shen Shen muttering together. What could they have to talk about that was so secret it was worth enduring the stench from the vegetable patch?

'Oh, Big Sister, you are back!' Formosa Boy saw me first.

'Ma! Su Lin is home!' Shen Shen called. So she hadn't told them Hideki Tagawa had driven me back in his car.

Ah Ma shuffled swiftly out in her kitchen clogs, thumping herself hard on the chest. 'Kus semangat. Pulang semangat!' she said over and over again. She was calling her spirit back into her body – it had been driven out by fear and shock. 'What happened? Where did that man take you? What did he want?'

'Ask her where her uncle is!' That was Shen Shen.

Was I imagining it or had I heard accusation in her voice? 'I don't know where Uncle is now. They want me to help them to find out who killed Mirza Ali Hasnain. They said they would let Uncle go if I help them to find the killer.'

'They are just looking for somebody to blame.' That was Formosa Boy. He was carrying a banana-leaf packet of charcoal-roasted peanuts and spoke with his mouth full. 'Better that you save yourself.'

'What do you know about this?' Ah Ma asked him.

'People say that Big Boss Colonel ordered him killed.'

'Colonel Fujiwara?' I asked.

'Yah. The guys say that Mirza was blackmailing Big Boss. Because he would do all kinds of things without permission, but Big Boss always said leave him alone. And when you want to check his house or his car, he would refer to Big Boss and Big Boss would say, "Leave my friend alone."'

'If they were friends, why would he order him killed? And why would the colonel order anyone to investigate Mirza's death if he was the one who ordered him killed?'

Formosa Boy spoke through a mouthful of roasted peanut:

'Maybe he wants to find out if anybody has any proof,' he said. 'So that he can get rid of it. If you find it for him, then he will get rid of you too.'

Shen Shen moaned softly and closed her eyes. 'We should not have moved back here to stay. Everything near you gets into trouble, Su Lin!'

'Can you just tell him that you have questioned a lot of people and nobody knows anything?' Ah Ma suggested.

'Much better if you just give him some names,' Formosa Boy said. 'That is all he needs. He needs to make the arrests and have public executions so that everybody can see that he is keeping order here.'

Formosa Boy was suggesting framing someone for murder, in effect murdering them. And Ah Ma was nodding as though she agreed. As though sending someone to be executed was just a practical business decision. It was the slippery slope from selling sweet potatoes on the black market to this.

'I think Hideki Tagawa really wants to find out who murdered Mr Mirza.'

'Better be careful of that one,' Formosa Boy said. 'If Big Boss ordered Mirza to be killed, he would have sent his snake to kill him.'

'His snake?' But part of me already knew who he meant.

'Hideki Tagawa. Tagawa is the only one who reports directly to him. If Big Boss wanted Mirza killed, he would get his snake Tagawa to do it. You should just pick a name and pin it on them. You will save many other people's lives if you can stop this sooner. I can give you some names, if you like. Even if they aren't collaborators, they deserve to be arrested!' He laughed.

Something about him reminded me of Uncle Chen. He was good-natured and ruthless. I wondered if Ah Ma had noticed that too. She seemed to like him. But she seemed to like all the people she found useful.

'Give them the names before they do anything to your uncle!' Shen Shen begged. 'For once in your life, think of somebody other than yourself and don't try to be too clever!'

I wondered if Madam Koh had been approached with the same offer: 'Give us some names and get yourself out of trouble.'

'I need to talk to Madam Koh.' I wanted to find out whether she had picked out Uncle Chen at random – or out of spite – or whether someone had told her to 'arrow' him. 'Is she back home, do you know?'

'Madam Koh is dead,' Shen Shen said flatly.

'What?' For a crazy instant I wondered if Shen Shen had snapped and killed her.

'Not our fault,' Formosa Boy said. 'They told us to let her go. So we let her go home. But then somebody pushed her into the canal.'

'Really?' I glared at Formosa Boy.

'That's what people told us. There were a lot of people around, but nobody saw anything,' Formosa Boy said. 'Nobody saw anyone push her. Some people say they saw the angry spirits of the dead come out of the canal water to grab her.' He shivered, 'I'm glad I wasn't there. I don't like ghosts.'

'Maybe it was an accident,' my grandmother said. 'Maybe she hit her head on something in the water and drowned.' She didn't seem sorry. After all, it was Madam Koh who had got us all into this mess, her and Mirza Ali Hasnain, who had started it all by getting murdered.

Formosa Boy finished his nuts and crushed the folded banana leaf of empty shells in a beefy palm. 'Chen-zong.' He placed his right hand over his left fist and raised them both towards my grandmother, then pressed them to his heart. It was a strange, old-fashioned gesture, almost as though he was paying respect to his ancestral altar. Also, I noticed he called her 'zong', a respectful way of addressing a boss. 'I should be going now. Thank you, Aunty.'

'You really didn't see your uncle?' Shen Shen asked me urgently, once he was gone, 'You were away for so long but you still don't know where they took him? What were you doing? What are they doing to him?'

'Why would I lie to you? Maybe you should ask your sister Mimi if she's heard anything,' I said.

Shen Shen's sister worked in a Japanese officers' bar. Her real name was Shen Mi. She had started calling herself Mimi to flirt with British soldiers. The Japanese soldiers had told her that 'Mimi' was a Japanese name so it worked even better now.

'Don't try to be too clever, Su Lin. You have already brought enough bad luck to this family!'

'People say daughters are bad luck, but daughters-in-law are worse,' Ah Ma said to the sky.

Shen Shen walked away. It was rude of her to turn her back on her mother-in-law but Ah Ma had been rude to her, too.

'That wasn't very nice of you,' I told my grandmother. But I appreciated her standing up for me.

'I said "People say". I never said "I say".' Ah Ma seized my wrists and gazed at me as though she was trying to convince herself I was really there and she was not dreaming. 'Maybe in today's world, smart granddaughters got better chance than strong grandsons. Are you really all right? They did not hurt you?'

'I'm all right, Ah Ma. Really.'

'You are going to get yourself involved again. You are going to get mixed up in all kinds of trouble. Aiyoh. If your father was alive . . .'

From all I had heard of him, my late father would have headed straight for trouble.

'I cannot stand losing you too,' Ah Ma said. 'Do you really think they will let your uncle go if you help them?'

I had no idea. But what choice did I have?

'At least we know he's still alive.' I wasn't sure if I was talking about Uncle Chen or Le Froy.

Kitchen Talk

———◆———

I remembered how Colonel Fujiwara had studied me and the questions he had asked about my family. Also that he had used me to tease Hideki Tagawa. Why?

He might know that Hideki Tagawa meant to use me to pressure Le Froy. But why, then, hadn't they taken me to the prison where he was being held and started cutting off my fingers and toes?

'Don't be too clever,' Ah Ma cut into my thoughts, 'and end up too stupid. That is what happens to people who try to be clever!'

That was how she talked. It would probably have confused anyone who didn't know her. But I knew exactly what she meant. And I didn't have any choice.

'Girl, have you eaten lunch?'

'What's the point of eating lunch?'

'If you think there's no point to anything, maybe we should all just go and jump into the river.'

Ah Ma went back into the kitchen to join Shen Shen.

They spent most of their time there because it took longer to feed people when there was so little food. Though Ah Ma protected her food stores fiercely, she didn't let anyone go hungry under her roof. That came from her Malay blood: you watch out for family, and everyone is family. It was probably what had started her feeding Formosa Boy.

Luckily, most traditional dishes had evolved through years of famine and flood. As long as there were weeds, you could make soup.

I wanted to be alone to think about what had happened and what to do next, but it was impossible to walk into the main house without disturbing people crowded behind partitions made of sheets over clothes lines for privacy. I couldn't stand by the stinking vegetable plots either, so I followed them to the kitchen.

'Here, eat.' Shen Shen slapped a plate onto the oilcloth-covered table. It was tapioca, of course. The rice ration was low-quality cracked rice thick with lime powder and dead weevils. Even the pig wouldn't eat it unless it was rinsed three times before cooking. But living on the coast helped: with sea salt we harvested ourselves, soft-shell crabs from the mangroves and razorback clams we collected from the seabed at low tide, we were eating much better than most people in Singapore.

Shen Shen had always fed me well – out of guilt, I suspect. It was as though the food she gave me would counteract all the bad thoughts she had about me. Or maybe she hoped to placate whatever demons she thought were living inside me, like people burn Hell money to keep demons away. She was the kind of woman who would go without food herself to leave offerings for the gods and ancestors. No one worked harder than her for her family, her husband's family and the descendants she hoped to give them. And she could work wonders with tapioca. No matter what happened, people had to eat. Keeping them alive by feeding them was the most important thing. It was part of the rhythm of life.

Ah Ma brought to the table the chilli padi she was working on and sat opposite me as I ate. In other words, she was ready to talk.

'Tell me everything you know about Mirza and his daughters,' I said. Even if they had lived on the other side of Singapore or across the waters in Johor instead of up the road, I would have asked Ah Ma first. 'What have you heard about them?'

'He was very rich. Stingy. His wife was a nice woman. Always paid her servants on time. But his daughters – you know his daughters, right?'

'Not really.' I didn't think reducing Safia to tears in under five minutes counted as acquaintanceship.

'The older one is serious and religious. Very sly and secretive.' That probably just meant she was shy and didn't like gossip. 'The younger one . . . I remember she had a boyfriend. Several boyfriends. Her father was furious. Don't know what happened to the boys. After he found out, he locked the girls up, wouldn't let them out of the house alone. The older girl and the mother didn't like Mirza drinking alcohol and doing funny business with funny people.'

'Funny business?'

'If you want to know about that you should ask Shen Shen.'

'Shen Shen?'

Ah Ma nodded. Shen Shen looked miserable.

If I was the nasty sort, I might have suggested that Shen Shen was the bad-luck magnet, not me. Her husband being taken away was only the latest in a long series of blows that had struck her family since the occupation had begun.

One of her brothers had been shot during the Sook Ching massacre. The other had died after he was beaten up by soldiers on patrol because he didn't bow low enough. Her father was among the men who had been taken away and not heard from since. Like many others who had had family members taken, her mother clung to the belief that he had been shipped out and put to work elsewhere. It didn't make sense that the Japanese would take an old man as forced labour after killing his younger, stronger sons but it was the only hope they had to cling to so they clung hard.

That was how the Japanese labour system worked. That was why Javanese men were starving and begging for scraps of rotten food around the market stalls. The Japanese had brought them in to use as slave labour and human shields. Then they had been 'freed' and left on the roadside with no way to get home. Some could barely sit up, and every morning the bodies of those who had died in the night had to be cleared away so they did not clog the drains.

'I heard one of the Mirza girls trained as a nurse and was going to run away with a British infidel but found out he was married. And the other wanted to marry a poor Malay boy and her father had the man killed, so she hates him. I don't know how true that is. Anyway, my parents owed money to Mirza,' Shen Shen said. 'One year, after the pigs got sick and died, he took their farm, but they still owed him money. Since they couldn't pay, he used to get my brothers to do things for him. Like report on the neighbours – were they doing business he didn't know about? And if the neighbours refused to pay, he would get my brothers to throw blood on their doors.'

I glanced at Ah Ma, who didn't look surprised. I wondered if she had ever hired Shen Shen's brothers for such jobs . . . I stopped myself thinking like that. If I didn't have to know, I didn't want to know. I tried to stay away from my family's black-market empire by closing my eyes to it.

'It was just work,' Shen Shen said defensively. 'That was how Mirza got people to pay him. But my brothers never hurt anybody.'

'I'm surprised Mirza couldn't protect your father and brothers from the Japanese if they were working for him.'

'He didn't need them once he started working with the Japanese. My mother and father went to him to beg him to speak for my brothers. But he refused to see them. He had found new people to do his dirty work. He must have told the Japanese to get rid of Ah Beng and Ah Zhai so that they couldn't tell what they knew about him. I'm not sorry someone killed him. I'm not even surprised!'

'Why did people pay him? Was it rent? Interest on loans? Was he a moneylender?'

'Mirza knew things about people. He knew who had debts and who was always getting drunk and who had the best durian trees and who was secretly making toddy.'

That sounded like my grandmother.

'And he knew how to twist that information and use it against people.'

Shen Shen wasn't looking weak and subdued now. A crazed rage in her eyes told me she would have killed Mirza herself, given half a chance and a sharp enough stick. And if what she said was true, I doubted she was the only one.

But the one thing that stuck with me was that Shen Shen's family was not rich. Even before the Japanese occupation the sons had been working for Mirza because they were struggling to survive. I had always believed Ah Ma arranged the marriage between Shen Shen and Uncle Chen because she didn't want Uncle Chen marrying into a poor family, like my father had. If Shen Shen's family was also poor, what had Ah Ma had against my late mother's family?

I couldn't even begin to guess because I had never met any of them. 'But if your brothers were working for moneylenders—'

'Looking for Miss Chen Su Lin!' a soldier, not one I recognised, called from just outside the kitchen. His bicycle was leaning against the side of the laundry tub. My grandmother and I froze, too startled even to bow.

'What do you want?' Shen Shen sketched a cursory bow. 'Is it about Mr Chen? Tell me. I am his wife. Tell me!'

The soldier looked doubtfully at her. I was afraid Shen Shen would grab him and shake him.

'I am Chen Su Lin,' I said. 'What is it?'

'I have something to give you.'

Copies of the stone codes Mirza had been deciphering, I thought. I was impressed by Hideki Tagawa's efficiency. And I was curious. Had Mirza just been stringing them along? Random arrangements of stones sounded like children from the fishing kampungs playing games.

No. The package the soldier handed me contained a book. Taped to the cover was a note, in English, from Hideki Tagawa: 'I am sending you The Tale of Genji so that you can read it to improve your Japanese instead of obsessing over British prisoners of war. Be ready at 8 a.m. tomorrow.'

Was there some clue in this book that he wanted me to figure out?

Ah Ma barely waited until the soldier had got onto his bicycle and left before making a sound of disgust. Then she muttered a prayer. You have to thank the gods for preserving you, in case you annoy them by taking them for granted, but sometimes you must let out your annoyance with them for sending so many trials that you need to be protected against.

'You and your books. Ang moh books not enough. Now Yappun books also you want!'

I opened it.

It was a children's book, with pictures. I had heard from Mrs Maki of Murasaki Shikibu, who was a prime example of self-taught women writers, and had composed the first Japanese novel, The Tale of Genji. In a diary entry Murasaki had confided that she had learned the Chinese classics from eavesdropping on her brother's lessons. This was in an age when Buddhism declared education dangerous for women so it was important for them to be discreet about their knowledge.

'It was always hard for women,' Mrs Maki had told me, 'It will always be hard.'

'Throw that book away! I don't want it in my house!' Ah Ma sounded angry but I could see she was afraid. Of the book?

I opened it and saw a name written inside the front cover.

Japanese traditional characters in careful childish brushstrokes: 'Ryoko'.

'This is all your fault!' Shen Shen shouted.

'I never asked for—'

I stopped because she was raging at my grandmother.

'You insisted on keeping her here. You sent her to school! You let her run around talking back so that people are getting us into trouble! I tell you, if your son doesn't come back it is your fault!'

And instead of defending herself, and me, Ah Ma let Shen Shen shout at her as though she agreed with her. That was the worst of it. It had been thus through all my childhood: despite all the good she had done for so many, Ah Ma was cursed at because she had kept me.

I would have walked away from the house and my family there and then if I could have. In fact, I turned to go, but someone else was standing on the kitchen path listening to the fight.

'You.' Heicho Han pointed at me. 'Come. I want to talk to you.'

Heicho Han

◆

Tall, smooth-skinned, broad-shouldered and slim, Heicho – Captain – Han was good-looking. He was also very smart, able to speak basic English and Malay as well as Japanese.

Heicho Han was the officer in charge of our division. He worshipped army protocol, and I'd heard he liked to drop hints that he was one of the kempeitai's top secret agents.

I doubted that. Weren't top secret agents far more likely to try to make people think they were of no importance? Like Hideki Tagawa? But I suspected Heicho Han's good looks were more appealing to women than the sly eyes and sloped shoulders of Hideki Tagawa. And it was the women in our district who whispered about Heicho Han being a top figure in the military police.

I stepped out of the kitchen. 'What can I do for you, sir?' I could tell Ah Ma and Shen Shen had turned into silent statues behind me.

'After that man took you from the sorting field this morning, I came to see whether you had been brought back.'

'That is very kind of you, sir. Yes, I am back. I am all right.'

I knew Heicho Han's real name was Han Jin Woo. He was an ethnic Korean who had grown up in Japanese-occupied Korea. His Japanese was fluent but limited: my first teacher, Mrs Maki, would have dismissed him as 'a low-class speaker'. His language, peppered with obscenities, had clearly been learned on the streets. But his enthusiasm for Japanese ways reminded me of the fervour of new Christian converts in the old days. I didn't judge him: those who dislike things in themselves make the most fuss about those traits in others.

'That man Tagawa who took you away. People call him "Rat Face", did you know?'

There was indeed something rat-like about Hideki Tagawa.

'What did he want with you? Where did he take you?'

'To the house of Colonel Fujiwara.'

'Why?'

'They asked if I could do translation.'

I wasn't lying. I would find out what I could in English, Chinese and Malay and present my findings in Japanese. You can't get through a day in Singapore without doing translation.

Heicho Han snorted. 'If I could speak Japanese as well as you, I would get a proper job at a desk instead of walking around in the sun. Are you going to be working for the colonel? You might recommend me. What is the use of planting vegetables that nobody wants to eat? Your old grandma only wants enough to fill her stomach. You should not let her hold you back.'

It was an old refrain. I had heard Heicho Han was full of big schemes for promoting East District 221, but most of the other soldiers posted to our district were Korean and Taiwanese conscripts from occupied territories. They were as suspicious of their captain as of each other and frustrated his schemes for advancement.

Besides, until now, the East Coast area had never attracted much attention from Central Command. And it was the first time I had attracted any attention from Heicho Han.

'Is Rat Face trying to muscle in on my territory?'

'I think he just wanted a local person who could translate Japanese.'

'Did he say anything about the murder case?'

'He said there had been a murder. I told him I didn't know anything about it.'

'Hideki Tagawa knows you. Out on the inspection ground, before he took you away, he knew your name. How come? Are you working for him? Have you been working for him all along? Spying on me for him?'

There was fear and suspicion in his eyes. It was not only the local population that lived in a state of constant fear. There were rivalries within the Japanese army ranks too. And Heicho Han, as an ethnic Korean, must have taken his knocks. Maybe I could have, should have, reassured him, but I found myself enjoying his fear. One way to survive terror is to pass it on to someone else. Not a good solution, but we were in the middle of a war, and I deserved to feel good just for a bit.

'I am not allowed to say,' I said.

Heicho Han's mouth tightened and he looked offended. I've noticed that those with less confidence are always the quickest to take offence.

He pulled his shoulders back, as though a senior officer was present.

'The death of Mirza Ali Hasnain is a local matter. We are handling it locally. He was helping us so the Chinese triads killed him. We have evidence and witnesses. Why is our esteemed Colonel Fujiwara so interested in finding out who killed a local informer?'

I had wondered the same thing. Locals were killed all the time. 'Maybe they were friends,' I suggested. I thought Mirza would have considered himself superior to the colonel, but the colonel was the one in power. 'They may have worked together. Or maybe he heard rumours that Mirza was killed by his soldiers.'

'How dare you?' Heicho Han raised his rifle as though preparing to swipe me on the side of the head with it. 'I am telling you, you lying fool, that it was the Chinese triads who killed him. And your uncle is involved with them. Don't think you can hide that! He is working for the British spies!'

My body flinched automatically. But I stood my ground and shrugged. 'My uncle is under protection. Like Mirza. That's why the colonel wants to find out if people are talking and, if they are, what they're saying.' My voice was surprisingly steady, though I could feel my heartbeat pulsing in my throat.

Heicho Han made a little twirl with his rifle and lowered it. 'Mirza was cooperating with us, that's true.'

I had guessed Mirza had been an informant and a collaborator. The kempeitai had established a network of informers to identify anti-Japanese locals. The informers were well paid and protected from random beatings and arrests since their loyalty was not in question.

'My uncle hated the British,' I continued quickly. 'He always said they treated us like dogs. Ask anybody. He had to serve them when they came to the shop, but he always sold them the low-class powdery rice. He wouldn't spy for them.'

'No difference to them. Pigs will eat anything,' Heicho Han said. 'Did your uncle know Mr Mirza reported him for being a traitor?'

'Of course not! He would have—' I stopped myself.

Heicho Han nodded. 'Exactly. Mirza had evidence that your uncle gave money to the fund set up to aid the British war effort. You didn't know?'

I shook my head.

'Mirza Ali Hasnain reported your uncle and your grandmother as undercover agents for the British.'

'That's impossible.'

'Your uncle must have found out somehow. He got so angry with Mirza that he killed him.'

'You don't know my uncle. He would have said something to Mirza's face in public. He would have told everybody, then gone to Mirza's front door and threatened to beat him up. He wouldn't have killed him in secret.'

But I wasn't sure. The upfront Uncle Chen of pre-war days was gone, replaced by a puppet doll that grinned and bowed like the rest of us, just to stay alive.

'We must punish someone for the murder,' Heicho Han said, 'or else the people will go around killing informers. They may come after you next. After they kill all the informers they will kill all the translators! There will be no more order. Everything we have done up till now to establish peace and order will be for nothing.'

I bowed and made to go past him to the gate. But he stepped sideways in front of me. 'In many ways, we are very alike, Su Lin,' he said. 'We have smart brains and we have ambitions.'

And he had a gun and a uniform, I thought. But I could tell he meant to flatter me and I tried to look flattered.

'You must tell me exactly what the colonel said. You must tell me exactly everything the colonel says to you. Hideki Tagawa is Colonel Fujiwara's rat. You cannot trust him to keep you safe,' Heicho Han said. 'I am the only one who can keep you safe.'

He put a hand on my shoulder and smiled. 'We are friends. If you trust me, I will try to help you. I will be your friend. But you must tell me everything. Do you understand?'

Was Heicho Han really interested in solving Mirza's murder? Because it had happened in his division and reflected badly on him? But that didn't mean anything. When it came to resolving problems, the Japanese prized speed over justice.

He was waiting for me to respond. I didn't know what to say so I bowed and said what was uppermost in my mind, 'Sir, forgive me. I desperately need to use the WC.'

Heicho Han finally let me go past him. It was the second time that day the lavatory excuse saved me. No matter what our station in life, humans are under the constant tyranny of needing to swallow and expel food to survive.

Inside the cubicle, I heard Heicho Han leave. He had a motorcycle with side-car, more prestigious than a bicycle but nothing compared to Hideki Tagawa's car.

Dr Shankar

———◆———

'Did you get the book? Do you like it?' was the first thing Hideki Tagawa asked when he turned up at seven forty-five the next morning. He had taken for granted that I would be ready and waiting outside our gate.

Getting into his car seemed almost natural now. 'Yes. Why did you send it to me?'

'It belonged to Mrs Maki's and my cousin.'

'Ryoko.'

He looked surprised. 'You know the name?'

'It was written on the inside cover of the book.'

'Ah. Yes. Of course. It is a good name. It means "wise child". We used to tease her and call her the Dragon because the characters sound like "dragon child". Poor Ryoko. Maybe we should not have. Names are important, don't you think?'

I couldn't think of anything to say to that.

'Ebisu is not a good name for you. I will call you Inori.'

'I don't need another name,' I said.

Hideki Tagawa seemed not to hear me. 'Inori means "prayers"

102

and is a beautiful girl's name. Living life as a prayer? That would suit you much better. If you ever decide to take a Japanese name, I will call you Inori. Usually a baby's name is announced at a celebratory dinner, the first ceremony of its life after it enters the world. Its name and the date are drawn in calligraphy. We have no such ceremony for adult children. So this book will have to do.'

He was a little mad, I thought, as I watched him take out his fountain pen and write in the front of the book before switching on the engine. Maybe we were all a little mad. It was the only way to survive in these mad times.

'Where are you taking me now?'

'You must see the autopsy results.'

He drove further east, and I waited outside as he went into the security-check building outside Changi Prison. The fence lining the compound was buffered with rolls of barbed wire and I was careful to keep my distance. No one paid any attention to me till Hideki Tagawa reappeared.

He had Le Froy's knack of blending into the background and not being noticed. It was a strange coincidence, especially since they were unusual-looking men. I remembered the way he had spoken of Le Froy and wondered if he had been studying my previous boss. He seemed to bear no grudge against Le Froy for branding him a spy. Perhaps if things worked out well – if I was still alive at the end of this – I would ask him.

But I forgot that after I followed him into the building.

'Dr Shankar!'

'Su Lin? Su Lin! Dear girl!'

I was thrilled to see Dr Shankar. We hadn't met for so long.

I ran into the room, completely forgetting Hideki Tagawa. 'I'm so glad you're all right! Have you heard from Parshanti?'

Dr Shankar was crouched by the table and got to his feet. He looked thinner, older and considerably greyer at the temples, but still himself.

I held out my hands to him and he took them in both of his. His eyes were wet with tears as he gazed at me.

'Su Lin. It's good to see you. You're even thinner than you were, poor girl, and you were always too thin. How is your leg? How is the pain in your back? You should be taking more calcium. But where to get . . . There isn't even enough rice. I hope your grandmother is well. What are you doing here?'

I had known Dr Shankar and his family for years. His daughter Parshanti had been my best friend ever since we'd met at the school for girls at the Mission Centre. Dr and Mrs Shankar, his Scottish wife, were my second family.

Though he was a qualified surgeon from the Edinburgh Medical School, Dr Shankar had never been able to practise in Singapore. The Westerners didn't trust an Indian doctor and the locals didn't trust Western medicine. But Dr Shankar had constructed braces to support and strengthen my polio-weakened leg, making it his personal challenge to enable me to walk without too much pain. And he had encouraged my dream – dead now – of going to university one day.

'Have you heard from Parshanti?' I asked again. 'Have they let you see Mrs Shankar? How is she?' The last I'd heard Mrs Shankar had been arrested for being a white woman, and Dr Shankar for being married to her. I glanced around, as though there might be some sign of Parshanti or Mrs Shankar.

Ridiculous, I know, but the delight of seeing him made me feel anything might be possible at that moment.

Of course they were not there. An old Indian woman sat on the floor holding a little boy with a large abscess on his leg. Some lint and a pair of scissors lay on a cloth on the stool next to her. Dr Shankar had been dressing the child's leg when we came in. I remembered the crowd of people in the corridor outside. They were all waiting to see him.

'What do you want?' After the first spontaneous flash of glad surprise at seeing me, he was now guarded and distant. 'As you can see, I am with a patient.' He might have been addressing a stranger on the street. Dr Shankar could not be rude. But he was clearly cautiously hostile. I understood. It was because I had come in with Hideki Tagawa.

Though he was treating patients in the prison clinic, he was practically a prisoner. I didn't know that he wasn't. But I was sure that if I could get a minute or two alone with him, I could talk to him as a friend and explain why I needed to know about Mirza's death. I was sure he would understand. Dr Shankar had always been a great help to Le Froy in the forensic department, since Dr Leask, the official pathologist, had disliked doing post-mortems.

'I can wait,' I said, 'or come back later.'

'Get out,' Hideki Tagawa told the old Indian woman, in English.

She shifted her grasp on the child, who started to kick and cry.

'No,' I said quickly. 'We'll wait. Please finish the dressing. Can I help you?'

Dr Shankar said something in Tamil to the woman. I could
tell he was telling her to wait, that he would come back to her.
But the woman did not intend to stay in the room with a
Japanese official. She picked up the struggling child and half
ran, half stumbled to the door, with him tangled in her sari.
When she opened the door, I saw that the corridor, so crowded
when we came in, was now empty.

'So. How can I help you?' Dr Shankar turned to Hideki
Tagawa.

'Show her the post-mortem report on the Mirza case.'

Dr Shankar glanced at me. 'Sir, you stressed that it was to be
kept secret. No matter what or who requested them.'

'I gave those orders. Don't try to be funny.'

Dr Shankar took his time in getting the file out of a box.
I remembered his immaculate office, how he maintained that
having things in order was the first step to putting people back
together. Now things were just laid out all over the place.

I went to his side.

'Don't get involved,' Dr Shankar said. He spoke in a quick,
low voice.

But I knew how sharp Hideki Tagawa's ears were and
answered clearly, 'Mr Mirza, who was killed yesterday night, was
my grandmother's neighbour. I'm just trying to find out what
happened.'

'They're trying to use you. Su Lin, this is not the time to
meddle and play detective. It's not safe.'

I was very aware it wasn't safe. But being alive in Singapore
wasn't safe.

'I'm not meddling. This wasn't my idea. They,' I nodded

towards Hideki Tagawa, 'asked me to work with them. I'm not bothering them.'

Dr Shankar shook his head. 'Here you are.'

The report he handed me was just one sheet of paper. I looked at it in disbelief. 'This is it?'

I remembered his previous autopsy reports. He had covered the birthmarks, moles, scars, even fungal infections and an ingrown toenail in painstaking detail. Not to mention the deceased's final meal and whether there was anything caught in their teeth or fingernails.

'Resources are limited.'

'I suppose I can't view the body?'

'Nothing to see. He was stabbed in the back with a blade. One stab through the heart. Fast. He was lucky . . . Is that all?' Dr Shankar asked Hideki Tagawa. 'I have work to do.' He didn't look at me.

For a moment I felt angry and humiliated that Dr Shankar didn't trust me because I was working for the enemy. Well, he was working for the Japanese too, wasn't he? Miserable as this room might be, it was better than being locked up in a cell like Uncle Chen was.

In that instant, I would have done a Madam Koh on him if I'd had the means to.

And in that instant I knew Dr Shankar was right not to trust me. I didn't trust myself. It was my own confused mess of feelings that I was projecting onto him. Hideki Tagawa must know about our friendship. He had done his research. This meeting had been set up to manipulate us.

'They have arrested Uncle Chen,' I said. 'If Mirza's murderer isn't found, it will be blamed on him. That's why I want to find out the truth.' I had to convey to him somehow that he could trust me with what he knew. 'You must have more than this.'

He unbent a little. 'It was not necessary to do more than a cursory autopsy. Cause of death was obvious. Besides, there are no resources to embalm bodies here.'

'But you can confirm the time of death?'

'Impossible to pinpoint. The body was outdoors, in warm weather. During the night, at least five hours before I examined the body.'

This man was a poor shadow of the Dr Shankar I had known, the Dr Shankar who had been so fascinated by uncovering strange modes of death and uncommon diseases. It was his curiosity and tireless work ethic that had drawn him and Le Froy into a close friendship.

I could understand how he felt, but Uncle Chen's life was at stake.

'A murder in Japanese-occupied Singapore isn't any less a murder than one in British-occupied Singapore,' I said. 'Mr Mirza had two daughters. He loved books and learning. Do you think it's right not to care who killed him just because the Japanese want to know? I thought you were a better man than that!'

I was trying to provoke him to anger, but Dr Shankar only straightened his lips in what might have been an echo of a smile.

'Clearly, I am less of a man than you think. Now, if you will excuse me, I have patients.'

'Patients? You're operating a clinic here?'

'He's treating his companions in the lock-up,' Hideki Tagawa said, 'some of our guards too, in fact. It was decided to give him a space to do his doctoring. But that is a privilege that can be withdrawn.'

Being allowed to work in these miserable surroundings was a privilege?

The room was small and smelt of bad meat, the worst stench coming from the row of bins by the door. Dr Shankar followed my glance. 'They are emptied once a week,' he said. 'I take them down to the disposal pit myself. You know how keen I am on physical exercise, and the guards are superstitious about touching discarded body parts. Mirza's remains are in there. But I wouldn't recommend trying to sort them out from the rest.'

I saw he meant to shock me. But I had calmed: I remembered the kind, wise man who had gone against everything in his society and everyone in his family to marry the woman he loved. And who had accepted me as a friend of his daughter and treated me as a daughter too.

If he was trying to push me away from him now, I knew it was for my own good. Or because something else was going on to which he didn't want attention drawn.

'Thank you,' I said, with my best attempt at affront or disgust. I would have done better if I had decided which to try first. 'Can I see the clothes he was wearing when he was brought in?'

'There may be danger of infection.' Dr Shankar raised his voice, speaking to Hideki Tagawa, who had stepped forward to take a look at the row of stinking bins. 'Contagion and infection.'

'I'm going to talk to his daughters.' I said. 'If I can tell them something about their father's death – for instance, that he died quickly and painlessly – they might be more willing to talk to me.'

'You can tell them that,' Dr Shankar said. 'But his daughters don't know anything useful. His clothes are supposed to go to the prisoners, but I doubt the prisoners will want them. Here.'

He handed me a cardboard box that was stained, damp and smelt like a dead rat in a clogged drain. 'What Mirza was brought in with.'

This drew Hideki Tagawa's attention and he abandoned the offal bins to join us. I looked around for a surface on which to open the box. Hideki Tagawa swept a box of bandages and ointments off a counter and I went over to it as Dr Shankar scrambled to pick up his supplies.

There were no gloves and there was nothing to protect the table surface. I carefully lifted out the contents of the box: a shirt and a sarong. A slight odour came from the cloth. But it was the smell of old, unhealthy sweat and body oils on unwashed cloth rather than the odour of death. The shirt was caked with dried blood. When I spread it out I saw what looked like an outline of a sprig of compound leaves stencilled in dark brown on the light cotton shirt. Some of the stalks were missing, as though they had been plucked off. Others remained, with only leaflets removed. On one, for example, there were only two racines, one with three leaflets on either side, the other with three on the left and four on the right.

Mr Mirza must have planned to meet someone: he would have been wearing an undershirt or a singlet at home alone on such a hot night.

'Were any tree branches found around him?'

'He was discovered in his garden. There were leaves and branches all around.'

'Can I see the weapon again?' I asked.

'You can see a photograph.' Hideki Tagawa had decided to find me amusing again. Apparently it was the proximity to dead bodies or Mirza's effects that made him uncomfortable. 'It's a dangerous weapon.'

'He would have died soon, anyway,' Dr Shankar said. He sounded as though it was an effort to produce the words. But his scientist-doctor side would not let him stay silent. 'He was riddled with cancer and heart disease. His liver was failing. His heart would have lasted another six months, a year at most. You can tell his daughters that.'

He was offering me a way to give them some comfort. But I wasn't sure I wanted to. The leaflets stencilled in blood on their father's shirt confirmed that the Mirza girls were lying.

Mirza's Office

The night before, I had lain on my thin mattress for hours listening to Ah Ma's wakeful breathing, both of us pretending to be asleep so there was no need to talk. So much had happened that day. What Shen Shen had told me about Mirza using and betraying her family ricocheted around in my head.

It was hard to reconcile that man with the Mirza I had been told about. The Mirza who had liked creating and solving codes, like I did. Languages, for instance, were just another code. I wondered about the Japanese children's book Hideki Tagawa had sent me. Was that some kind of code or test too?

Le Froy always said, 'Do everything you can do, then don't worry about what you can't.' Now it seemed there was nothing I could do except worry.

I hadn't realised I had fallen asleep till I woke out of a strange dream of trying to find my way home in a world where Singapore didn't exist. I had to choose between China, Japan and England. I had just decided to go to England, to let Le Froy know that I was all right, but suddenly Dr Shankar was there, blocking my way, warning me that I would destroy Le Froy's life as surely as my mother had destroyed my father's if I tried to find him.

The dream had come back to me when I met Dr Shankar. I was glad he was alive, but there was such a change in him, such a barrier between us. Until now, all I had hoped for was that everyone I knew and loved would lie low and stay safe until the war was over. Once peace came and there were no more stabbings and beheadings in the streets, whether Singapore remained in the Japanese Empire or returned to the British, I assumed things would go back to normal.

But the war was changing us. Now I knew that nothing would ever be the same again.

Colonel Fujiwara and Hideki Tagawa were trying to create a new normal, a system in which Japanese authorities sought justice for locals. Where murderers were tracked down and punished. Why was it more wrong to help the Japanese than the British?

'Good! Come!' Hideki Tagawa stopped the car with his usual grind and jerk and was halfway out before I realised we had stopped outside Chen Mansion. Some of Ah Ma's lodgers were bowing to him in their singlets and sarongs, looking terrified.

'Come where?'

'To talk to Mirza's daughters. Obviously.'

'Do they know we're on our way?'

'It is morning. It has been morning for some time.'

He left his car in front of Chen Mansion and we walked over to the Mirza house. I wondered if Hideki Tagawa was a member of a martial-arts cult that believed in early-morning exercise.

Probably not, or he would have been doing high kicks or twirling bamboo poles instead of terrifying the poor guard he found drowsing in the morning sun in front of the gate.

Neither of the girls was around when we got to the house, but the guards let us in without question. Hideki Tagawa left me in Mirza's office while he went to find out where they were.

Of course I looked around while waiting. And of course I started sorting and ordering the books and papers scattered everywhere. I couldn't help it. Mess makes me feel physically uncomfortable.

And that was when I found out what Heaven looked like. For me, at least.

I'd never thought much about it. I assumed the Western Heaven was full of missionaries and bureaucrats, white people with white beards and white robes sending the rest of us to Hell for swearing or speaking Malay or Chinese. And their Hell was probably the Chinese Heaven, run by bureaucratic minor gods taxing offerings of Hell money, oranges and joss sticks.

My idea of Heaven was Mirza Ali Hasnain's private office.

I could hear raised voices coming from elsewhere in the house but ignored them and lost myself in the work. Most of the books were not seriously damaged. Whoever had searched the room had shaken and dropped them. Some people hide money between the pages of their books. But since there was a safe I doubted Mirza had done that.

I fell in love with that room. Even given the state it was in. Not just because it smelt faintly of lemongrass and furniture polish and books. Not just because of the wooden bookshelves standing against three of its walls. Although some of the back planks had been knocked in, to check for hiding places, I started putting the books back on them, just to get them off the floor. Once upon a time someone had put this room together with love and respect for books, and that feeling was still in the room.

I had never seen so many books in one room before. It had to be three or four times larger than the Mission Centre library, where all the books were in English and at least half of them could be classified as Bible stories for children or 'improving tales for heathens'.

Mirza's books were in several different languages, and I didn't think any of them were 'improving tales'. On one shelf I stacked English, Arabic and French titles, and what I guessed were Russian and Dutch. From where they had been dropped, the books were classified by subject matter: history, poetry and mathematics. And there was a row of atlases, geographical papers and maps.

The shelf behind the enormous desk contained books on linguistics, codes and puzzles, and on the floor beside it stood the largest globe I had ever seen. It must have been three feet in diameter, set within a wooden frame on four wheels within which it rotated freely.

I had heard so many things about the dead man from so many different people. But among his books and dictionaries, his framed maps and that enormous globe, he came alive for me. Until that moment, I hadn't thought much about who he had been while he was alive. Or, rather, I'd imagined I knew what he was – an informer and a moneylender who had inherited riches from his family of pawnbrokers – and had never thought further about him.

Now, for the first time, I felt the full injustice of Mirza Ali Hasnain's murder. He had created this haven of knowledge and learning and had been ripped from it. Now, for the first time, I wanted to solve and avenge his death for him, regardless of any game the Japanese might be playing.

I only realised I was holding my breath when I felt dizzy. I exhaled and walked around the room. It was airy, because of the huge windows and high ceilings. There were the two comfortable chairs with a standing lamp between them, the only seats other than the chair behind the desk. It didn't look as though Mirza had entertained business visitors in there. He might have sat in one of the armchairs with a daughter, or the two girls might have sat there reading while he worked. The combination safe stood behind the chairs, its door ajar.

'My grandfather designed this house,' Safia Mirza said, startling me. 'Thanks for helping to clear up.'

'It's beautiful,' I said, though I hadn't seen most of it.

'It's old,' Safia made a gesture of dismissal, 'but my father designed this study. As you can see, he was very interested in his books. He wanted to write the history of these parts before he died.'

'Maybe you will complete it for him one day,' I said. I meant only to make polite conversation and was taken aback to see the flash of anger in her eyes.

'No. Never!'

'Miss Mirza?' Hideki Tagawa appeared in the passage behind her. I wondered how long he had been standing there.

Safia pointedly ignored him. 'Writing is not my thing. And I doubt my father would want me – or anyone else – poking around in his precious papers.'

'What was on those shelves?' I pointed to two empty ones behind the desk. There was nothing on the floor in front of them.

'The kempeitai took them. I don't know why. I think they were his crossword-puzzle books.' She threw a disdainful glance in Hideki Tagawa's direction. 'They probably thought he was working with codes and ciphers.'

'Your father did crossword puzzles?'

'He liked making them up. In multiple languages. You had to deduce from the clues what language the solution was in.'

'Golly.' I was impressed. Now I understood the many dictionaries and the alphabet grid on the desk. I had never understood why people did crossword puzzles any more than why they did jigsaws. You didn't come up with anything new, just unravelled an artificial complication. But I could totally understand the challenge of creating puzzles, putting together clues and encoding them.

'Did he use this too?' I held up the alphabet grid I had found slipped under the desktop blotter. It was a five-by-five grid hand-drawn on squared paper, except with twenty-five squares it could not cover all the letters in the alphabet. I saw that the Z was missing.

'Probably,' Safia said. 'Father loved codes, ciphers and cryptograms. The kempeitai took away all the charts he was working on just before he died. There were a lot of diagrams.'

'The stone codes were our property. Mirza was merely helping us with them,' Hideki Tagawa said. 'But some of his most recent papers are missing, also his account records and appointment books,' he added.

'Are you accusing us of taking them?' Safia asked sweetly.

'Things are misplaced,' Hideki Tagawa said. 'As long as they are found and returned, no harm done.'

'And if they are not found?'

'I wish I'd had a chance to try his multilingual crosswords,' I said. I didn't want Mirza's daughter to smart-mouth herself into a death sentence in front of me. 'Are they published in magazines?'

'No. It frustrated him no end. Father used to say that he was the only person who could truly appreciate how clever his clues were, and he couldn't appreciate them because he already knew the answers. He used to hide his puzzles in books so that he could come across them later, trying to catch himself off guard. But it never worked. He had the kind of brain that never forgot something once it had registered.'

'That's a gift.'

'He called it his curse,' Safia said. For a moment the mask slipped and her face twisted in memory and loss. 'He used to get bored and frustrated and he would drive our mother out of her mind because he wanted something new, something different, something out of the ordinary. She used to tell us that she had been so happy as a girl, and so happy to marry such a clever man. But that meant she was reminded continually of how stupid she was. She told my sister and me that she would do her best to find us stupid men for husbands because they would treat us better than clever ones.'

'Your father didn't treat your mother well?' I thought of angry relatives out for revenge. 'Did her family know about this?'

'Ah, my mother's family thought the world of my father. He took over their affairs completely when he married her and he helped them pay off their debts. If my mother dared to complain to them, they would have laughed at her.'

'So, your mother had nowhere to turn?'

But I had gone too far.

Safia shook her head. 'I don't know what stories you've been listening to, but my father didn't treat my mother badly. Not by any standards. He gave her a generous allowance and wasn't interested in taking any other wives. But he wasn't very interested in her either. She was a renowned beauty as a girl, the flower of her generation, she was called. That was why my father married her, even though she was from a local Indian-Persian family and everyone thought he would go back to Hadhramaut to find a bride. He liked to have the best of everything. Poor Mama. All she liked to talk about was who did the best embroidery and where to buy the best-crafted gold or silver bangles and necklaces. Father paid for whatever she wanted to buy. But he never told her she looked beautiful in her expensive clothes and jewellery. My mother was used to being admired by all who saw her, but her own husband barely noticed her.'

I tried to feel sorry for the late Mrs Mirza, but I couldn't. It sounded to me like she'd had a pretty good life. And I wasn't interested in embroidery or gold and silver trinkets either. Not when there were all these books and codes to play with.

A row of traditionally dyed ikat cotton shirts hung on a rail behind a curtain. Emergency formal wear to be pulled on over an undershirt for unexpected visitors, I guessed. The bulk of his wardrobe was probably elsewhere, but these were beautiful. Ikat fabric is patterned by resist dyeing: repeatedly shielding different parts of woven fabric from the dye to create intricate designs.

I looked around the room again, paying attention to more than the books this time. I noticed there was dust everywhere. Dust on the bookshelves, dust on the intricate frames encasing maps and beautiful geometric patterns. There were no photographs, but some quotations in English, French and what might have been Arabic.

There was much less dust on the desk. And almost none on the enormous globe.

'Father didn't like having anyone in the room to clean.' Safia had noticed where my eyes had gone. 'My mother used to say, "What will people think?" But Father never allowed visitors in here. In the old days, the maids were allowed to come and clean once a week, after he had locked away all his precious papers. But since the British left ...'

She didn't have to finish. Dusting in the morning was the least of your problems when you didn't know if you would be alive at night.

'They searched all the books. Do you know what they were looking for?' I asked.

'I don't think they knew. In the end, they took only his puzzle books and the charts he was working on for them.'

I looked at the large safe that stood empty with its door open.

'What did your men take from the safe?' I asked Hideki Tagawa.

'Mirza held money in several different currencies. And a selection of valuable items. We took them for assessment.'

'Will his family get them back?' I don't know where the courage of foolhardiness came from, but I heard a surprised giggle come from Safia.

'His family made their money as pawnbrokers. It would need to be assessed.'

I could tell Hideki Tagawa was amused and it made me more cross. What would the Mirza girls live on, supposing they survived the war, if their father's property was not returned?

'It doesn't matter, Su Lin.' Safia touched my arm lightly. It was the first time she had used my name. 'He is gone. Nothing you can do will bring him back.'

'But we can try to get justice for him.'

'You are taking this seriously, then,' Hideki Tagawa said. His face was a mask of calm, expressionless. But I knew enough of him to sense his amusement. It was in those darting snake eyes he was now fixing on me.

'I already agreed to try to help you find out who killed him,'

Hideki Tagawa shrugged elaborately as though to say agreement and commitment were two different things. And, yes, standing among the dead man's books, I felt totally committed.

But did I begin by accusing his daughters of lying?

'There's no point you going through all this twice with each of us. Nasima is upstairs. I'll go up and tell her to cover herself before coming down. Because of him.'

Mirza's Daughters

───◆───

S trictly speaking, the Mirza girls had not lied to me. Only to the kempeitai, which was a different matter. I decided not to take it personally.

After Nasima joined us, with just a loose scarf over her head, I told them what Dr Shankar had said about their father.

'So you're saying our father would have died within a year?'

We were in the dining room where the sisters sat side by side on two upright seats facing Hideki Tagawa and me across the table. The girls had their eyes cast modestly down, though Safia kept glancing around as though she was not used to sitting still.

'That's a medical estimate. And his health would have deteriorated drastically.'

'Doesn't that make it worse instead of better? He had so little time left. And even that was taken away from him!'

To my surprise, it was the religious Nasima who was more upset. Or maybe it wasn't surprising. What little I knew of Islam suggested sinners' souls were extracted in the most painful way while the righteous transitioned smoothly and easily to the afterlife.

'If someone stole a purse from you with five cents in it, wouldn't it hurt less than if the purse stolen from you contained fifty dollars?'

'Not if it was my last five cents!'

'You are right. I'm sorry.'

'Sorry for trying to give us comfort?' For the first time Nasima smiled at me. 'No. It is I who am sorry. Thank you for trying to help. But there is really nothing you, or anyone else, can do to help.'

We were speaking in English, which Hideki Tagawa could follow without trouble.

'What time did you find out your father was dead?'

No matter how much small-talk you pad a bombshell with, it's still a bombshell. I wanted to trigger it and rule out the sisters as quickly as possible.

Safia glanced at Hideki Tagawa before answering. He seemed content to leave things to me. 'Our father did not take his tea with us that morning. But it was not out of the ordinary when he was working on something. And he was working hard. At such times he worked day and night in this room. He locked the door to the hall and the door to the garden from the inside. We would bring his tea to him and knock on the door and he would open it. Usually Nasima. She would worry when she thought he wasn't eating or sleeping enough.'

Nasima was elegant and beautiful even in the shabby clothes she wore. She was clearly the elder sister, not because of anything she did, but because Safia deferred to her. I was surprised.

Not having had a sister myself, I wasn't sure how such relationships worked from the inside, but Safia deferred to her sister almost as a soldier might defer to a commanding officer.

And, yes, all the stories I had heard of Nasima Mirza's beauty were true. Even though she was not wearing any make-up to cover the dark shadows under her eyes, and in a pale grey long-sleeved dress, her mixed heritage gave her the kind of looks that appealed to both Asian and European men. Her apparent lack of concern over her appearance only added to it.

'But yesterday morning she knocked on the door and got no answer. She was afraid he might have fallen and hit his head, or had a seizure, like our mother. So she called the guard outside the gate to come in and break down the door. But Father wasn't in here.'

'When did you last see him?'

'When we went up to bed. That must have been around nine p.m.'

'How did you find out he was in the garden? Dead?'

'The guard went to check and found him . . .' Safia's voice wavered. Then she pulled herself together and bowed in Hideki Tagawa's direction. Her bow, like her manner, was perfectly proper, yet there was something mocking in both . . . almost as though she were acting the part of obsequious servant – and undercover spy. I recognised it because I felt that way myself.

'They – he – questioned us so many times already. I'm sure they can tell you more than we can. We're both still in shock.'

I remembered Safia was friends with Parshanti Shankar. Parshanti might have been my best friend but she and Safia had a lot more in common. Like Parshanti, Safia had been interested in Western fashions and music. Her mixed ancestry had given her shining dark hair with ivory skin and long-lashed green-black eyes. And those eyes were now looking at me with a mixture of suspicion and contempt.

All right, I might have imagined some of that. But it definitely wasn't affection and friendship I saw.

Maybe Safia was just frightened. In her position I would have been. Every time she spoke she glanced at her sister first. If she was hiding something, I wanted to find out what it was before I let Hideki Tagawa in on it.

I wondered what it had been like for them, growing up in this house, surrounded by all this culture and parents who encouraged them to read and learn. I thought they were lucky. And until the war they had been much luckier. Now, if you talked about luck, we were all in such a bog of bad luck that there was no competition.

'If you won't co-operate, we'll have to take you to the station for questioning,' Hideki Tagawa said.

'We are co-operating,' Safia said. 'If we're not telling you anything useful, it's because we don't know anything useful.'

Nasima remained silent, gazing at her fingers. She was surprisingly calm, given there were strangers in her house investigating the murder of her father.

'You say you last spoke to your father at nine o'clock. What did you talk about?'

'We said we were going up to bed.'

'And what did he say?'

Safia rolled her eyes. 'I don't remember. Whatever people say at such times. "Good night", I suppose.'

She was not a good liar. She would say anything other than the actual words. Nasima, sitting quietly detached, was more in control.

'Do you remember?' I asked her.

Nasima gave a gentle shrug, 'We didn't see him. He never liked to be disturbed when he was working, so we just called to him through the door.'

I saw Hideki Tagawa shake his head slightly. I didn't know why, but he didn't believe them either.

'I don't think they can tell us anything more. I want to look at Mr Mirza's study again,' I said.

'There is nothing more to be found there,' Hideki Tagawa said.

I could see he thought I was stalling because I wanted to look at all those books again. 'You wanted me to investigate this my way? This is my way.'

The girls looked at each other. 'So you don't need us any more?'

When I shook my head and Hideki Tagawa said nothing, they wasted no time in disappearing back upstairs.

Hideki Tagawa followed me into the office. Once the door was closed behind us, I walked over to the globe and beckoned him to me. Bending over it, as if I was pointing something out to him, I whispered, 'You have to let me talk to them alone. They won't say anything as long as you're around.'

I had already examined the room and found no spy-holes. But there was a foot-wide gap at the top of the walls for ventilation, and the office space extended upwards to the second-floor roof, with no rooms above it.

'They don't trust you either,' Hideki Tagawa said, matching my low tone. 'They know you're helping us, and they don't trust us, so why would they trust you?'

He was clearly frustrated. I don't think he thought either of Mirza's daughters had murdered their father, or he would have taken them in for questioning. But he was finding their behaviour strange. Why weren't they more upset? Why didn't they cry and demand revenge? And he believed they were lying.

'It's hard for girls to talk together when there's a man around.'

I guessed a Japanese man would be as uncomfortable as a Chinese when it came to female company, unless the woman in question was a mother, grandmother or prostitute.

'There are things I can't bring up in front of you. They will be too conscious of you listening to speak openly.' I hoped that a mixture of my awkwardness and male vanity would work in my favour. 'I want to ask them about boyfriends, for example, and find out what kind of men are attractive to them. Just give me half an hour. If I get any information, it will be worth it. If not, you will only have wasted half an hour.'

'If you learn anything—'

'If I learn anything relevant to their father's murder I will tell you. But I'm sure you don't want to hear female gossip about boyfriends.'

'There is no guarantee they will tell you anything.'

'Trust me.' I put a finger to my lips and stepped away from him.

From the desk I picked up a heavy brass paperweight and brought it down with a hard thump on top of the leather-bound dictionary. At the same time I gave a desperate little cry of pain such as a girl might give when she is punched hard on the head, and fell – carefully: I didn't want to rip my dress – pushing the desk chair so that it fell with a loud clatter. I made enough noise to be heard inside the house, but not enough to reach the sentries outside.

Hideki Tagawa watched me in amazement. His mouth opened as he moved to help me up, but I put my finger to my lips again and he remained silent. I was watching the door and he turned to it too. It took less than ten seconds.

The door slammed open and both girls were there, Safia in the lead, making her way towards where Hideki Tagawa stood over me. Nasima followed more slowly and much better equipped. She was carrying a small deadly dagger as though she knew how to use it. It was a beautiful piece, with a jewelled handle and wavy blade. But it was a weapon, not an ornament.

As I had guessed, given the design of the house, most of what went on in one room could be heard in the corridor and probably upstairs. If the girls had rooms on the floor above, they had been able to hear most of what happened in Mirza's office downstairs, which probably explained why Mirza had held his private meetings outside.

They had heard what was going on in the office and I had learned they were willing to risk arrest to help me.

'Just give me thirty minutes,' I said. 'It will help all of us.'

Hideki Tagawa didn't like it, but I saw he was impressed by my ploy. 'You will tell me what you find out.'

'If it is relevant to the murder,' I said.

Hideki Tagawa left the room and closed the door behind him.

For a moment I thought Nasima was going to follow him. The cold contempt in the look she gave me made my insides twist with guilt and I wouldn't have been surprised if she had used her dagger on me. I would probably have deserved it.

'Wait. Please,' I said. 'Just give me thirty minutes. I know you're lying about the time your father died. Just tell me why. If I can, I will clear you of suspicion. And then I will go away and not bother you again, if that's what you want.'

'Thirty minutes?' Safia Mirza glanced at her sister. 'It can't hurt. After all, we don't know anything. Why do you say we're lying?'

She was nervous and talking too much. Nasima looked at her fingers and said nothing. But she stayed.

'Are you familiar with the mimosa tree? There are several in your garden.'

'What? Why are you talking about trees? Have you gone crazy?' Safia was overreacting. Again, she turned to her sister. Nasima, beautifully impassive, said nothing.

'The most interesting thing about the mimosa tree is that its leaflets open during the day and close at night. I saw your father's clothes at the mortuary. He had a mimosa branch with him when he died. And the leaflets were still open. That means he died some time in the afternoon, when the sun was still in the sky. You couldn't have spoken to him at nine o'clock.'

'There are so many trees in the garden. What makes you think it was the mimosa? Some leaflets stay open for days after the branches are cut down,' Nasima asked conversationally.

'I saw the shirt your father was wearing when he died. The leaf pattern on the shirt was smudged. But only slightly.

It showed that the blood had already clotted when he was found. The pattern on his shirt – where it had pressed against blood-soaked grass, then where the closed branch brushed against almost dried blood – shows someone discovered your father's body, turned him over, saw the branch and pulled it out from under him.'

Neither girl spoke. They reminded me of two suspicious cats, watching and waiting to see what I was going to pull out of my bag next.

'You lied about seeing your father alive that night. He was dead long before dark. I'm not saying you killed your father. I'm not even saying you know who killed your father. But I want to know why you're lying about talking to him shortly before you went to bed. Unless you went to bed in the middle of the day, you're lying.'

'You think you know so much,' Safia said. 'You don't know anything!'

'I'm trying to find out what I don't know,' I said. 'Why don't you want them to find out who killed your father? What difference does the time of his death make?'

'They're only going to make a big show of searching until everybody forgets,' Safia said.

'Even if they find his killer, it won't bring Father back,' Nasima said.

My thirty minutes, measured by the clock on the wall, were ticking by loudly. I looked around the room in frustration. Maybe because of the children's book Hideki Tagawa had sent me yesterday, I spotted some I hadn't noticed before on the lowest shelf by the door.

'Your father kept children's books? From his childhood?'

'Not his childhood.' To my surprise it was Nasima who volunteered this. 'Some are stories Safia and I loved when we were children. Father always gave us books, even though we were girls and most of his relatives said it was a waste of time to teach us to read. He made sure we had a good education. Languages, poetry, mathematics . . . He never had books of his own when he was growing up. That was why he always bought us books.'

'And some were our mother's,' Safia said. She seemed glad of the change of subject. 'Our mother never had books when she was growing up either. Her family was more traditional and didn't believe in educating daughters. It was Father who encouraged her to learn to read. When she was expecting us, he bought her children's books. To encourage her to read to her sons when they were born, he said. And even though we were girls, he helped her learn enough to teach us.'

This showed yet another side of Mirza.

'That's nice,' I said. It was a lame word but the best I could come up with. 'I really mean it. It's the nicest thing I've ever heard of a father doing for his daughters or a man for his wife.'

Nasima smiled. Safia cried.

'You love books too, don't you?' Nasima said. 'I've heard about you. You're the girl who should have been put down a well but might end up running this island.'

'What?' I looked at her blankly.

This time she relented enough to laugh. 'Dr Shankar,' she explained. 'He treated us as children, and he talked about his daughter's best friend. We were quite isolated here, so any titbit of information was welcome. We used to ask him all kinds of questions about you and Parshanti.'

I hadn't realised Dr Shankar knew Mr Mirza.

'Then why didn't Dr Shankar tell your father he was sick?'

'We haven't seen him, or anybody, really, since the Fall.'

'Why are you working for the Japanese police?' Safia blurted out accusingly.

'I only want to find out who killed your father.'

'You are working for the Japanese police,' Safia repeated, as though I had not spoken. 'Why?'

Well, two could play at that game.

'Why don't you want to know who killed your father?'

'Why do you care? It's none of your business.'

'Let's have some music,' Nasima said, standing up. 'We can talk in the schoolroom.'

In the Schoolroom

———◆———

The schoolroom, where the girls had had their lessons growing up, was on the ground floor at the back of the house. It was comparatively small and no inch of space was wasted. The single bed in one corner, covered with a counterpane, cushions and books, clearly served as a sofa. A small upright piano stood in another corner. There were two small chairs, and a few tons of books and portfolios occupied the shelves and tables, and were stacked on the floor.

They had an electrified American 78-rpm record player. To my surprise a Japanese song started playing. '"Sendo Kawaiya" by Kikutaro Takahashi,' Safia said. She turned the music up much higher than I found comfortable. 'It should keep your Japanese friend and his men happy for a while. That and Masao Fujiwara – no relation to the colonel, before you ask. Why did you decide to become a collaborator?'

'I am not a collaborator,' I said. 'There are many different ways of fighting for the survival of our people.'

Much later, Nasima told me it was the way I said 'our people' that persuaded her to give me a chance.

'What are you really after?' Nasima asked me. 'What are you trying to do?'

'If I don't find out who killed your father, they will kill my uncle,' I said. But I was distracted by a new question. 'Did your father know you were listening in on meetings in his office?'

'It was his idea,' Safia said. 'He said it would show us how difficult it is to run a business, any kind of business. Of course, that was before the Japanese time and all this.' She made a vague gesture around the room as though its shabbiness spoke for the situation we were living in.

'Did your father also meet with Hideki Tagawa? The man who brought me here?'

Nasima seemed confused.

'You must have seen him from upstairs.'

'They all look the same from above,' Nasima said. 'If Father didn't want us to listen in, he would take his visitors for a walk in the garden. Then, after the Japanese came, when he was meeting people he didn't want to be seen with, he would tell them to go round to the back gate where there's no guard. The Japanese think it's a big secret, but of course we knew. Everybody knew. When we still had servants, they would use the secret gate. They even put down a plank over the drain to make it easier to cross.'

'He got more secretive when he started working with the Japanese,' Nasima said. 'He didn't want us to know anything that might get us into trouble. That's why all the windows on this side of the house have shades nailed in – so that from upstairs we can't see who he's walking in the garden with.'

'I thought it was for modesty,' I said, 'I thought gardeners or something . . .'

'Then it would make more sense to cover the windows on the street side of the house,' Nasima said. 'Father was not that conservative. When our mother was alive, he would make her go out with him to meet clients, even though she felt uncomfortable about it.'

This seemed to remind her I had lost both my parents too, and she touched my arm. 'Remember, Su Lin, when this worldly life comes to an end, our lives continue in another form. Death is the gateway to the afterlife and predetermined by God. We should not grieve over deaths we cannot undo but live the best we can.'

Nasima's words irritated her sister, who fidgeted and said, 'You wanted to ask us questions. What sort of questions? Why don't you just come out and ask us, "Did either of you kill your father?" And we'll say, "No, we didn't." Then you ask, "Does either of you know who killed your father?" We'll say, "No, we don't," and that settles it.'

'It may settle it for you,' I agreed, 'but, as Mr Tagawa told you, I am here to investigate who killed your father. And that is no way to do it. What if I wanted to ask whether your father had any enemies before the war?'

I stopped because Safia was laughing. I didn't think I had said anything funny. Nasima didn't seem surprised. Safia looked like a girl who was always laughing. Current circumstances had dampened her but the laughter was there, waiting to burst out sooner or later, no matter how feeble the trigger.

'If you knew anything about our father, you would have grasped that any number of people hated him and would have been glad to see him dead. Even before the war. It wasn't all his fault, of course. Sometimes people just hate you if they think you're doing better than they are. Or just because you're different from them. If our father was a night-soil collector, they would probably have ignored him. But because he was successful and rich and worked with powerful people, they hated him and called him a devil and a manipulator.'

'What people?" I asked.

'You know – Chinese people.' Safia stopped herself. Now she looked awkward. She glanced at her sister but Nasima was studying her fingers again.

I wasn't offended. It was a perfectly reasonable thing for her to say.

Besides, we Chinese are highly skilled at discriminating against others. Or, rather, we are very good at discriminating. Children are warned that, if they are naughty, the Malay and Indian bogeymen or the ang moh witch women will catch them and take them away. When there aren't enough others to discriminate against, we discriminate against each other: Hokkien versus Teochew, and Straits-born versus 'pure' Cantonese or Shanghainese. When even that is taken away, it's boys versus girls, first wives versus concubines and so on.

But all this is mostly to keep in practice, like athletes practise fencing or boxing. People support different sides in long-running inter-family feuds just as Westerners support their sports teams and Japanese their martial-arts schools. I had always taken it for granted.

But Safia had been brought up differently. For one thing, she had probably been taught a great deal more about propriety and civilised manners. For another, she had grown up as a minority race. No matter how superior you may feel when you have been raised with money and power, there is constant tension when you are surrounded by people who look different from you, when you don't recognise yourself in the faces of the people looking at you.

I was aware of that because my great friend Parshanti Shankar grew up with Indian-Scots features in a sea of Malay and Chinese faces, and I had my polio-withered leg. Parshanti's beauty had not helped her fit in any more than my intelligence made up for my limp.

'I'm sorry,' Safia said. 'I didn't mean that.'

'Don't be,' I said. 'And I do mean it.'

'I swear to you,' Nasima said, 'that neither of us caused our father's death. Do you think we wouldn't have told them? Even them? With his body lying goodness knows where, still unburied? What more do you want from us?'

'I want to know if there is any truth to the stories I've heard about you,' I said. 'I don't mean to offend you but you can tell me what is gossip and what is true.'

'Gossip can be true,' Safia observed flippantly.

'I heard you had a boyfriend who was killed at the Bukit Timah battle.' I hadn't really believed this story, which had come from Shen Shen via Ah Ma.

I was sorry I hadn't phrased it more tactfully because she gasped and her face crumpled.

'Not her boyfriend.' Nasima addressed her sister as well as me. 'Ghufran was a friend of the whole family. He was only one of many who died at Bukit Timah. Father cried when we heard the news.'

She made clear that, whatever Ghufran and Safia might have meant to each other, it was not to be discussed now.

'And I heard that you were both angry with your father because he would not let you go to university or even finish school. And that you,' to Nasima, 'didn't approve of your father drinking alcohol.'

'It was Mother who stopped our schooling, once our female cycles started. Father would have let us study. He wanted us to. But Mother was afraid that if we continued it would be impossible to find us husbands.'

They saw my surprise and Safia managed a shaky smile. 'Father wasn't the monster people say he was. He was interested in psychology and sociology. That's why he was so interested in studying the Japanese and British. Yes, many local people may have resented him for being Muslim and for being rich. But for years he gave money to hospitals. And he always donated to the temple-food kitchens as well as to the mosques. There was no reason for any of them to kill him.'

'He was working for the Japanese,' I said.

'Because he didn't want to register us to work in a Japanese factory. And he said he worked better sitting at his desk than standing at a conveyor-belt.'

When the Japanese reopened the factories and needed workers, it was announced that every household had to send at least one member to work for them. The former tenant farmers and shopkeepers staying at Chen Mansion had registered, so we were all right. But Mirza had no sons and would not have wanted his daughters working for them.

'He helped the Japanese with translations because it was

something he could do,' Nasima said. 'He thought that would satisfy them.'

'Could the Japanese have killed him?'

I saw they had already considered this. Their only surprise was hearing me mention it.

'What makes you say that?' Nasima asked carefully.

'I'm just considering all possibilities.'

'The Japanese soldiers came even before we knew he was dead,' Safia said. 'That man you came with – Tagawa – he did. They were looking for something and they took his papers and his books – even things that had nothing to do with what he was working on for them.' Her voice trembled. 'I hate them! I hate all this!' At least she had the presence of mind to scream softly.

Of course she was upset. I wanted to scream too. But if I allowed the despair and misery inside me to surface, I wouldn't be able to control it. I would go mad, ranting and crying, like the woman wandering and wailing in the pineapple plantation carrying the bodies of her dead children, begging them to come back to life to avenge their murdered father.

But I couldn't afford to go mad until after I had done what I could for Uncle Chen – and found out what had become of Le Froy. And Parshanti. And my colleagues and friends from the Detective Shack. And Dr Leask. And Shen Shen's brothers. After that, I didn't care what happened to me. Maybe that showed I'd already gone mad without realising it.

I would press on until I could indulge in madness. I seized on the name Safia had mentioned. 'You think Hideki Tagawa had something to do with your father's death?'

'He's one of the men Father used to have meetings with, in

his office at first, then out in the garden. I don't like him. I don't like the way he looks at us and everything here. I can tell he hates us.'

'I don't believe Tagawa killed our father,' Nasima said. 'If it was him, he would have shot Father in front of us after telling everybody what he was going to do. After making sure Father knew he was going to die.'

'I think so too,' I said. Stabbing a man in the back didn't sound like something Hideki Tagawa would have done. But how well did I know him? Years ago, Le Froy had called him one of the most dangerous men in Asia.

But I couldn't let myself be distracted. And my time was running out.

'I don't just know you lied about the time your father died. I know that someone – maybe one of you – found him and pulled a branch out from under him. The smudge on his shirt shows the blood had clotted but was not dry. Then someone went out through the garden door. It was padlocked because one of you pulled the chain through and locked it on returning. But the door itself wasn't locked. Your father always locked it automatically, even when he had a visitor in the garden with him. He might have locked the door without putting on the padlock, but he would not have put on the padlock without locking the door.'

'Oh, so now you think you know our father better than we do,' Safia said. But there was no conviction in her sneer.

I saw she had known about it. But that she hadn't touched her father's body. Did that mean Nasima had found him? Or had Safia been with someone else? I couldn't read Nasima's feelings.

'I just want to know who might have had reason to silence your father. I'm not trying to get him or you or anyone he was working with into trouble. I want to find out who killed him. I don't believe you did.'

'My father was an egotistical, egocentric and arrogant man,' Nasima said. 'He could be rude and selfish and difficult to live with because of his vanity and impatience. But my mother was married to him for over twenty-five years and some of those were happy. She was not educated, but she was not a stupid woman, Miss Chen. And while she was alive, I believe he was happy, an indulgent husband and father.'

'But he changed after he learned the Australians were responsible for Operation Jaywick,' Safia said.

Operation Jaywick

———

Hideki Tagawa rapped on the door, 'Thirty minutes over! What are you doing in there?'

Something in his voice suggested he had been shouting for some time and was on the verge of doing something terrible to the locked door – and probably to us once he got through it. We hadn't heard him with the music so loud.

The good thing was, even with his super eavesdropping skills, he wouldn't have been able to hear us either.

'You locked the door?'

'Automatic,' Nasima made a key-turning gesture, 'like my father.'

I spoke fast. Hideki Tagawa was still banging on the door. 'You went out? After you found your father dead? Why?'

'I was at the Alexander Road mosque the day the Japanese took over Alexander Hospital. I told my father we saw them killing the doctors who tried to surrender. Sometimes I go to the mosque and help prepare female bodies for burial. They are washed up on every tide and there are never enough people to help. Islam teaches us to be merciful to the entire world and all in it, not just Muslims. My father didn't like it. He was worried for me, but he didn't stop me.

'He knew I didn't like him working for the Japanese. He said he was doing what he had to for us to survive. It was his only purpose. He was lonely after our mother died and went into a depression. Surviving the war gave him purpose.'

I thought of the stories that the war had been provoked by warmongers in nations that had built up armies and arms factories for the Great War and needed another to keep profits coming in. In that instant I understood how either Safia or Nasima could have killed their father, and not out of anger. Killing the man Mirza had become might have been the only way to save the father they had lost.

The record reached its end again. Safia restarted it. Hideki Tagawa's voice, which had paused in the sudden silence, rose over the music. Again.

'Operation Jaywick?' I asked quickly. 'How did that change him?'

We all jumped as the door burst open, slamming back against the wall. Hideki Tagawa crossed the room and tore the record off the turntable with a horrible scratching sound. He stood by the machine, glaring at us.

Nasima continued talking to me. Her soft voice was clear in the sudden silence. 'Initially, after the attack on the port, Father deduced the Australians couldn't have come so far unnoticed, so it had to have been locals who attacked the Japanese battleships. This was what led to the Double Tenth killings. That was bad enough. But then, as more and more information came in and he decoded some intercepted messages, he told the Japanese that Australian Z Special Unit commandos were responsible for the attack. The commandos came into Singapore waters using a captured Japanese fishing boat, then approached the warships in three collapsible canoes and attached time-delay explosive mines to their hulls.

'After that Father fell into a depression. Especially when the Japanese believed local civilians had given the Australians information and stepped up their interrogations, tortures and killings. He changed. Wouldn't go out. Wouldn't let us go out. We thought we were going to be locked up for ever until the day he suddenly demanded breakfast and ate a huge meal.'

Nasima glanced at Hideki Tagawa. He looked grim, but he was listening.

'That was after Father got interested in finding out all the details of how the Australians had carried out Operation Jaywick. He said it took them forty-eight days, from the time they left Western Australia to when they returned on the nineteenth of October. But what he really got worked up about was how the commandos had chosen those warships and transport ships to attack. He had lists of all the ships that had been bombed and he wanted to know where in the harbour they had been docked, how many men were on board, where they had come from and so on. For a long time, the Japanese wouldn't tell him.' She turned to Hideki Tagawa. 'I suppose they thought he was trying to get information out of them to plan another attack.

'Anyway, he managed to get some details on all the wrecked ships. He was particularly interested in the timing of the explosions and the last ship that had been attacked. It was difficult, because he couldn't get anyone to confirm the details, but eventually he managed to talk to a couple of Japanese soldiers who had helped to put out the fires.'

'When was that?' Hideki Tagawa demanded. 'Who were the soldiers? They had no business talking to him without authorisation.'

'Two days before he died. He was so excited. He didn't sleep that night. He was poring over his documents and his timing charts and his maps.'

'Where are they now?'

'The Japanese soldiers took them all.' She gave Hideki Tagawa another hard stare. 'They wanted to know who Father had talked to, but of course we didn't know. We heard them talking in Japanese, but we couldn't understand.'

'They didn't speak very good Japanese,' Safia put in, 'but that just makes it harder rather than easier to understand.'

'Then he called for breakfast. But, really, he ate enough for lunch and dinner. It wasn't easy finding enough food for him. We were so relieved. We thought the worst was over. He told us to stay in the house for one more day and sent the front-gate guard off with a message.'

'To whom?'

'To Colonel Fujiwara,' Hideki Tagawa said. 'You told us you didn't know what your father wanted to tell us.'

'We don't. He didn't tell us anything. But we could see he was very excited. He had some big news.'

'He can't have,' Hideki Tagawa said. 'At the time, he hadn't left the house for three days. And no one else had been in or out with any information. Mirza was bluffing. He must have been cooking up more lies.'

'He hadn't left the house in three days?' I echoed.

'It was for his own protection. He asked for protection,' Hideki Tagawa said. 'We had someone watching the house, both the gate and the secret door. He was afraid of being targeted by local vigilantes. Like your uncle.'

'If you sent men to protect him, why didn't they see who came in and killed him?'

'Father became nervous of the men sent to guard him after Operation Jaywick,' Nasima said. 'It threw the Japanese off balance not only because of the damage to their ships but because of the blow to their supposedly impregnable defences.'

'What else was Mr Mirza working on for you?' I asked Hideki Tagawa.

'Who told you he was working on anything else?'

It was hard not to look exasperated. 'If Mr Mirza was only working on solving the stone codes, you wouldn't be wondering what he wanted to tell you.'

'That is none of your concern.'

'He was trying to help the Japanese find some missing stuff. He said it was probably misplaced rather than stolen,' Safia said, 'but that they would still have to blame someone for it.'

Safia clearly meant to blame Hideki Tagawa for the blaming. Even if she was right, I thought she was being reckless.

'There were some missing supplies,' Hideki Tagawa admitted. 'Of some value. Mirza believed he could track them down.'

'Supplies?' My mind went uncomfortably to the black market. Soldiers like Formosa Boy weren't above a little back-door trading. 'Like food?'

'Like contributions to the war effort,' Safia said.

Oh. 'Contributions to the war effort' covered everything the Japanese took from museums, temples and the homes of wealthy individuals.

'Here are the codes Mirza was working on.' Hideki Tagawa gave me a paper binder. Inside I found carbon copies of crudely drawn circles on grids. For some reason, the papers reminded me of the grid I had seen on Mirza's desk.

'The alphabet grid in his office. Did he make that to work on the codes? When did he draw it up?'

The girls looked blank.

'Doesn't seem likely,' Hideki Tagawa said. 'The copies were made on hiragana writing sheets but all attempts to map the original stone arrangements on a grid failed.'

'These are black and white. Were the stones all the same colours? And was there always a tree branch? Was it stuck in upright or pointing in a particular direction? Did it always point in the same direction or different ones? Was it always the same size? From the same kind of tree?'

'Mirza asked the same thing.' I saw curiosity and new respect in Tagawa's eyes. 'In fact he asked for the branches, but the men hadn't kept any. Damned fools, the lot of them. There were different numbers of stones. You can see for yourself in the diagrams. The number of stones in each is indicated, but there is no pattern as far as we can tell. As for what kind of tree they came from, what difference would that make?'

'Did you ever see your father with mimosa branches?'

Safia looked at me strangely. 'He preferred his trees dead and turned into books.'

'When he died he was holding a branch of the mimosa tree.'

'He wasn't holding anything when he died.' Safia shook her head. 'At least, not that they told us about. The Japanese soldiers came and cordoned off the area. They searched it and took away everything suspicious, even the stones lining the path. They wouldn't even let us go and collect the mangoes that fell in the night. Can you imagine the waste? Of course the monkeys and squirrels ate them. Even their guards can't keep out the monkeys!'

Safia was suddenly talking too much. She was lying. And the hand she raised to brush back her hair shook slightly.

Was she covering up for whoever had killed her father? Had she killed her father after all?

I saw Safia was waiting for me to say something so that she could contradict it. I waited too. If there's one thing I'm good at, it's waiting for someone else to make the first move. You learn how to do that if you grow up as a girl in a Taoist-Buddhist family that worships money. Everything you say will be shot down at first. But if you persist long enough, when they've forgotten it came from you, your point will be considered.

'What about the globe in his office?' I was sure that enormous globe meant something. Had he had an escape plan? Had the Japanese learned Mirza was sending money and 'war-effort contributions' to the Middle East, hoping to buy a new life there?

'It's nothing to do with any of this,' Nasima said. 'Father had had that for years. He had it made after he and our mother went on Hajj. It shows the three holy cities.'

That was that, then. But I still felt certain I was missing something.

Their grief seemed genuine but I could tell the Mirza girls were lying. Still, I didn't think they had killed their father.

'I want to see Mr Mirza's notes about Operation Jaywick.'

Anything to do with Japanese sea traffic was at the highest level of top secret, so I doubted I would get the information. But at least I hadn't been shot on the spot for requesting it. After all, Hideki Tagawa had trusted me with copies of the stone codes.

But he hadn't stopped the Mirza girls talking about Operation Jaywick: he wanted to find out what they knew. What more was there to know? The Aussies had meant well and done well. But the locals had been punished for something they hadn't done. Unless there was something more to Operation Jaywick than Australian marines sneaking in and sabotaging seven Japanese ships.

One Dead Soldier

◆

This time, on leaving, I was allowed to walk back to Chen Mansion on my own. Hideki Tagawa stayed at the Mirza house. The last I saw, he was examining the books I had re-shelved. I wished I'd thought of spelling out some kind of message with the first letters of authors' names or different-coloured spines.

I meant to shut myself up in Ah Ma's bedroom and go through the stone codes papers. Anyone can devise difficult, 'unbreakable' codes. The problem is creating codes simple enough to be understood by the intended recipients with access to a shared key. If there was one, it would have to be something both parties had access to – like the Bible, for example. Or a copy of a newspaper on a certain day. But given that the only English-language paper available was the Syonan-To, and it was unlikely that prisoners or rebels could get hold of copies, that was unlikely.

When I reached Chen Mansion, it immediately became clear that I wasn't going to get any time to myself. Formosa Boy was waiting on the front drive looking highly upset.

'Please. Tell your relatives to let me go inside the house. I need to stay near to your Guan Yin statue so that it can protect me from the Buddha statue!'

The Guan Yin figure stood just inside the front door. Frightened faces of people camping in the front room were staring unwelcomingly at him.

The Guan Yin figure might already have saved my family once.

When the first batch of soldiers came round to inspect the neighbourhood after the Fall of Singapore, their Japanese captain had stopped on seeing it. He and his men bowed and paid their respects to 'Kannon'. And they had left our house without stealing, smashing or stabbing anything or anyone. Since then, other soldiers had stopped by to touch the statue for luck and protection, and I had learned that Kannon, the Japanese incarnation of Guan Yin, was the goddess of mercy and protection for them too.

'Have some tea. Made with pepper-plant leaves but not bad. Calming and cooling.' Ah Ma appeared and offered him a cup. I suspected it also contained some of the soothing leaves that lulled Little Ling back to sleep after nightmares.

How long had Formosa Boy been carrying on in this way? What would the other soldiers think if they saw him looking so upset? A fat tear rolled down his cheek. Worse, if they knew we had seen him crying on our property?

Formosa Boy shook his head. 'Tea is no good. I must go inside and stay there. Or the Buddha statue will kill me too.'

'What Buddha statue?' I wondered if the other soldiers were playing a trick on him.

'I cannot say. It is secret. If I say I must kill myself!' He was really scared, ignoring Ah Ma's tea and the soothing noises she was murmuring to him. 'Please let me stay here! I will work for you!'

'What happened?' I asked Shen Shen, as she joined us.

'Didn't you hear? A soldier was found dead with his truck.'

'Well, what does it have to do with him?' Then I noticed that Shen Shen was full of suppressed excitement. 'And why are you so happy?'

'Next thing you know they'll be rounding people up again,' Ah Ma grumbled. 'Another death in our district. And this time a Japanese soldier!'

'Yes – but this time they can't blame Liang.' Uncle Chen's name was Tou Liang. 'He's in prison so he can't have done it!'

I couldn't blame Shen Shen for hoping. 'They think this soldier was killed by the same people who killed Mirza?' I wondered if the soldier had killed himself. I doubted any locals would have found a lowly soldier boy worth the risk of killing him, given the likely reprisals. Though that didn't mean we would escape them.

'Since you are working with the Japanese, can't you tell them they were killed by the same person? That's all you have to say. Find some clues and show them!'

It seemed to me that the only thing worse than Shen Shen thinking I was good for nothing was Shen Shen thinking I could pull off something as crazy as that with the Japanese. 'What happened to the soldier? Was he stabbed too?'

Shen Shen jerked her head towards Formosa Boy. I turned to him.

Formosa Boy's smudged face, and the fact that the plate of tapioca on the ground next to him had not been touched, showed how upset he was.

More than anything I wanted to shut myself up in Ah Ma's bedroom to look through the papers Hideki Tagawa had passed to me but he was such a lump of misery it would have been like kicking a hurt dog. Besides, he was so huge that I might not have been able to move him to get into the house.

'Sorry, Big Sister. I am in your way.'

I had meant to find a polite way to get rid of him. I would have too, if he hadn't called me Big Sister.

I sat next to him, on the folder of carbon copies, though Formosa Boy had shown no interest in it. 'It isn't the worst thing.'

'Yes, it is! I knew Ree! We were on the same team! He was my friend!'

'The worst thing is if the dead soldier is our Formosa Boy,' I said. 'But Formosa Boy is alive, so it is not the worst thing.'

That got a small smile out of him.

'What happened to your friend?'

'I don't know. They found the truck on the roadside and he was outside it, dead. They say he must have stopped to vomit, then couldn't drive on. And he died.'

'Maybe he was sick?'

'He wasn't. He wanted me to meet them last night. He said if I joined them they could get more money. I was scared, but he said if we stuck together it would be all right. I was supposed to go with them. I didn't know who they were going to see. But yesterday I found a nest of saltwater alligator eggs with sixty eggs. I took thirty and brought them here for Ah Ma and forgot all about it.'

We had feasted well last night. Though we were close enough to the breakwater to harvest shellfish and small fish, eggs were a precious rarity. The alligator eggs had a slightly fishy taste that went well with the clams and crabs. Formosa Boy had been hailed for his find. He had eaten enough for two or three men and slept the night under our porch, blissfully drunk on food.

But that wasn't the point.

'What were you going to do? Who were they going to get more money from? Were you going to blackmail somebody?'

'I don't know. He didn't tell me. But he said we would get more than the official offer.'

I knew the Japanese paid locals for information. I hadn't known their soldiers got paid for it too. But blackmail was still a possibility.

'Whoever he tried to get money from might have killed him. You must have some idea who it was, if he thought you could help them.'

'I think he was killed by the spirits!' Formosa Boy wailed, upset again. 'We were warned not to make the spirits angry! But Ree said that was just to scare us. He laughed at me because I was scared. But now he is dead. It must have been the spirits!'

Many of the Japanese soldier-conscripts were no more than boys.

'Was Ree also from Formosa?'

'He was Korean.'

'You were supposed to meet him and other men? Do you know who the others are?'

Formosa Boy nodded. 'At first we were all in the same unit. But they were transferred out except for me. They said it was a sure thing. We would get money and we would get them to send us home. Then we wouldn't have to be scared of Hideki Tagawa any more.'

Bells rang in my head. 'Did you work for Hideki Tagawa?'

'Yes. No. Sort of. Only for a short while but not really.'

That was a mess even for Formosa Boy.

'What exactly did you do for Hideki Tagawa? Was Ree working for him too?'

'I – I don't know. Yes, I think so. Heicho Han told us to work for him and watch him. I'm so stupid. I don't know anything. I shouldn't have forgotten to meet him.'

'If you had, you might be dead too. Tell me. How long did you work for Hideki Tagawa?'

'Not long. Maybe a week, ten days. He needed somebody to drive him around. But his drivers didn't last long. The one before me, he lasted less than a day. In the end Hideki Tagawa said he wanted to drive himself. I was scared. Because when he gets angry he shouts and throws things. What if he got angry when he was driving and started banging into people and chickens?'

'So he's violent. Has he ever hurt anybody?' That was a stupid question to ask about a Japanese intelligence officer, 'Has he ever hurt any of his assistants? Any soldiers?'

'He whacks himself on the head sometimes. And I saw him slam his fist into the wall shouting, "Stupid! Stupid! Stupid!" but I think he was yelling at himself, not the wall. He thinks very fast. So, compared to him, I'm even more stupid than most other people.'

'But he never actually attacked you?'

'No. He just threatened to throw me into the river and run

155

a tram over me.' Surprisingly, Formosa Boy grinned. 'After he'd finished shouting, he'd call me useless, give me a cigarette and tell me to take the rest of the day off.'

'Did you see or hear anything while you were working for Hideki Tagawa that might be worth information money?'

'Hideki Tagawa didn't kill him.' Formosa Boy answered the question I hadn't put into words. 'It was the spirits. It was the Buddha spirit taking revenge.'

Bad Luck and Spirits

◆

Analysing their behaviour, preferences and conscious or unconscious rules had helped me get along with lady missionaries and British officials. Now I was trying to figure out how best to survive the Japanese. But in all the years I'd known her, I hadn't managed to figure out Shen Shen.

Uncle Chen and Shen Shen had longed for a child for years. It was more than a personal matter. Uncle Chen was my grandmother's only surviving son, my father having died before I was three years old. That, and the polio that left me alive but crippled, had labelled me 'bad luck' where Shen Shen's superstitious family were concerned. For years, her mother blamed me for everything that went wrong, from pigs not breeding to Shen Shen not bearing sons. That was why I had moved out to stay in their shophouse when Shen Shen had kept a pregnancy past six months. She and my uncle had moved back into Chen Mansion and the baby was born there.

After our last encounter I expected to find Shen Shen still angry with me. Instead, she was all smiles. When I went into the kitchen the next morning, I found her and Ah Ma cooing over a large, unripe cempedak. Growing up, I'd hated it. It had sticky sap that was so hard to get off skin and clothes. And its belly had so many compartments, all crammed with seeds. But I had to admit it was good food. Its drive to produce offspring fed ours to stay alive.

'Where did that come from?'

'Shen Shen found it.'

It would ripen in the kitchen, safe from birds and monkeys. There were not many trees left because the British had hated the smell of ripe cempedak even more than that of durian. Le Froy once told me that most Europeans thought it stank of stale urine. Remembering the expression on his face made me smile. He, who could face the worst smells of the opium dens and night-soil trucks, winced at the smell of a fruit.

Le Froy had come to love cempedak, just as he had learned to appreciate and enjoy durian. I had been stopping myself thinking about him – or Uncle Chen or Parshanti or the other people who had disappeared – but the memories inspired by that smelly fruit ambushed me. Why were so many of my memories tied to food? And would we ever eat together again?

'What's wrong?' Ah Ma looked closely at me.

'Nothing. It's a big one. Where did you find it?'

'I went out to get paku pakis and saw it.' Paku pakis was the wild fern that grew abundantly around streams and drains and supplemented most of our meals. 'It was high up in the tree but I climbed up and cut it down. At first I thought of leaving it and coming back with a ladder, but what if somebody else had found it first? Once it's ripe all the monkeys and crows will come!'

Sweaty from exertion, Shen Shen was triumphant. The forested area was a trove of food if you knew where to look for it. Even if you didn't, you just had to follow the monkeys and the birds and you'd find papayas, guavas, cempedak, chikus, mangoes and rambutans in season.

'When it's ripe I'll fry strips of it for Little Ling. That was my favourite when I was her age. Have you ever eaten fried cempedak? And we'll keep the seeds for boiling. Your uncle loves boiled cempedak seeds.'

Her face twisted. Much as mine had, I suspect. And most likely for the same reason.

'Your uncle will be all right,' Shen Shen said firmly, more to herself than to me. 'He will come back to us. Maybe not in time to eat this cempedak but he will come back.'

I was surprised. Had Shen Shen changed overnight? I wouldn't have been surprised if she blamed me for Uncle Chen's detention. Out of habit, if nothing else. I wondered if Ah Ma had said something to her. She said something now: 'You are the mother of a Chen child. Whatever happens to my son, you will always be a Chen wife or widow. Like me.'

Shen Shen nodded. She was no longer the scared daughter of a superstitious family. She was a Chen woman. The Chens did whatever they had to do to survive. And we had survived better than Shen Shen's relations. So far, anyway.

'Wait. Sit down. I will make you something to eat,' Shen Shen told me.

But I had heard a motorcycle stopping on the driveway in front of the house. Only the Japanese would come straight in rather than calling from the gate.

The empty clam bucket was a good excuse. 'I'm going out,' I said, picking it up.

At the side of the house, I saw Heicho Han taking his bayonet out of his side-car. It was part of his outfit. I didn't think he meant to use it. But it was too early in the day to be polite in Japanese, so I cut across the chicken run and climbed over the breakwater to the beach. Unlike the barrier around Mirza's house, with its glass shards, this low granite wall was purely to protect us against nature. A freak wave at high tide, especially when there was a full moon, could soak and kill a growing crop of tomatoes or chillies.

It was less than ten minutes later that I heard, 'Hey! Come back! What are you doing out there?'

I was not happy to see Heicho Han coming after me. I wanted to process thoughts that had nothing to do with him and the Japanese. No – my thoughts had everything to do with the Japanese. But I had to be polite to him, because keeping him happy was part of our survival strategy. He liked to drop hints that, as district commander, he was the only one keeping us safe. But right then, if he killed every single one of us, I wouldn't have cared. At least it would have stopped my twisting thoughts.

'Hey! Stop! Your feet are getting wet. Are you mad? Come back!'

I smiled and bowed, to hide how much I resented him crowding me like that. I held up the clam bucket to show him I was collecting food. Living in occupied Singapore was hard on the face muscles because you had to smile when you bowed to the Japanese or you would be accused of 'bad attitude'. I think that was the greatest difference between life after the Fall and under the British: they had never bothered to look at our faces.

'Come back! It's dangerous!'

I stayed where I was. I could use the excuse that I hadn't been able to hear him over the distance and the sea breeze. Heicho Han was an impatient man. I doubted he would wait for me for long.

I bent back to my work. The sea was still retreating and the gentle waves were warm. Then I saw him awkwardly walking towards me, trying to maintain his dignity in boots that were sinking into the soggy seabed.

'Let me help you back to safety.'

I wiped off my smile, in case he thought I was laughing at him.

'Easier if you take off your shoes,' I suggested. I had left my slippers above the tide line and was ankle-deep in the fresh, cool mud.

But he would not. Anyway, they were boots, not shoes. And he was a soldier, who was clearly unfamiliar with walking on that surface. He looked pretty disgusted but he continued until he reached me.

I wondered who cleaned his boots.

Beach

———◆———

'What are you doing?' Heicho Han had been polite to me since he saw me driven home by Hideki Tagawa instead of being dragged into a truck, my wrists locked in barbed wire.

'Looking for clams. There are lala and tua tows here.'

I needed more than the handful I had found so far. Formosa Boy loved Ah Ma's stir-fried clams with wild ginger or her home-preserved sambal chilli. I wanted to question him again about the murderous Buddha spirit he was so afraid of. Heicho Han wouldn't approve of his men's fears.

'You don't have a net,' Heicho Han said. 'How are you going to catch them?'

'I don't need a net.' I put a finger to my lips. 'Ssh. You just need to keep quiet. Then when you hear a hissing sound the clams are squirting. Look for little holes in the mud and you'll find clams underneath.'

'You can't eat what you dig out of the mud. It's dirty!'

'We'll soak them in fresh seawater back in the house before cooking.'

'In that bucket?'

'No. They'll drown in a bucket! We use a tray and put in just enough water to cover them. You can see each one sticking out its tube to breathe and using it to expel sand. The water gets dirty very fast. We keep changing the water until it stays clean. And then the clams are ready to be cooked!'

I had learned all that as a child, when clam hunting was a game that meant a special dinner treat. Now it struck me that we were keeping the clams alive only to be eaten later. Like the Japanese were doing with us, perhaps.

I shook myself. I was being ridiculous. There's an old wives' tale that clams get plumper and more plentiful after bad shipwrecks. These days they were probably juicier and tastier because of all the bodies the Japanese had dumped in the sea.

'Didn't you catch fish and prawns when you were a child?'

'I'm from the mountains,' Heicho Han said. 'I don't know about the sea.'

I didn't hush him again. If he wanted to talk, he would talk. I squatted and scraped my hand through the surface layer of mud. Yes, there were the hard shells.

Heicho Han remained standing. Every time he moved, his boots muddied the water, making it difficult to see. But clams don't move very fast. I put my little trophies in my bucket.

'I never saw the sea until I joined the army. I joined the Japanese Army because there was no other work at home and because I had no family left alive. My parents, my grandparents, all gone. I thought, if the Japanese were going to force everybody to join up, I might as well go straight away and get a higher rank, right? I decided that the best thing I could do for my ancestors was to survive. So now I'm here. I have a good position and I'm going to do well and get rich.'

Was he telling me his life story? Why? I made listening sounds as I filled my bucket. Maybe the man was lonely. Given Heicho Han's Japanese pronunciation (already mocked by Colonel Fujiwara) I didn't think his chances of advancement within the Japanese Army were very good. But maybe he had other plans.

'It was hard growing up in Korea under the Japanese. I hate the damn Japanese. I hate the damn army. I hate the damn rich people, always showing off. I hate the damn poor people, always asking for things. Han was a good name in the old days, but now it means "injustice". All we get now, under the Japanese, is injustice. I only joined the Japanese Army to stay alive and save lives,' he said. 'I think you are doing the same thing. I can see that in you.'

What was that? I pretended to study a dead clam intently, then turned to toss it far out to sea without answering.

'We are both smart and survivors and can help each other,' he said. 'I warned you about that lying rat Hideki Tagawa, didn't I?'

He wasn't the only one. It seemed to me that everyone was warning me against Hideki Tagawa. It was almost enough to make me trust the man. I've never been very good at going along with majority opinions.

I straightened my knees and stood up, even though my bucket was barely half full. I was tired of listening to him. 'Why are you telling me this?' I tried to sound curious rather than condemnatory. Heicho Han was still the enemy in charge.

'Don't worry. I won't pass on the lies Rat Face has been telling about you. Nobody in your family needs to know. We are both outcasts. We must help each other stay alive through the war.'

I looked blankly at him. I wasn't acting. I really didn't understand what he wanted from me.

Heicho Han lowered his voice, even though, where we were, no one could hear us.

'Did you know that Colonel Fat Belly sent Rat Face Tagawa to see Mirza at his house the day he died? Rat Face reported back that Mirza was not there. But if Rat Face knew he was expected and he found the garden gate was locked, surely he would have gone round to the front of the house.'

Of course he would have. No man could have got over that wall if the door was locked. And even if Mirza had refused to see him, Hideki Tagawa would have made the guard in front of the house let him in. He would have seen Mirza, whether dead or alive.

Safia Mirza said her father had had an argument with a Japanese man the day before he died. If that had been Hideki Tagawa, had he come back to finish the argument once and for all? Then had he returned with his men to ransack Mirza's office, to make sure the dead man had left no trace of evidence?

'I must tell you. I have no choice.' Heicho Han jolted me out of my thoughts when he put a hand on my shoulder.

'Sorry, what?' I bent to refresh the water in my pail, dislodging his hand.

'Rat Face Tagawa wants everyone to believe the locals killed Mirza for being an informer. He doesn't want people to think the Japanese also had reason to kill him. Mirza took money and gave false information, making them look stupid. Worse than that, Mirza had blackmail material on Colonel Fat Belly. Why do you think he got away with so many things?

'And Rat Face Tagawa! He is the worst. You cannot trust him! Rat Face Tagawa must have stolen Mirza's information. That's why the colonel lets him do whatever he wants. Everyone knows that man has done terrible things. He just barges in everywhere and throws his weight around. And now he is taking you as his local woman, but he is not even paying you. He is making the office pay for you.'

I started to correct him, to tell him what Hideki Tagawa had really said and what our arrangement was, even though it was none of his business. But Heicho Han was still talking,

'Your face is quite pretty,' he said. 'If only you were not crooked, you could look quite good. Also, you are too short and your skin is too dark for real beauty. And you should cut your hair more stylishly and dress better. You locals don't know how to make yourselves look good. But if you can take a photograph showing only your face, people might call you pretty.'

I was one of the few unlucky – or maybe lucky – girls who had never flirted with British and Australian soldiers or local boys. But I recognised the overture because I had watched young men angling for my friend Parshanti's attention since she'd turned fourteen or fifteen. Some had been as awkward at flirting as this man standing in the mud in his boots.

In other circumstances I suppose I should have been flattered. Or, rather, if I had been any other female I would probably have been flattered. Heicho Han was tall for an Asian man. In fact, he was probably as tall as most of Parshanti's

British and Australian admirers. He had a muscular build and an almost pretty face …

I knew I could do worse. And I was determined to do much, much worse.

In the old days, soldiers gave local girls imported chocolate and lipsticks to persuade them to 'walk out' with them. 'Walk out' usually meant a film, a meal and an hour together in a rented room. The inside information Heicho Han offered showed he knew me better than I'd realised. Or maybe he had as little dating experience as I did.

'So. What do you say?'

I heard his exasperation. Luckily for me, Heicho Han expected a girl like me to be overwhelmed by a gift like him.

I looked at him as though he was too good to be true, and said, 'Sorry? What?'

'We team up. Partners. You help me, I help you. I am good at business. I am better than your uncle at making profits. It will be good for your family.'

Moving my lame leg in the mud, my toes felt more clams, but for once I let them be.

'But there must be give and take. So, tell me what else the colonel said to you. What is he asking you to do?'

'He asked me to talk to Mirza's daughters. But they didn't know anything.' I dipped the edge of my bucket of clams and swirled fresh seawater in, then started to walk back up to the tideline.

'And Operation Jaywick, what did he say about that? Did he ask you to track down the workers who were at the port that night?'

That might be a good idea, I thought.

'He said only that Mirza may have given them false information. Were you there that night? Did you see anything?'

'That is no business of yours!' Heicho Han snarled, suddenly angry. 'Did they tell you to question me? Stop lying and tell me!'

My brain was too overloaded for me to feel scared. We had reached the shore by now. I rinsed my feet with water from the bucket and put on my slippers. 'They asked if any goods missing from the damaged ships had appeared in the local market. But I don't even know what was on the ships, so I couldn't help them. I thought you might know, if you were there.'

Ignoring his anger worked, just like it worked with a toddler throwing a tantrum.

'Why would I be there? The port is in the Central District. I am in charge of East District 221.'

'Checking on who was there that night is a good idea. You should suggest it. Maybe they will put you in charge of doing it.'

'Oh. Okay. Here.' He handed me a piece of paper. 'I was going to leave it at the house if I didn't see you. But since I wrote it, you might as well take it. It will help you to remember my points.'

It was a marriage proposal, written in English, with spelling and grammar errors. It was the first and last I was likely to get. Even if the war ended tomorrow, most of the men in my generation were already dead. I should probably have felt sentimental. Instead I was struggling hard not to laugh. Seriously struggling. I knew laughing could cost me my life but it was bursting out of me. Stress was exploding in hysteria. My shoulders were shaking and I put my fist in my mouth, biting down hard on it. The sounds that came out didn't sound like laughter, but what else could they have been?

Heicho Han didn't seem put out. In fact, he seemed satisfied. 'Women are too emotional about romance,' he said. 'When all this is over, I will explain to you how we will live. If you are willing to learn, we can work together very well.'

The way he strode up to the breakwater, scraping mud from his damp boots, and climbed over without a glance back at me, limping with my bucket, made me suspect any courting was already over. If I ever write the story of my life in a book, one thing I know for sure it will not be is a romance.

I was Singaporean, after all. For us, marriage was not a romantic but a practical arrangement. I only existed because my ancestors had been practical enough to survive famine, make the sea journey out to this island and find mates. Love and romance applied only to white people.

I turned back to my clams. In difficult times there is always work. It was what Le Froy would do. I wished I could tell him about Heicho Han's proposal. How he would laugh—

Heicho Han had stopped. He turned and looked at me and, for a moment, I thought he was coming back. No! Anything but that, please! My mad fit of laughter had passed and I felt exhausted.

But instead he stopped and saluted another figure on the other side of the breakwater.

It was Hideki Tagawa.

Hideki Tagawa's Real Quest

———◆———

'I won't go into the house,' Hideki Tagawa said. 'I just came to see if you— Have you had a chance to look at the stone-pattern diagrams?'

A muscle twitched in his cheek and he seemed tense. Still reeling from Heicho Han's offer, I wondered, absurdly, if I was about to receive my second marriage proposal from a Japanese man.

My grandmother always said that, as a child, I made straight for whatever I was warned against: 'Don't taste that curry, it's too hot'; 'Stay away from that dog, it bites.' Maybe her warnings had triggered curiosity rather than fear.

Now I knew I ought to be afraid of Hideki Tagawa. But I wanted to hear what he had to say. Maybe it was his obsession with Le Froy that made me think he couldn't be all bad. Or maybe I was just hoping to hear something about Le Froy.

After climbing clumsily over, I rested the clam bucket on top of the breakwater and pressed my knuckles into the back of my hip.

'What's wrong?' he asked.

'Nothing.' But Hideki Tagawa looked even more worried, so I explained, 'Sometimes it hurts when I walk. No,' I said, as he tried to ease me to sit on the grass. 'It also hurts when I sit too much.' With my lopsided gait and crooked hip, I must have strained my back, standing while Heicho Han talked.

'Here. Just stand here, facing the breakwater. Put your arms and weight on it.'

Standing behind me, he put his fingers on my back. I had heard stories of the terrible things Japanese soldiers did to female bodies, but I had never heard of one using pressure points to ease back pain. I had heard of acupressure, of course, but thought it was something only rich people wasted money on.

'The study of pressure points started with a Japanese samurai.' Hideki Tagawa's fingers traced out and massaged tense cords of pain in my lower back. 'Minamoto no Yoshimitsu – he was a distant ancestor, if you believe the family stories – used to dissect the bodies of his men after battles to understand muscle and nerve connections and triggers. I know it hurts, but bear with it. It will be worth it.'

'It feels like there's a stone in the back of my hip,' I said.

'Your muscles have been knotted up for so long they've forgotten how to release. The parts of your body without good blood flow will get a build-up of waste, and sickness will develop.'

'I never knew the samurai understood healing.'

'If you want to fight long battles you have to learn to heal fast. Besides, healing was only a side product to the art of disabling and killing using pressure points and nerve meridians. With the use of knives and guns, not many take the trouble to learn the old ways. But sometimes it is useful to understand which points in the human body can heal or harm when pressed at the right angle.'

I thought he was talking to distract me. If so, it worked. I was definitely interested. 'You can kill people just by pressing these points with your fingers?'

'Try standing straight again.'

'It's much better.' I stretched upright. If I sounded shocked, it was because I was. 'Can you show me how to do that?'

'How to kill people with your fingers?'

'No – but I wouldn't mind learning how to do that too.'

'Of course you wouldn't!'

He was laughing at me, I saw. I couldn't help laughing too. Learning to kill was just part of learning to survive, wasn't it?

'Here. Some of the food that Tagawa-san brought. Ah Ma said you'd better eat outside. The kitchen is so hot and crowded.' Shen Shen bowed low to him, then put her cane basket on the stone table further along the breakwater and started unpacking it. Formosa Boy had followed her, carrying a laden tray.

'You brought food?'

'I am only the messenger. The food is from Colonel Fujiwara.'

They laid it on our folded banana-leaf dishes. The situation was clear: my family could not eat in the kitchen without inviting Hideki Tagawa to join them. But if he went into the kitchen, they could not sit down or eat in his presence. Neither could I imagine him sitting at the stained wooden table on one of the wobbling stools.

It was real food. In addition to the white steamed rice, mushrooms and tofu in sauce that Colonel Fujiwara had sent, there was one of the charcoal-roasted wild chickens Formosa Boy had brought last night. He had a real talent for scavenging and hunting food. If only the Japanese had set him to sourcing provisions rather than manning guard posts, they would have been much better off. But I wasn't going to say so. Now Formosa Boy ate in the kitchen with the rest of my family. In a strange way it felt as though he belonged there more than I did.

'It's been years since I ate this well,' Hideki Tagawa said. 'The latest in modern food is powdered milk and powdered egg and powdered protein. Supposed to be scientifically good for us and faster to prepare. But this is real food.'

The smart thing would have been to enjoy it – after all, I had real chicken, slivers of mushroom, peanuts and fragrant white rice in front of me – while trying to get on this man's good side.

'Why are you here?' I demanded.

'Why am I here in Singapore? Why am I here in your garden?'

'Both.'

'I came to ask for your help . . . An organisation, *Kin no Yuri*, Golden Lily, is intended to finance Japan's war effort. This is secret even to most in the Japanese military. It is run under the direct guidance of Prince Yasuhito Chichibu, Emperor Hirohito's brother.'

I looked at Hideki Tagawa, remembering how the soldiers had bowed to him. 'You are not a brother of the . . . or are you the prince?'

'Oh, no. Connected, yes. We are from a completely different line. But just as honourable. An old samurai family.'

His cousin Mrs Maki had told me that. She had been very proud of her family.

'Of course, these days, some call us yakuza and gangsters. When there is no war, it is very difficult for warriors to survive. Yet for the sake of the nation, they must.'

'So you're here to get money for the war.'

'The contributions are collected by others.'

In other words, they were looted or 'confiscated'.

'I arrange transport of the contributions. Singapore – Syonan – is the collection point of the region. From here they are transported to the Philippines and from there to the Japanese Home Islands.'

He stopped, as though he had explained everything.

'Why are you telling me this? And why were you investigating Operation Jaywick?' My thoughts sped on. 'Mirza told you the local resistance staged that attack, so you punished them. But what about the Australians? If they sent men into the harbour to plant bombs on your ships, why not into Mirza's garden to kill him?'

'Some contributions were getting . . . lost. Such things are always difficult to keep track of. You need a man on the ground.'

'Mirza was your man on the ground?'

'According to his reports over the last months, pirates running a smuggling operation had been caught. A massive amount of goods and narcotics had been confiscated. They were to go to the Golden Lily project. Also gold and silver objects, including a giant solid-gold Buddha, brought down from Malaya and Siam. They disappeared after reaching Singapore harbour.'

'The Buddha was one of the "donated" treasures?'

'It was not taken on my watch.'

'Because you don't take religious objects?' I knew very well they did.

'Because even if it was taken as a tribute, it didn't end up among the prince's tributes. Again.'

'Again?'

'Along with stacked crates of gold bullion. That was why I was here before Operation Jaywick. They could only have been taken by someone who knew of the Golden Lily project.'

'Mirza knew.'

'And he knew he was under suspicion. He was under pressure to expose the leak or take the blame.'

'So you think he found out who stole your gold and they killed him? Where did he get his information from? Did he just make it up? Because you said yourself that some of the information he gave you was false. Like about locals bombing your ships.'

'Some of it was deduced. Based on insufficient data.'

'What do you want me to do?'

'Deduce,' Hideki Tagawa said, as though it was the most obvious thing in the world. 'Based on the additional information around Mirza's death. Find out who killed him and who stole the Golden Lily tributes.'

He looked at me expectantly. 'What would your Chief Inspector Le Froy do?'

Ah, yes. But Hideki Tagawa's Le Froy fixation might be all that was keeping Uncle Chen alive. 'He would ask questions, I guess.'

'So ask questions.'

'No. Those stone arrangements your men found, I've seen only line diagrams. Were they always the same kind of stones? Always the same colour?'

'Stones are stone-coloured. Why would that matter?'

'If they used different colours, it could be like morse code.'

He nodded. 'That was looked into. No.'

'Can I ask you a personal question too?'

He inclined his head.

'Did you find Mirza dead in the garden that day? Is that why you knew the girls were lying about talking to their father at night?'

'Is that your only question?' Hideki Tagawa asked. He wasn't going to answer it, and he didn't give me a chance to ask anything else. 'Why was Heicho Han here?'

'Maybe he likes the sea air.'

Hideki Tagawa snorted. 'Be careful. Your mother also fell for unsuitable men.'

At least, that was what I thought he said, which didn't make any sense. While I didn't know anything about my long-dead mother, her people could not have considered my father 'unsuitable'.

Dream Solutions

◆

Ever since the Japanese came, I'd had nightmares when I managed to sleep. But I couldn't complain. They weren't as bad as what was happening to some people in real life.

I must have been thinking of what Hideki Tagawa said because I dreamed he was telling my mother she was in love with an unsuitable man. I couldn't see her face, but she was wearing a kimono patterned with mimosa leaflets stencilled in blood, like on Mirza's shirt: there were different numbers of leaflets on different sprigs.

And then I knew. I turned to look for Le Froy to tell him but he wasn't there.

I was angry with the British for letting us down, angry with Le Froy. The British had promised we would be part of the British Empire for ever and now they were gone. They had abandoned us to fight their own battles. Just like my parents had abandoned me by dying.

Then Hideki Tagawa was there, telling me to hold out my hands. I did so and he emptied a bag of gold coins into my palms.

'You are one of us. We'll look after you,' he said.

But the gold coins slipped through my hands and fell, digging themselves into the ground, like clams, and disappearing.

Solving the Code

———◆———

Le Froy was alive. The thought came up every time I wasn't monitoring my mind.

First thing this morning, for instance, I woke out of a turbulent dream of which I could only remember snatches. Yet I felt strangely comforted and I knew I had been dreaming of him. I couldn't be in love with him because I didn't believe in Western romantic love. Love at first glance. Love as your eyes meet or you hear his voice. If they really believed in such things, Westerners would be stricter about segregating the sexes than the most orthodox Muslims.

'What's wrong?' Ah Ma came in. She always said she had an instinct for change – changes in mood included. 'Why are you still in bed?'

'Why not?'

'Shen Shen made peanut biscuit. I cut some for you.'

'I'm not hungry.'

'Just eat it.'

The tapioca-peanut square was surprisingly tasty. 'How did Shen Shen get sugar?'

'Cane. The children collected yesterday. They ate most of it but we boiled some for sugar.'

Ah Ma left the tin dish with me. I stayed in her bedroom and went through the papers Hideki Tagawa had brought me. And I thought of the man who had made these careful notations.

I tried to remember everything about Mirza and his office. People leave clues to themselves in their surroundings. And when I discovered who Mirza had been I would find the key to untangling what he had been doing.

Le Froy had always reminded us to collect as many facts as possible when investigating a crime, rather than fixing on a culprit and working backwards to find out how he or she had done it.

Le Froy had stressed, 'Ask yourself questions. It is the formulating of the questions as much as the answers that lead to solutions.' He said I helped him most when I was asking questions, not trying to answer them, because he considered himself handicapped by his English education, despite his years in the east.

Well, that didn't help me now. I had so many questions, all of them leading to more questions and no answers.

I remembered how he would cover desks, the floor, with scribbled pieces of paper, shifting and studying possible links between them. Le Froy had said I was helpful to him when it came to that: most of the time we don't know what we don't know, since our brains fill in gaps with what we expect to see.

I lay on my mat moving pieces around in my head and testing possible links, then testing the truth of the links, of the pieces. Hideki Tagawa: why had he involved me? Had he really known my mother or was that another story? I told myself I didn't care, that having a grandmother like Ah Ma more than made up for any number of dead mothers.

I thought about the hand-drawn alphabet grid I had seen on Mirza's desk, its twenty-five squares, the missing Z. Was that a clue? Of course, that depended on what you were using the grid for. If it hadn't looked so recent I might have thought he'd used it to teach his daughters the alphabet.

Mirza had worked his crossword puzzles and poetry in the two comfortable armchairs under the floor lamp. He had done his work at the desk. If the grid had had anything to do with his crosswords it would not have been on his desk. But what work would require an alphabet grid with a missing Z? It had to do with his helping the Japanese figure out the codes that the resistance and the PoWs were using.

I studied the grid. I compared it with the patterns of stones Hideki Tagawa had given me. I tried different permutations, different alignments . . . Nothing. I remembered Le Froy saying that a code was useless unless both parties understood it. He had been warning me against over-sophisticated ciphers. Something simple was best. And codes that depended on a reference key, like a verse in the Bible or a column of a newspaper, were useless unless both parties had access to the key. And given that the PoWs were shut up in Changi Prison behind barbed wire, and the resistance movement was in the jungles up north . . .

It was unlikely that whoever had passed the messages between the two groups had a camera. Had they stopped to sketch the positions of stones as the Japanese soldiers had?

I didn't think it likely. But there had to be a message in the stones. Or why would anyone have gone to the trouble of reaching through the fence to pile them up?

Could they have arranged for there to be messengers outside the fence? As some kind of signal to the prisoners inside? None of the villagers living around the area had admitted to knowing anything. What was surprising was that none had reported anyone for carrying messages, despite the rewards the Japanese offered. Either they really knew nothing, or loyalty was stronger in the kampong than it was in the city.

My thoughts went back to my dream. Le Froy had been in my dream, drawing something in the sand. I sensed his urgency and frustration. He was trying to show me something and I couldn't see it.

Instinct told me I was close. I trust my instinct on such things. This has nothing to do with the supernatural: our bodies are always sensing things we can't put into words, like remembered smells and temperature, the moisture of the wind. All the subtle signals link up until we feel impelled in a certain direction or distrust of an individual. Some say it is our guardian spirits watching over us, but I don't see why I should trust spiritual advisers any more than colonial overlords. I prefer to believe it is our own senses, far more powerful than we are aware of.

I thought about Mirza Ali Hasnain.

On the last day of his life, Mirza had gone into his garden and cut branches off the mimosa tree. He had not been interested in gardening. He had paid so little attention to the trees and tools in the garden that he had left a mess in the shed after he had looked for the tree trimmer. Given the precision with which he arranged his books, something big must have been on his mind.

Why? He hadn't brought the branches into the house. What had he been examining them for? I had thought he must have been bored. Some people pluck petals off flowers, which makes less sense than plucking feathers off chickens. But if he had gone out of his way to find the tree trimmer and cut down those branches, he must have had a good reason.

Yes, he had been meeting someone in the garden – the man who had killed him. But he had been killed with a mimosa branch in his hand. If he was meeting someone to pass on vital information or to blackmail them, why had Mirza cut down those branches?

A flowering sprig might have indicated something to do with a woman. But I could remember only leaves, the symmetrical leaflets on tiny parallel stalks . . . but some of the leaflets had been missing, hadn't they?

I closed my eyes, trying to remember the blood stencil on the dead man's shirt. Which leaflets had been missing? He had trimmed off most of the sprigs so there had been only two left at the top and four beneath.

I could ask to see the bloodied shirt again, but I didn't want to let Hideki Tagawa think I had found something before I knew for sure. Even more, I didn't want to pass on the message before I knew what it was. I wanted to confirm Mirza had solved the puzzle, as well as find his killer.

I opened my eyes and drew what I remembered of the leaf pattern stencilled on Mirza's shirt. What if his time of death was not its only message? There was a secret here. I was so close I could smell it. And I was sure it had to do with the leaf print on the shirt. Almost as though, in his last moments, he had tried to leave a message.

'Why are you drawing?'

I jumped, startled, and dropped the sketch I had been staring at.

Little Ling seldom sought me out. Her mother, believing she might be infected by my bad luck, kept her away.

'Can I draw too?'

'Of course.'

It wasn't as though I was getting anywhere. Little Ling plopped down on the mat beside me, and I went back to staring at the diagrams of stone patterns.

'Look! Do you like it?' Little Ling had drawn in the missing leaves on the stalks. Because mimosa leaflets are evenly paired, it was easy to see where they should go. 'You should pay me for drawing your leaves for you. I know exactly how many leaves I drew. Three and three on this one. Then three and four on this one. Do you like it? Can I keep the paper to show Mama?'

Midpoint: Mimosa Leaf Code

———◆———

I showed Colonel Fujiwara and Hideki Tagawa my rough sketch of the print on Mirza's shirt. On the left, one sprig with three leaflets on both sides, on the other, three on one side and four on the other. On the right, the first of the four sprigs also had three pairs of leaflets. Then five and one, two and five, three and four.

Then I showed them my copy of the alphabet grid I had found on Mirza's desk.

3-3. 3-4
3-3. 5-1. 2-5. 3-4

When I matched the top leaflets to the horizontal axis of the grid and the lower to the vertical, this spelled out, 'No news.'

But what kind of message was 'No news' to die for? Or to kill for?

'The mimosa branches are the ideal medium to transmit messages, because the leaflets stay open for some time after the branch is cut. And because the leaflets grow in pairs, it is easy to see the number of leaflets for each alphabet letter. Then, because the leaflets close in time, just as they do at night, the message is hidden. The branch looks like just another withered branch until you spread out the leaflets to count them. That's why they had to stick it into a pile of stones. To make sure whoever collected it found the right branch.

'They may have learned that you were trying to analyse the stone patterns and had people arrange stones in different places and in different patterns to confuse you. That's why there were so many strange stone arrangements.'

'You broke the code based on a bloodied leaf print and that crudely hand-drawn alphabet grid?' Colonel Fujiwara looked at Hideki Tagawa. He seemed more interested in rubbing in Tagawa's failure than in what my discovery might mean. 'In how many days only? How long were you and your men working on that code, Tagawa?'

'Those idiot soldiers threw away the branches they found. Said they were dried up,' Hideki Tagawa fumed. 'Fools! But this shows that they were transmitting codes via the branches stuck in the stone structures. If I had those branches now . . .'

'This shows the resistance must have had Mirza killed to prevent him revealing their secret,' Colonel Fujiwara said. 'He must have been in on it. Otherwise why did he have the branch with him? He didn't get it from our men, did he? Or from you?'

'No. I never saw it.'

'Perhaps one of your men passed it to him along with the stone drawings. They wouldn't have mentioned it to you. You didn't think it was important, did you?'

'That wouldn't have been possible because Mirza must have

cut down the branch just before he died,' I said. 'That's why the leaflets were still open in the print.'

But Hideki Tagawa ran over my words. 'Those soldiers who found the stones, they must have been in on it. Otherwise how can anyone be so stupid? Time and again, they said there were branches pointing in a particular direction. But did they pay attention? Did they bring them back? No! They copied the useless stone patterns and drew an arrow for the branch. Fools! Dolts!'

He stormed out of Colonel Fujiwara's office and we could hear him barking orders and imprecations in Japanese. I could think of a lot more questions he should have been asking. Like, how had Mirza discovered the branch code if Hideki Tagawa, who provided him with material to decode, hadn't given him the branches?

Instead I seized the opportunity to plead my case with Colonel Fujiwara, 'By solving the mimosa code, I have shown that my family are not traitors. Please free my uncle. He has nothing to do with Mirza's death or the codes.'

'Of course you solved it. You are half Japanese so of course you are smart!'

'No, sir. I am not. I am Straits-born.'

'You really don't know?' Colonel Fujiwara was clearly far more interested in this than in the code. In fact, he looked delighted. 'Sit down. Tagawa! Tagawa, get back in here! You must explain things to your cousin! Tagawa!'

I sat. Or, rather, I took a step away from the colonel's desk and my legs gave way. I felt a chair pushed in behind me.

And as I tested the information just thrown at me, I realised I wasn't altogether surprised. At some level I had known this all along. Suddenly many things made sense: whispered snippets I had heard, narrowed eyes following me, the way my grandmother would not answer any of my questions about my mother and forbade anyone to speak to me of my parents because of 'bad luck'.

Yet I had heard stories about my father. Things slipped out, such as his favourite food as a boy, how he had loved fishing, and the tricks he had played on Uncle Chen when they were children.

Of course they had no stories about my mother's childhood. But even if a girl leaves her own family when she marries, I thought it surprising that no one could tell me even which family she had come from. Yes, there was an altar to her and another to my father in the Chen Mansion, and a third to the little brother who hadn't lived even a day. But that was just to feed and appease their ghosts.

'This is not how I wanted to tell you,' Hideki Tagawa said.

Japanese Mother

———◆———

'You are the thing that Tagawa-san came here to hunt down!' Colonel Fujiwara said.

'One of the things,' Hideki Tagawa said.

He switched back to English. That wouldn't give us much privacy as Colonel Fujiwara understood basic English and Emily Bennington-Smith had followed Hideki Tagawa back into the room. But I was beyond caring.

'Just tell me,' I said.

'With your permission,' he said to Colonel Fujiwara, who nodded vigorously.

'I grew up with a family name, Tagawa, as well as my clan name, Sakanoue. The Sakanoue clan was dying out. The last true generation came down to three sisters. My mother, the mother of my cousin, Mrs Maki, and the mother of your mother.'

'My mother is long dead. And she had no family.'

'Your mother's mother was the youngest of the sisters. Your mother was only five years old when her father died. She and her mother came to stay with my family. My earliest memories are of her wanting to play with me and my brothers although she was much younger.'

I shook my head. He was talking nonsense.

'It was a difficult time for Japan, yet it was a happy childhood. We didn't know any different. Ours was an old samurai family, which supported the growth of Japan against the Western powers. We boys learned samurai skills and sword fighting, also poetry, calligraphy and healing. There was nothing unusual in this in families like ours. It had nothing to do with war then. It was part of bushido, the warrior spirit.'

'The warrior spirit sounds like it has to do with war,' I said. I was surprised by how calm my voice sounded. My head was spinning as pieces of new information banged around inside it, looking for hooks to anchor to. For a moment I felt dizzy and wondered if I was in another dream.

'The warrior spirit is about being fearless and selfless under attack. Bushido also emphasises care for the weak, loyalty to one's family, responsibility, kindness and honesty.' Hideki Tagawa closed his eyes and rubbed his knuckles into his temples. 'I didn't know it would be so hard,' he said. 'I assumed you knew where your mother came from, even if your father's family didn't want you to have anything to do with us.'

It was a good act, I thought. The distress and weariness. The appeal to family. He would have checked up on me enough to know I had no information, no memories of my mother. If he had dug deeper he would be aware that I felt no need or desire to know anything about her.

But why was he taking the trouble to do this? What could they want from me?

'Who my mother was means nothing to me.'

Of course I had always wondered if the family rift might have been mended if my parents had not died of cholera so soon and so fast. But there was no point in thinking about that. My grandmother had done her best for me, despite her disapproval of my mother and their marriage.

'Your mother wanted to study and learn sword fighting, like the boys.'

'She did?'

'It was forbidden, of course. She was a girl from a well-to-do family. She had a good dowry and would have made a good marriage.'

I dismissed that. Even if Ah Ma forbade mention of my mother, I had heard plenty from other sources to have an idea of where and how my parents had met.

'Your mother read and wrote poetry. She read magazines like Seitō, which carried articles on women's equality, chastity, and abortion. Our cousin, Mrs Maki, still has some of those magazines, marked in your mother's hand.'

Anyone could make up stories about a dead woman no one remembered, I told myself, but something painful was twisting in my stomach, in my bladder.

'There was a family discussion. It was agreed that she must be married off before she disgraced herself. I was very young when this happened. Still in my first apprenticeship. All I knew was that when I returned to the family home at the end of the week she had disappeared. I was told she had been sent to stay with her future in-laws.'

'But?'

'But she had run away. She wrote under my father's name to change the date and time of her betrothal ceremony. Then she walked out of the compound and disappeared. All she took were the shoes on her feet and the clothes on her back.'

He had been staring at the opposite wall as he talked, almost as though he was looking into the past. But now he turned to me again. This time his eyes were not calculating and rat-like but wet, glazed with emotion. 'She was so beautiful. So shining bright and beautiful. You remind me of her. And not just because you look like her.'

'I am not beautiful.' I was not fishing for compliments, but it was the only thing I could think of to say.

Hideki Tagawa took me seriously, 'You have the same eyes. The same shape of face and chin. She was small and slim too. Your skin is darker than hers was, but that is because she was kept indoors most of the time. And when she was in the sun, her skin bronzed to gold, like yours.'

'My mother was a prostitute,' I said. That was what the old women, the neighbourhood children, Shen Shen's family had whispered to each other in my hearing. Deliberately, no doubt. Though I blocked the words, they stayed with me. My grandmother resolutely denied my mother had ever existed. 'My father met her in a whorehouse on Japan Street. When she got pregnant with me, he bought her contract and married her.'

Although, as all the rumours went, there was no way of telling which of her clients was my true father. But I couldn't bring myself to say that.

Hideki Tagawa's voice was quiet. 'I don't know what happened

to her after she left Japan, but your mother was one of the last
of the Sakanoue clan. She was destined for a good marriage
with a family behind her. She had a fine education. Too good,
perhaps.'

'Too good?' Against my will I was drawn to defend this
unknown woman.

'Certain obligations and agreements are understood in the
old samurai code. There are connections – financial connections
– with politicians and major business, but there is no selling
drugs, no excessive violence towards civilians and no committing
rape, murder or amputation unless under instructions.'

'Instructions! Instructions to rape, kill and cut off body
parts?'

Hideki Tagawa smiled. 'And that is almost exactly how your
mother reacted. But we were the guardians of our neighbourhoods
in an age when the police could not be depended on. We offered
the only justice the weak could turn to. And in times of disaster,
we were strong for them. We set up systems to provide water,
shelter, food. We helped keep people alive, because we put
ourselves in a position where we could do so.'

It sounded like what what my Chen family had done in
Singapore.

'But your mother would not accept that. I don't know how she
ended up in Singapore, or what she was doing here, but she was
not a prostitute. Mrs Maki traced her to a boarding house where
she was helping women – slaves and prostitutes – who wanted
to return to Japan without their families knowing. That must
have been where she met your father.'

'So she did meet my father in a whorehouse.'

Hideki Tagawa leaned forward. It wasn't anger I saw in his face. It was passion. 'Wherever they met, if I could only be sure that your father was worthy of her I could die in peace. But for your mother, one of the last of the Sakanoue clan, to end up with a small-time moneylender in Singapore?'

'My father was not a small-time moneylender.' There was a huge pressure in my chest, making it difficult for me to breathe.

'No. As my cousin found out when she came to Singapore. Your father, Big Boss Chen, pretty much ran the black market in Singapore. He was the big boss of all the local triads. Ironic that your mother should run away from her own life and end up with him. Maybe that was her destiny.'

I nodded: a polite nod, which said that while I acknowledged what he had said it was nothing to do with me. Mrs Maki, his cousin, had never asked me about my parents.

'My cousin paid Mirza for research on your parentage. Mirza was good enough to tell her much of the information came from confidential police documents. There should be a record in Mirza's files. I looked for it among his papers, but I have not yet found it.'

Le Froy must have known about me, then. The British would have gone thoroughly into my background before I was allowed to join the Detective Unit. What information they found would have been given to my superior officer, if not to me, so that he could assess whether or not I was 'safe'. Was that the reason Le Froy had taken me on as an apprentice? Keep your allies close and your enemies closer, he always said. Had he, with his extreme Japan-phobia, seen me as a potential enemy all along?

'The book I gave you belonged to your mother.'

I had already guessed that.

'She had an intuition that was almost supernatural. That was why she found it so difficult to deal with the lies – the necessary deceptions – our family used. That is the other way you remind me of her. You know what I am saying is true, don't you?'

'I read people,' I said flatly. 'It's not intuition. I study people and I can tell what they are likely to do. What their type is likely to do. There is nothing supernatural about that.'

I was good at it, too. The fantasy the man was weaving had to be a manipulation tactic. It had to be. So why was pain stabbing, like a sword, through my gut?

'I have to go now.' I got to my feet and started towards the door without asking permission to leave.

'Wait.'

Hideki Tagawa took out his wallet. For an instant I thought he wanted to give me money and, in my mind, I was already pushing it back at him, throwing it in his face. But he held out a small photograph. 'This is all I have. It was taken before I left for school. The last time we were all together. Only two of us are left now.'

I saw five children posed for the camera. I recognised Hideki Tagawa at once. Sitting cross-legged in front, he was pulling a face. I guessed the little girl beside him, who looked about to cry, was Mrs Maki. Of the three remaining children, only one was a girl. Standing at the centre of the group, on the cusp between girlhood and young womanhood, she was the tallest of the children. She wore a light-coloured shirt with a broad waistband over a darker skirt. And her face, though still with

the round softness of childhood and confident eyes that knew
and asserted her place in the world, was my own.

'That is Ryoko. She was your mother.'

Family Confession

———◆———

'Is what Hideki Tagawa said about my mother true?'

I don't remember how I got back to Chen Mansion. I was still holding the old photograph when I pushed Shen Shen aside to confront Ah Ma.

Ah Ma reminded me now of an old temple medium who doesn't want to give you news he knows you will be too angry to pay for.

That was enough for me. Her eyes went to the picture in my hand. I had meant to ask her if she recognised the young girl in the photograph but now I didn't want her to see it. I turned to go, though I wasn't sure if I was walking out of the kitchen or leaving the Chen family for ever.

'Of course!' Shen Shen said. 'Everybody knows. Your mother was a Japanese whore who couldn't find a husband, or who ran away from her husband and ended up here selling herself. And your father was one of her clients. He couldn't find any other woman willing to marry him, so he had to marry that dirty woman whom nobody else wanted!'

That was certainly not true. Ah Ma had talked to me about my father, Big Boss Chen, the first son of the Chen family.

My late father had been the smartest, handsomest (and richest) man on the island. He was known for his speed, both in how fast he could run and how fast he could calculate numbers in his head. He would calculate your interest for you. And if you challenged him, figuring out the numbers more slowly on the abacus and finding him wrong, he would give you a five-dollar bonus as well as cancelling your debt.

But he was never wrong, and his only challengers were people who had never met him before. I had inherited my skill with numbers and languages from him.

I knew any woman Big Boss Chen chose to marry would have been deemed 'not good enough' for him. I thought my mother had just been unlucky in dying with him so soon after their marriage. Because clearly (in superstitious local eyes) that showed even the family gods disapproved of the marriage.

I wasn't surprised Shen Shen chose to ignore that. Most people who remembered my family in the old days talked about how much smarter Big Boss Chen was compared to his younger brother. Since he was in his teens, Big Boss had run the family businesses alongside his widowed mother. It was thanks to him that the Chen family had maintained its position and preserved the triad hierarchy so that the British assumed there was no trouble.

And that was why Uncle Chen, despite his size (huge for a Chinese man) and his having run the Chen family businesses alongside Ah Ma for years, was still known as 'Small Boss Chen'.

I hadn't thought Uncle Chen minded. From childhood, he had been his elder brother's most fervent admirer and most loyal lieutenant. But Shen Shen, who had married into the family after my father's death, had not known him. She clearly resented it.

If my father had married a local-born Chinese girl – even the daughter of pig farmers like Shen Shen was – without Ah Ma's permission, Ah Ma would have got over it in time. There would have been no point in holding on to such a grudge after they were both dead, especially as she had taken me into her family under her special protection despite all the fortune-tellers' warnings.

My grandmother had loved my father enough to keep me. But she had never allowed any mention of my mother. I knew that over the years servant girls had lost their jobs and tenants their shophouse businesses because something they had said about my mother reached Ah Ma. And all these years I had believed it was because of her fear of bad luck.

'Maybe I made a mistake,' Ah Ma said heavily. 'All those years ago.'

Shen Shen's eyes flashed in triumph. 'You see? So many years I could not have babies because she was living in your house. The temple told my mother she is the curse on the family, blocking my womb. After she moved out, finally you have one granddaughter. If only you had done the right thing and sent her away when your son died, who knows how many grandsons we would have given you by now?'

My grandmother seemed about to say something, but Shen Shen hadn't finished.

'And she was not just born bad luck. She is bringing more bad luck into the family. Look at how she was hanging around with the British. Now even worse! Because of her, the Japanese are coming to the house. Because of her, the Japanese took away your only living son. Don't you see? You cannot let your memory of your dead son blind you to what you have to do. You have to get rid of her or the whole Chen family will be destroyed for ever.'

'I made a mistake,' Ah Ma said to me. 'I remember. It was just after your father came and told me he had married your mother without permission. I was so upset and angry. And I knew that my second son always copied his big brother. If his big brother jumped into the sea, Ah Liang would follow him. Whatever his big brother did, that must be right. So, yes. I rushed to arrange a proper marriage for him. That was my mistake.'

'You should have disowned him!' Shen Shen said, not taking in Ah Ma's words. 'Then, no matter what happened to him, you would not be responsible for his daughter. You should disown her now. Make her leave!'

'I didn't want to disown my elder son,' Ah Ma said. Her voice was full of pain but steady. 'But I wanted to find a good wife for my younger son. That was my mistake.'

Shen Shen froze. Her mouth was open, ready to deliver her next volley but nothing came out.

'One of my tenant farmers owed me a lot of money. He was a pig farmer, who had big ideas about expanding. He wanted to create a dynasty for his sons to carry on. I normally don't allow long-term loans. I will not lend money to gamblers, drinkers and opium smokers. But I lent money to this pig farmer because he said he needed it to set up a new farming system. He wanted to use pig dung to fertilise his vegetables. After selling his vegetables he would use the roots and stems to feed his pigs. And after butchering his pigs, he would put what was left back into the earth for his plants.'

'I thought your family was rich,' I said to Shen Shen, who was still staring at Ah Ma.

'My father had rich ideas,' Shen Shen said numbly. 'He always said that one day—'

Ah Ma went on as though Shen Shen was not speaking. 'I learned that men who have big ideas but refuse to learn what needs to be done step by step are the worst gamblers of all, because they are gambling with their own and their families' lives.

'He offered me his elder daughter as *mui chai*, a bondmaid, because he could not afford to pay me. He said his elder daughter was beautiful enough to become a rich man's valued mistress or concubine. He said if any man wanted her, the money he paid to buy back her bond would come to me.'

I believed it. Many poor families sent daughters away young because there was no point in feeding a girl who would bear children to another family.

'But the elder daughter was at work when I went to see the family. They wouldn't tell me where, but of course I knew. Shen Mi worked at a bar, serving drinks to *ang mohs*. I would not have such a woman in my house. Instead, I asked about the younger girl, Shen Shen.'

'Shen Shen poured tea and served snacks to me. She wasn't the eldest daughter and she was wearing a drab samfoo and no make-up. I thought she was the servant girl until the pig farmer said she was his second daughter, only thirteen years old.'

'You were only thirteen?' I knew Shen Shen had married young, but thirteen?

'I know I looked like a servant,' Shen Shen said. 'My mother hoped that Chen Tai was looking for one and would protect me from the men servants. My father told me that if I went with Chen Tai as a *mui chai* I would earn him more money than all my brothers put together. He promised that, when he made his fortune, he would pay back the bond price and bring me home. My father even asked whether Chen Tai would take Mimi instead, but she said no. She wanted me. Mimi wouldn't have minded, because she had seen Big Boss Chen in town and thought he was very handsome. At that time we didn't yet know he was married. But Mimi wouldn't have minded that.

'I was scared, but Chen Tai asked me if I was willing to go back to Chen Mansion with her and learn to make rempah for the Chen family. I liked cooking, so I nodded.'

Rempah was a spice paste, made with shallots, garlic, chillies and candlenuts: the heart and backbone of home cooking. There was no fixed recipe, because even in Ah Ma's kitchen the ingredients varied depending on what was in season, what was being cooked and who it was for. The only constant was the backbreaking pounding of the ingredients, followed by slow, gentle frying to draw out the fragrance and release the oil.

Every family has its own secret rempah blend. It is said that women pass their rempah secrets to daughters-in-law but not to daughters who will marry out of the family. So Ah Ma asking

Shen Shen if she would come to learn to make rempah was pretty much an offer of marriage.

'I engaged Shen Shen to work for me for three years as a kitchen girl,' my grandmother said, startling us. Engrossed in Shen Shen's story, I had forgotten she was there. 'So that she could learn everything she needed to know about household management. After that, she could decide whether to return home to her parents or marry into the family. After three years, she decided to stay. So we had the wedding.'

'Of course she had to stay!' I said. 'If she didn't marry your son after all that time, everybody would say you sent her back because she wasn't good enough. If she didn't want to stay and marry Uncle Chen, she would never find another husband.'

'I stayed because by then I knew your uncle was a good man and would be a good husband,' Shen Shen said. 'I knew after the first month – after the first week. He told me he wouldn't come near me until I was ready. And he said that even if I decided to leave the Chen house my parents' debts would still be forgotten. That was when I decided I would marry him and be the best wife I could. Anyway, if I left, where would I go? I couldn't go back to my parents' house. All I ever wanted was to be a good wife and give him many sons.'

Ah Ma had chosen well, I thought. Shen Shen might be the uneducated daughter of pig farmers, but she was smart, humble and hard-working. And Ah Ma had taken her when she was still a child, young enough to shape and influence.

'I thought you would be a good wife. I thought you would become part of the Chen family,' Ah Ma said. 'But you are still an outsider.'

'No, I am not!' Shen Shen protested. 'I have only given you one granddaughter. When your son returns, we will give you grandsons!'

'I have two granddaughters,' Ah Ma said. 'If you cannot accept both my granddaughters, you have no place in this family.'

Evil Within

———◆———

When I got up the next morning, after little sleep, I almost stepped on my breakfast tray on the floor outside Ah Ma's bedroom.

Ah Ma had got up before dawn as usual, slipping out of the room in silence. My presence was clearly not wanted in the kitchen. I could understand Shen Shen avoiding me after Ah Ma had stood up for me, but even Ah Ma was keeping away from me now.

I had spent so long hating the Japanese it seemed impossible that I had Japanese blood in my veins. I didn't feel any different, but I couldn't get away from it. It was possible even that my father was not really my father and I was not really a Chen. But I couldn't escape my mother having been my mother.

I had naively thought that, once I had figured out the mimosa-leaf code, the Japanese would believe that Uncle Chen, and our entire family, had had nothing to do with Mirza's murder, that they would release Uncle Chen and leave our family alone.

Instead, Uncle Chen was still in detention and there had been more arrests. The previous day, anyone found near mimosa trees or around suspicious branches was detained, and soldiers were cutting down trees outside the PoW camp. I felt almost as guilty for the poor trees as I did for the people. Shen Shen would have said it just showed how warped I was.

And I had received a note from Emily Bennington-Smith asking me to submit articles for the Syonan-To. They would not be able to pay me, but my name would be published and my contribution to the Japanese Empire's war effort would be appreciated.

Once upon a time my biggest dream was to be a news journalist. I'd thought I would do anything to get such a job. But I couldn't see myself writing about how good the Japanese invaders were being to Singapore and Singaporeans. I had seen the kind of articles the Syonan-To carried. Previously it had written about how swiftly and easily 'the invincible imperial army' had destroyed the supposedly 'impregnable island fortress' but now the Japanese propaganda department was focused on softening the image of Japanese soldiers for civilian acceptance.

In her note, Miss Emily suggested I write something about how soldiers interacted with the children in my family or played battledore and shuttlecock with them. I could write about any interactions I wanted, she said, as long as I stressed how we were all living with 'vim and vitality in perfect harmony', now that we were part of Japan's Greater East Asia Co-Prosperity Sphere.

I assumed the obligatory phrases had come from the Japanese propaganda department. As far as I knew, Emily Bennington-Smith had had no interest in politics before the war. The only previous writing she had done was for fashion magazines, talking about the best way to walk or accessorise with scarves.

I could understand her doing whatever she could to stay alive. But I wasn't sure if I wanted to do the same.

Then again, how could I say I wanted only to write what I believed was the truth when I had just realised I had lived all my life not knowing the truth about myself?

Yesterday I had called Hideki Tagawa a liar. But if I insisted on believing he was a liar, that would make my grandmother a liar too, a liar who had hidden the truth from me for years.

I understood better now why there had been so much pressure on my grandmother to send me away or put me down a well. That might have been the best solution for everyone involved.

Someone pushed open the door. 'Su Lin?'

It was Shen Shen.

I turned away from her. 'I am not going to leave my grandmother alone here. At least, not until the war is over and I know she is safe. I know you blame me for what happened to Uncle Chen, but you can't leave the house, however much you want to get away from me. At least, not until Uncle Chen comes back and you find somewhere safe to go. So can we just pretend we get along? Or at least pretend we don't know each other and go on living here?'

'Su Lin, I want to say I'm sorry.'

'What? Oh. Don't worry. Ah Ma isn't going to throw you out. She's just feeling bad because every time people blame me for something, she thinks they're really blaming her for keeping me. I suppose she hoped no one would find out that little detail about my mother.'

'I was scared of you,' Shen Shen said. 'You are the daughter of this rich family and I am a nobody. Your uncle is a very good man. He wanted us to take you as our daughter, but I refused. I thought you would bring bad luck to our children. And then when we didn't have children for so many years, I was afraid the gods and your ancestors were punishing me for rejecting you. I even believed you would curse us so I tried to stay away from you.'

'You always fed me,' I remembered. 'You always made me peanut candy and egg cake.'

'You were so small.' Shen Shen smiled a little, also remembering. 'And so smart. You learned things so fast. When your grandmother said she was sending you to school to learn to speak English, I tried to warn her you would turn into a modern girl. Then, as though that was not bad enough, after I tried to help your grandmother find you a good husband, you went and got a job working for the police with an ang moh and Indian men!'

'There were Chinese policemen too,' I pointed out.

'You think it's all a joke. It's not. You aren't old enough to remember what it was like in the old days. In those days, if one person disgraces himself, the whole family suffers.'

I didn't know if Shen Shen had meant what she said. She might just have been delivering a propaganda speech so that she could continue living in Chen Mansion with her daughter. If so, I had to respect her for that. In the old days, in the old country – China, India or Indonesia – survival and getting on had been controlled by the triads and family connections. But that was what our parents and ancestors had come to Singapore to escape from. On this island, what you were willing to do counted for more than which family you had been born into.

At least until the Japanese came.

When the Japanese first arrived, not only did they target all family associations that might have connections with China, they also targeted the families of soldiers. After the Malay Regiment's 1st Battalion had fought to the death in Pasir Panjang, resorting to hand-to-hand combat when they ran out of ammunition, the Japanese took it out on their family members. Wives who had already lost their husbands in battle were driven to destroying any evidence they had that their men had ever existed in a desperate attempt to save their children.

And in the middle of all this loss, I had discovered new relatives.

I was curious about my mother, I admit. I didn't want to have anything to do with her Japanese relations. They – especially Hideki Tagawa – meant nothing to me. But I did want to know more about her.

'I know your uncle better than I know anyone else. And I know he is alive and coming back,' Shen Shen said.

'How can you know that?'

'Your uncle must come back,' Shen Shen said. 'Or what is the point of me and Little Ling staying alive? Look. I was shocked to find out you are really half Japanese. I thought it was just gossip. But now I see it is a sign. Don't you see? If you have Japanese blood, maybe they will trust you. If they trust you, you can help to bring your uncle back alive.'

'I don't know what I can do,' I said.

'You are the only one who can do anything to help us now.'

'I don't know where to start.'

'You can start by talking to that man standing in front of the house. Take him somewhere else to talk. Your Ah Ma wants to go to market but nobody dares to walk past him.'

Long-lost Cousin

<hr />

I have no idea how long Hideki Tagawa had been standing across the road, leaning against his car and staring at our front gate. Certainly he had been there long enough to frustrate Ah Ma and our neighbours' wish to go out: they didn't want to draw attention to themselves by walking past him.

They weren't the only ones. The Japanese sentries at the road-junction guard post, about twenty yards away, were standing to attention in the sun instead of sitting on their wooden stools in the shade. Later they would be in a worse mood than usual, thanks to Hideki Tagawa.

'He wants to be your boyfriend. Is that it?' one of the children asked me, as I joined the group peering out at him.

'No, Didi. He says he is a long-lost relative of my dead mother.'

'My ma says long-lost relatives only come to look for you when they want money.'

I didn't think Hideki Tagawa wanted money from me, but he certainly wanted something. Not that he'd said so.

'I was just passing. In the neighbourhood, you know,' Hideki

211

Tagawa said, in his posh British English, when I asked who he was waiting for.

'Good morning, then.' I made to walk past him but he stopped me.

'I wanted to give you enough time to accept the news. If you really didn't know.'

'I really didn't know.'

'Well, then, now you do. But we still have a murder to process. Have you anything to report on who might have come up with the mimosa codes? I didn't want to rush you.'

He had given me less than twenty-four hours after my breakthrough with the mimosa leaflets to process my new parentage. Maybe I should have been flattered that he thought me as cold-blooded as himself. But I was feeling contrary.

'You are a man of great patience,' I said sarcastically.

'I know I am. If you have no questions, we will proceed with the investigation.'

'What was she like?' I asked.

Hideki Tagawa opened the car door and gestured that I should sit. I did so, my feet dangling above the road, and felt like a child. He returned to his position with his back against the car. But now his attention was on me, people started to slip out of their gates and go about their day.

'Your mother was an arrogant young woman. Arrogant, confident and careful. But she was also a romantic. I'm sure she wanted to prove herself and return home. She would never have cut herself off from our family for ever. She would have wanted to come back and change things. But she never had the chance.' His jaw hardened.

'It wasn't my father's fault.'

'Of course it was! If your father was Japanese, there would have been no difficulty.'

That was true. But then I would be Japanese: my only problem then would have been how to conquer the rest of Asia.

'I tracked you down for your mother's sake,' Hideki Tagawa said, 'and for my own. I wanted to know if there was anything of her in you.'

'How could there be? You can't be influenced by what you don't know. My family brought me up to be Chinese so that's what I am. There's nothing Japanese about me.'

Maybe I blamed my grandmother for keeping information from me, but I wasn't going to say so.

'You know now that you are half Japanese. Growing up is all about gaining wisdom and discarding childish beliefs. Because a child has seen so little of the world, its view of life is limited. But you cannot crawl like a baby for ever. Now you know who you are. There may be a reason why the knowledge came to you only at this time.'

That was close to what Shen Shen had said. But it didn't feel like the right time to ask for a favour.

'I am also my father's daughter. If my father was alive, you would put him in prison. And if my mother was alive, you would arrest her for being married to my father!'

'I don't think you understand what your Japanese family connection could mean for you.'

'My connection with the family she ran away from?'

'Perhaps you need more time,' Hideki Tagawa said.

'Earlier you said you wanted me to help figure out who killed Mirza and stole the Golden Lily tributes, among them a large golden Buddha. You wanted to know what Chief Inspector Le Froy would do. Was that true or was it just an excuse to study me?'

'You're not so important that I would make the effort to lie to you. Your mother was good at understanding people and Le Froy was good at understanding motives. You're not stupid and you know the nature of the people here. What can you tell me?'

When the world goes mad around you, it's probably mad to stick your head out and answer questions you know nothing about. But this was the first time anyone was appealing to me as my mother's daughter.

And, yes, I was flattered that he thought I had learned something from Le Froy.

'I doubt either of the Mirza sisters killed their father. Or had anything to do with his death.'

'So you don't think there was a personal motive. I agree,' Hideki Tagawa said. 'It feels like a business killing.'

'A business killing?'

'I'm not saying someone was paid to kill him. If that was the case, they would have been more efficient and professional. At least, a professional Japanese assassin would have been.'

'I'm sure local assassins are efficient and professional too.' I felt driven to defend them.

'Besides, no proof of death was taken. All Mirza's body parts were present. I say this was not a personal killing because if the motivation of resentment or revenge was strong enough to drive murder, they would have wanted to tell him to his face why he was being killed. Stabbing him in the back after knocking him down from behind would give no satisfaction.'

'But this was in the man's own garden with his two daughters at home. Maybe the murderer was in a hurry.' If I ever hated someone enough to kill him or her, I was pretty sure my priority would be to get the job done as fast as possible. Why bother telling somebody to his face why I was killing him when he was going to die anyway? I could always gloat in private later. If I got away with it, I could gloat in peace for years.

But Hideki Tagawa was going on: 'Mirza was in the garden, which suggests his killer made an appointment to see him. If that was the case, there should have been a record in his office. He always kept records of meetings. Even if his daughters know nothing of his death, it is possible he told one of them who he was meeting. It's also possible one of Mirza's daughters took his record books. We searched the whole house for them, but they've gone.'

'Maybe he promised to keep the meeting secret.'

'Why? If I were his killer, I wouldn't trust the word of the man I was going to kill.'

'Agreed. But not all killers are so rational.'

'This killer was rational enough to set up the meeting, to get Mirza to let him in without telling anyone about it, then to walk out calmly, closing the door behind him.'

Hideki Tagawa didn't seem to realise that someone inside the garden must have closed the padlock. I remembered asking the Mirza sisters about this. How had they deflected me? Very skilfully, for sure. It showed me how much more they might be hiding. But I wasn't going to mention that to Hideki Tagawa until I had been able to speak to them again.

'Mirza was a smart man. He wouldn't trust somebody he

didn't know. This had to have been someone he'd been working with for some time. Someone he either had reason to trust or to fear,' I said, 'Maybe someone he was working for.'

'You think he was killed by a Japanese official?'

'Mirza was working for your people. And he knew it was to be kept secret. You can't really believe that he would have let some local triad members into his garden and turn his back on them, especially with his reputation as an informer.'

'Why don't you come out and say you believe Colonel Fujiwara sent someone to kill him?' Hideki Tagawa asked.

'Because you could arrest me for saying that.'

I waited. So did he.

Eventually I said, 'And because you already suspect him yourself, don't you? You just want someone like me to accuse him so that you don't have to. Then after I get arrested for treason and executed, you can investigate him.'

'Nobody is going to execute you.'

Even if he meant that, spoken words were no guarantee.

'You came to investigate treasures missing from the Golden Lily organisation. Do you suspect they disappeared so successfully because someone in a position of power was helping?'

He did not answer. I suspected he wouldn't say anything till he had enough evidence to confront the perpetrator. Then again, he might skip the confrontation and just take care of it. Without taking proof of death or gloating over the kill.

Maybe we were related after all.

While Safia and Nasima had distracted my attention with Operation Jaywick, they had generated other questions for me.

'Mirza's daughters said he was interested in the timing of the Operation Jaywick explosions, and in the last ship attacked. Why? Which was the last ship attacked?'

'We don't know why. In Operation Jaywick, seven large warships and one small cargo ship were attacked. It was the last that Mirza was interested in but it was not important. It was probably targeted by mistake.'

'What was the cargo ship carrying? Where was it bound for? Who knew where it was docked? Did all the explosives go off at the same time?'

Hideki Tagawa held up his hands to slow down my questions. 'As a matter of fact, no. I know this because I followed up on Mirza's questions. According to several of the men trying to put out the fires, the last explosion took place when they were already in action. We believe the last was a deliberate attempt to target men assigned to put out the fires, but it didn't work.'

'Why not?' I asked.

'It was too far away from the main site of damage.'

'Why? If the purpose was to target men responding, why didn't they set the explosives closer? Was the explosive used on the cargo ship the same as what was used on the battleships? Was the same amount used?'

'What makes you ask that?'

'If the cargo boat was closer to the dock than the larger ships, they could have blown it up just to use up the rest of their explosives before making an escape – on land.'

'But we've established that the Australian marines escaped out to sea, not onto the island, so that isn't relevant.'

The last thing I wanted to do was set off another round of

home inspections. But I had one last question: 'People would have been rushing into the docks area to help, but could you ask if any of your men saw vehicles leaving it at the time?'

I still didn't know how far I could trust Hideki Tagawa, but if he had any sense he would grasp my point.

'What do you think happened that night, Miss Chen?'

'What if the first responders found something on the cargo boat and took it to a safe place with good intentions, then later saw the advantage in not reporting it? What if Mirza found out and they thought he was going to report them?'

'How would he have found out?'

'Mirza knew secrets. He paid small people to feed him information so that he could put the squeeze on big people. If anyone tried to sell anything on the black market, or ship anything illegally in or out of Singapore, Mirza knew about it. The dock workers and labourers would sell him the information.'

Lying Sisters

———◆———

After he'd left, I walked over to the Mirza house. It was an unofficial visit, as I hadn't told Hideki Tagawa I was going. Of course I knew it would get back to him, but I didn't have to tell him everything I learned from them.

Most of all, I wanted to ask Safia and Nasima why they had lied about the time of their father's death and how their father had got hold of a fresh mimosa-branch message. I still didn't believe they had had anything to do with his murder, but they were hiding something. And this time I wasn't going to be distracted by talk of Operation Jaywick.

Besides, I didn't think it had had anything to do with the Mirzas: it was a useful distraction that would keep Hideki Tagawa occupied for a while.

'What do you want now?' Safia asked ungraciously, when she finally came to the door.

'Can I come in?'

She looked over my shoulder to where two Japanese sentries were talking. It was clearly a change of shift. The Mirza murder was at least a week old and didn't merit more than one guard at a time. They were probably deciding which of them would report my visit, but since I had been brought there before by Hideki Tagawa, they weren't going to stop me. But if she refused to let me in . . .

Safia stood back and held open the door for me. Then she swung it back quickly, cracking it hard on my crooked hip. 'Sorry,' she sang out insincerely.

'No problem.' I smiled at her, managing not to wince. Yes, it hurt. But I wasn't going to let her see that.

'This door always slips,' she said. 'Do you want to see Nasima?'

We went back to their schoolroom.

Nasima brought in a ceramic pot and cups on a rectangular tray, with a dish of what looked like sesame balls. Where would they have got sesame seeds? I was starting to think like Formosa Boy. 'You didn't have to,' I said.

'You are a guest,' Nasima said. 'It is these little customs that make us civilised. Besides, we so seldom receive guests without boots and bayonets these days.'

'What are those?' I asked. The smell of freshly fried dough made my stomach rumble.

'Lukaimat,' Nasima said, 'but made without saffron and using tapioca flour instead of wheat. In the old days we used to have them only at Ramadan, but now, when each day may be our last, we decided we would eat what we like most whenever we can. Try it. It's sweet, but not too sweet.'

It was delicious. A little like a dough fritter, but lighter and moist. Being poisoned by it would be worthwhile, I thought.

Though I hadn't been there for several days now, the room and the whole house seemed familiar. It didn't feel as though anyone else had been there since my last visit. My thoughts went back to Mirza's beautiful office, and I wondered what Safia and Nasima would do with all those books in all those languages.

'Why did you come back?' Safia asked.

'The last time I asked you why you lied about the time your father died. You didn't answer. I've come to ask you again.'

'We didn't lie. How do you know we lied?' Safia said.

Nasima watched me silently.

'Because of the mimosa branch.'

'What mimosa branch?' Safia burst out. 'What has that got to do with anything?' I saw her glance at her sister. They knew the branches were messages but didn't yet know that I did.

'The mimosa branch found under your father's body wasn't the real message. If it was cut down by someone else, the leaves would have closed by the time he received it. They could not have left such a clear print on your father's shirt unless he cut that branch down and plucked the leaves himself, just before he was killed.'

'A print on his shirt?' Safia's confusion seemed genuine.

I wondered if it was possible that they didn't know about the blood stencil on Mirza's shirt. Yes, it was very possible. Mirza had died face down, stabbed through the heart from behind. That was the only way the leaflets, caught beneath him, would have marked the front of his shirt. It was lucky Mirza had not been wearing one of his beautiful ikat cloth shirts or the bloodstains might not have shown up so clearly against the pattern.

But wouldn't the branch and leaflets have stuck to the dried blood on his shirt? Had it been the killer or the kempeitai who had turned him over and removed the branch?

It might have been tossed aside, of course. After all, who would pay any attention to a fallen branch in a garden full of trees? Unless they knew about the mimosa-leaf code.

'What do you know about the mimosa branch?' I asked Safia.

'Nothing,' she said quickly. Her eyes darted again to her sister. 'Nothing at all. I don't know what you're talking about,'

'You took it from under his dead body, didn't you? And you delivered it. But you didn't deliver the right message. Your father created a new one on the branch he cut down.'

'Nonsense. Why would he do that? And even if he did, why would we take it?'

'This is just a hypothesis,' I said. 'Maybe one of you had a friend or a fiancé in the resistance. Maybe he came to see you. Maybe your father caught you together and was going to tell the Japanese authorities. But your friend couldn't let him compromise the rest of his unit and in trying to stop him, perhaps without meaning to, he killed him. Then maybe you or your friend took the branch from your father's hand.'

Now they were both staring at me.

'This is your fault!' Safia shouted at her sister, and ran out of the room.

Nasima sat, looking at her fingers.

'What's your fault?' I asked gently.

'Everything. If you believe my sister.'

'I would rather believe you.'

'I had a husband.'

'*Had* a husband?'

'We performed the *Akad Nikah* the day before he left with the Malay Regiment to defend Singapore.' Akad Nikah was the formal binding marriage contract between a man and a woman.

'I never saw him again. My father ordered me to burn all photographs of him, and all letters from him. He said that the Japanese were killing the relations of the men who had refused to surrender.'

'I am so sorry.'

'He did what he had to do. His family lost three sons in the battle.'

So many families had lost so much.

'But why does your sister say it's your fault?'

Nasima shrugged. 'Who can understand sisters?'

She told me a little about her Dawud and I had the impression she enjoyed the chance to talk about him. 'We had our betrothal ceremony a year ago. When he signed on to serve under Lieutenant Adnan Saidi, he wanted to break our engagement because he did not want to leave me a widow or burden me with a cripple for a husband. It was I who insisted we marry. In Paradise, we will finally be together. You don't agree?'

'I'm glad you can still believe in Paradise,' I said, 'with all that's going on here.'

'The world is like Paradise compared to the womb. And it is like a garbage dump compared to Paradise,' Nasima said.

I learned nothing useful. Again. I'd always thought I was good at coaxing information out of people, but there's only so much you can get if they slam out of rooms or talk about Paradise.

Safia was waiting for me outside the Mirza gate, under a roadside tree away from the solitary sentry. 'What is Rat Face Tagawa investigating now?' She seemed to have forgotten her earlier upset. 'Come on, tell me what's happening. Nobody tells us anything. When are they going to stop putting guards in front of our house?'

'They may be trying to protect you,' I suggested.

Safia snorted.

'Why did you say it was your sister's fault?'

'What?'

'When I asked about the mimosa branch. I upset you – I'm sorry, I didn't mean to – but why did you say it was your sister's fault?'

Safia rolled her eyes. 'My father was murdered. I have a right to be upset about things. But come on. Tell me what Tagawa's really after. What did he send you to find out from us? And what have you got on him?'

'What?'

'You must have something on him. Nobody believes this cousin business. I have cousins and I hate them all. Look, I have a right to know. The colonel sent Hideki Tagawa to meet my father, and the next thing anyone knows, Father is dead,' Safia said. 'Hideki Tagawa killed my father. And now he's sending you to spy on us, trying to find out how much we know, so he can decide whether he wants to kill us too.'

'Hideki Tagawa doesn't even know I'm here today. He wants

to find out what happened to your father. He thinks it has something to do with some missing gold and a missing statue.'

We heard the motorcycle before it appeared. Heicho Han, I guessed – and I was right. He stopped by the gate sentry.

'I'd better go. I have to get home,'

Safia was patting her hair and moistening her lips and I don't think she heard me. So I learned something that day after all. She reminded me of my friend Parshanti – how I missed her – falling for men because they were handsome, clever or charming. I didn't think Heicho Han was any of those things but in wartime some standards rise while others fall.

I started walking homewards quickly, hearing Safia greeting him chirpily. I didn't think she would be slamming any doors on him.

'I hear that you solved the code that Rat Face was too stupid to crack.' Heicho Han jogged to catch up with me, then slowed to match my pace. 'Colonel Fujiwara should sack him and hire you instead.'

'It was just a lucky guess.' I glanced back and saw Safia standing where I'd left her. She was scowling.. Heicho Han had hurried past her without stopping. I felt a petty spark of satisfaction.

'I heard that Rat Face Tagawa said you got the answer from Le Froy because he invented it. And he was so angry with you and Le Froy that, in revenge, Tagawa had Le Froy's foot cut off!' Heicho Han laughed as though this was the best joke he had ever heard.

I managed a smile, but didn't believe it.

'Have you heard anything about my uncle Chen? Do you know if they'll let him go?'

'Tagawa is keeping him locked up. You'd better not make him angry or he will cut off your uncle's hands and legs as well.'

Buddha's Curse

—◆—

When Ah Ma sent me to learn English at the Mission Centre school, I learned that different languages followed different rules. Once you understand the rules about nouns and verbs, you can work out the rest. The same thing applies to understanding societies and organisations.

The problem now was not just that we didn't understand what our new Japanese rulers wanted from us but they were trying to figure it out and each other too. They weren't consistent because some weren't Japanese.

I didn't know what kind of joke 'cutting off his foot' was in their culture. At least, I was almost sure it was a joke. It had to be.

At home I found Formosa Boy on our front porch, as usual. He looked upset, as was also usual these days.

'Who died?' I made a lame attempt to joke with him.

'Another one of my soldier friends.'

Something else that was becoming usual in our neighbourhood.

'He was cursed by a Buddha statue,' Formosa Boy said. 'We all were.'

'You mean there was a curse on this Buddha statue or that this statue cursed him?'

'I can't talk about it. I'm not allowed to.'

'You can go to the temple to ask for a protection paper.'

'You know things like that don't work in real life.'

Indeed they didn't. But, then, I didn't believe in bad-luck statues either.

'The bad luck is because we were disrespectful of the Buddha statue,' Formosa Boy whispered. 'That's why I dare not go to the temple. They will know. That's why I'm staying close to the house with the Guan Yin statue so it will protect me.'

'Fine. Good.' I would leave it to the non-paying front-room guests who shared the front room with the Guan Yin statue to handle him.

'I cannot tell anybody or I must kill myself. The vow is that serious. When I go to the factory I will apologise to the god before moving him. But if I die, please look after Chen Zong, your Ah Ma, for me. I think of her as my own grandmother because when she cooks for me I can pretend that my whole family isn't dead.'

I didn't have the energy to tell him to stop.

'You'd better watch out for Hideki Tagawa, you know. He is dangerous. I will tell you what I'm not supposed to tell anybody.' Formosa Boy lowered his voice to a whisper. Somehow I knew what he was going to say before he said it. 'Hideki Tagawa had Le Froy's legs cut off so he can't escape.'

It was true, then. Le Froy was crippled and that, too, was my fault. All because I had wanted to show off how clever I was.

But all I had wanted to do was save Uncle Chen's life.

Would Le Froy ever forgive me for crippling him? And given his prejudice against the Japanese even before the occupation, what did he think of me being half Japanese? Had I only imagined the bond between us? All that time had he been watching me, suspecting me of being a spy? Was that why he had given me a job in the Detective Shack – to keep an eye on me?

Even my dream of becoming a reporter was warped. Once upon a time, in what seemed like a different life, I had believed news reporting was a noble calling. I liked the idea of rigorous investigation and analysis, then telling the story to help others understand what was happening. I had picked up some vague ideas about people's 'right to know' from the American women reporters who followed soldiers into battle to inform their readers on what war zones were really like.

But looking at Emily having to pick and choose facts that presented a distorted view of a situation made me think again. I understood she had to please the Japanese. It was an extension of us bowing and addressing them as our lords and masters. And I realised that I had been writing propaganda all along without knowing it. Anyone who's ever written a piece for a newspaper is only presenting their own opinion – even that is just my opinion.

Did I still respect Emily for her independence and making a living from her writing?

I couldn't blame her for writing propaganda for pay. It wasn't much different from writing advertising copy. It was a job. My problem was that until now I had thought of my writing as a vocation. Maybe going to work in one of the Japanese-run factories would be more honest. At least I couldn't do as much harm there.

Mother Dream

———◆———

Dreams were worse during the war: all the things we didn't let ourselves think about while we were awake tortured us at night. That night was one of the worst. I felt like I was tossing and turning restlessly, yet I must have been dreaming.

I felt like I had lost my parents all over again. Now everything I'd thought I knew about them was a lie.

'I couldn't stand my family, so I left them. I couldn't stand your family either, so I left again and took your father with me. No one can treat the Chinese people worse than other Chinese people. Why do you think so many of you left China? I gave you a crooked body to save you from crooked men.'

I couldn't see her face but I knew the woman talking to me was my mother. She was wearing a hood over her head, like the one Madam Koh wore in the inspection field. And I knew she was a liar, just like Madam Koh. Also that it was my fault she was dead . . . she and everyone else.

'You have to find where he kept his secrets. Men like him always record their secrets!'

Then she was gone and I was alone in Mirza's office. I had a duster and I had to get rid of all the dust without moving anything. But there was so much dust. Only his desk and the huge globe standing on the floor were free of it. And to make it worse, there was blood dripping on the books. I pulled out the huge dictionaries from their shelves to try to save them and saw all their pages were blank.

Where was the blood coming from? I looked up and saw huge sprays of leaves were painted across the walls in blood.

And the blood was running in three large streams towards the globe.

I woke, thinking of dust and blood.

Until the Japanese came, my grandmother's greatest hatred was directed towards dust, which made me super-aware of dust in my surroundings. I had seen dust everywhere in Mirza's study, except on his desk and on the large globe next to it.

I tried to focus on that because I didn't want to think about how it was my fault that Le Froy had had his foot cut off.

But now I knew that Le Froy had been crippled, I understood why he had not wanted anyone to tell me anything. He knew the Japanese would use it to manipulate me. Le Froy had never seen the point of loading people with information they could not use.

But he was wrong there because sometimes people would rather know the worst. I would always prefer to know exactly how things stand. You can only play a good game of chess if you know how many pieces you have. And sometimes it is not the number of pieces on the board but the brains manipulating them that determine how things turn out.

For now? I directed my thoughts back to blood and dust. Or rather, to the room and the globe they had coloured in my dream.

I heard Ah Ma moving quietly as she dressed. I kept my eyes shut. I wouldn't rise till my familiar, protective anger woke and reclaimed me. It felt safer to be angry than scared. But what if it was true? What if Hideki Tagawa was torturing Le Froy while he was pretending to be nice to me? What if he was using me to manipulate Le Froy?

When I got up, I made Ah Ma's bed. Then I sat down on it with my notebook. I knew she had gone to the kitchen to give me some privacy but also to start boiling water for morning tea and Little Ling's wash. She would be on the go all day and only return to her bed after everyone else had.

I wanted to ask the Mirza girls to let me back into their father's office. It was still too early to go over to their house, but at a decent hour I would go to see them again. They had no reason to believe me, but I just had to talk my way in, and then they would either see for themselves or I would be wrong. But no worse off than before.

I must have dozed off because I was startled when someone banged on the door.

'Safia Mirza is dead. She hanged herself in the garden last night.' It was Shen Shen, calling on the way to the kitchen.

I jumped out of bed and went after her, 'No! I saw her yesterday!'

'They say she committed suicide because she killed her father,'

'Don't say such things in front of Little Ling,' Ah Ma scolded.

Little Ling, who had not been not paying attention till now, pricked up her ears at this. 'What are you talking about?'

'Nothing to do with you,' Ah Ma said. 'This one is growing up just like you,' she told me, which might have annoyed Shen Shen.

'They say it's your fault, you know,' Shen Shen said. 'Her sister said you went over there yesterday, asking questions, busybodying and accusing them of things.'

'I never accused her of anything!'

'How did you hear?' Ah Ma asked her.

'There are police in the garden and on the road outside. They say she killed herself in the same place where her father was killed. That shows something, doesn't it?'

'What do you mean? What does it show?'

'Sometimes committing suicide is not shameful. Sometimes it's to make things easier for everyone else.'

'You hate me enough to want me to kill myself?'

'I don't hate you. You are Chen Tai's granddaughter. I will never forget that again. It's just that every time I look at you I think how much easier it would be if you didn't exist.'

'That sounds like you hate me.'

'No. I just wish you didn't exist.'

I could understand how she felt. I didn't want to exist either.

Little Ling threw a five stone at my foot, then another. I squatted down to pick them up and challenge her to a game, but Shen Shen snatched the little cloth bag away from me. 'Even if you don't believe it has anything to do with luck and gods, everybody who comes near you dies. I don't want my baby anywhere near you.'

I couldn't blame her. Shen Shen had tried so hard last night. But the suicide of a young girl had shaken her. It had shocked us all. I couldn't help thinking that, after all, I was part Japanese. I was the enemy that was making all this happen.

I walked out of the house to give them some relief from my presence. Heicho Han was standing with some of his men outside the Mirza gate. When he saw me he left them and came over.

'You heard? Terrible thing to happen,' he said. 'Was she your friend?'

'Yes. No. We weren't really friends but, yes, it's terrible. I wanted to ask you – what you said yesterday about Le Froy, that his foot had been cut off. Is that true?'

He deliberated on how to answer me. 'Le Froy is your friend?'

'Not really. Sort of, but not any more. I just want to know if it's true. He is a prisoner of war. He surrendered. Are you really doing things like that to the PoWs? Just tell me.'

'I heard you solved the code Hideki Tagawa could not solve. Is that true?'

What did that have to do with anything? I nodded.

'That made Hideki Tagawa angry because you made him look bad. So, in revenge, he had Le Froy's foot cut off.'

'What did it have to do with Le Froy?'

'He thinks Le Froy came up with the code. And he gave you

the solution just to make him look bad in front of the colonel. Excuse me, I must go.'

I hated the thought of being related to Hideki Tagawa. But I wasn't going to kill myself, like Safia. At worst, I would make him kill me. Like the soldiers of the Malay Regiment who fought to the last to force the Japanese to use up their ammunition.

Had Safia really killed herself? Why?

Singapore has been described as an island with no natural resources other than determination. Well, I had buckets of determination. If Singapore could survive the occupation, so could I.

And if Singapore didn't survive, it wouldn't matter what I did, so I might as well do everything I could.

I remembered Le Froy laughing at me, in the middle of a case, for saying, 'Do something – anything. If you do it well it should either show you the next step so you move on or show you that it was wrong so you move back and start again. Either way it's better than doing nothing.'

He had laughed at the energy I wasted, acting before I'd thought things through. But he had tried something. And later Le Froy agreed that making a move had triggered reactions that had helped solve the case, so it hadn't been a futile waste of energy.

How could I go on living in such a situation?

The same way I would live in any other situation: day by day, moment by moment, doing anything I had to do to survive.

Now I wasn't investigating facts to write a piece for some

weekly paper. I needed to find out for myself what the story was. I took a deep breath and walked towards the Mirza gate. The soldiers looked curious but did not stop me as I passed them, opened the gate and let myself into the Mirza compound.

Mirza's Office

———◆———

'I have to look at your father's office again, I'm not here officially but it's really important. I just thought of something. Because of the dust.'

'You're not here officially? Meaning you don't want them to know you're here? That soldier outside isn't just a decoration, like Father's sentries. He'll report to them exactly what time you came and left.'

'Maybe I was just visiting,' I said desperately. 'We're neighbours, after all.'

I had to look at that office. I was almost a hundred per cent sure I knew where Mirza had hidden his most private documents.

Nasima stared at me. She was probably thinking of her dead sister. If she thought as everyone else seemed to, she probably wished I was dead instead.

'Please,' I said.

Nasima looked over my shoulder and backed away. The Japanese sentry had come up the drive and was watching us. He looked as though he was about to offer to get rid of me for her.

However much Nasima hated me, she hated the Japanese more.

'Come into the office,' she said.

'Heicho Han used to come to see Father,' Nasima said, 'not just as the district commander. He was one of Father's sources of information. And he also used to come to see Safia. That was what Father really hated. He despised him for being unable to read his own language, Korean, not Japanese. He said that in Korean "han" means unresolved resentment against injustice with no exact English equivalent. Han creates acute pain in one's guts and bowels, making the whole body writhe and squirm, combined with a drive for revenge.

'But Heicho Han used to bring Safia treats and he made her laugh. I thought that was all right. I could see she didn't take him seriously. Not in that way. And I didn't want her to go into a decline, like Mother did. I should have stopped her. Safia mentioned going to meet Heicho Han in some factory, and I thought if she was playing at being a factory girl, the reality of the job would soon wake her up. With our parents gone, I should have looked after her.'

Mirza might not have been a devout Muslim, but there were no depictions of people or animals on the walls. Instead there was Arabic calligraphy, some bright geometric shapes in a kaleidoscope of colours, and one small grid showing the English alphabet. The alphabet looked handwritten with a brush on canvas and I guessed Mirza had done it himself. A Chinese brush pen and an ink stone lay on his desk.

But that day I was there to see the globe.

Even now there was little dust on it. The windows and door had been closed, after all. Whatever preserved the dead man's books and papers had also preserved the condition of the room. But that just showed how long the pictures and lamps in the rest of the room had gone without cleaning. What had drawn Mirza to this globe? What had it meant to him?

It turned under my hands, a well-oiled mechanism. But slowly. It was a heavy, stolid object. I wondered what it was made of. Two metal rods ran through it, fixed to the rotating wooden frames so you could turn it all the way around, getting a clear view of the whole world. Like most globes and maps I had seen, this one had rested with the North Pole at the top and Antarctica below. I couldn't see anything at either pole. But I felt a slight irregularity under my fingers. I looked more closely. It was in the Middle East. Was it Mecca? That would make sense. I could feel the slightest depression, smaller than my fingertips could fit into. There was a slight give when I pressed my finger down on it, but nothing happened.

The golden flower stood on his desk. The tiny beads encased in the tips of its three petals gave me the idea. I picked it up and slid it over the globe. It should have been obvious – was blindingly obvious once the tiny ball bearings slid into place at Mecca, Medina and Jerusalem. Holding my breath, I pressed gently. Nothing. Then I tried rotating the golden flower and felt a lever within the globe slide into its release position, and the two halves of the globe sprang apart along the Equator.

This was the secret safe Mirza had protected with his locked doors and curtained windows.

'Who told you?' Nasima sounded angry, but I could tell she was afraid. 'How did you know?'

'I didn't. I guessed – deduced.'

'We had no idea, and it was right here all the time.' Nasima reached into the globe for something, but I had seen it, too. I grabbed it. It was a withered, shrivelled branch of the mimosa tree. And if I was right, this was the last message to have come through.

Thanks to its own defence mechanism, the leaflets were folded close against the dried bark. With luck their fibres would keep them safely in place. I held it gingerly by its base, protecting the closed dried sprigs against my forearm. Nasima stared at it. So she did know about the mimosa branches. Knew enough not to risk damaging it. I put it carefully on the desk top and looked around for something to lay it on before I tried to prise open the leaflets without damaging them.

But first I reached into the globe again and lifted out a vellum-bound notebook.

'That's his appointment book,' Nasima said. 'He had them specially bound. I thought the soldiers took it. It's private.'

Of course it was, private from her and the rest of his family, given how carefully he had hidden it within his own home. That meant he had commissioned this beautiful book for his own pleasure, not to impress others. I felt even more in sympathy with the man. But a note of warning sounded in my brain. It was possible he had been too caught up in his books and cleverness. There were other things in life, like duty and responsibility – but to whom?

I put the book on the desk and spread it open. Mirza's appointments were recorded up to the last days of his life. He had used his secret safe until the end. I was so close to finding out whom he had met that day. The book showed appointments with 'Colonel Pig', 'Golden Bat', most recently 'Rat Face'. Besides the names, there were amounts in the ledger ...

'Rat' had been coming to see him the day he died.

Who was Rat?

Colonel Fujiwara and Heicho Han had called Hideki Tagawa 'Rat Face'. If Hideki Tagawa had been coming to see Mirza on the day he died—

'Get out,' Nasima flared. 'Get out of here!'

So it was Nasima who had been involved, I thought. I wondered who she was in contact with. Someone in the mosque? A contact with the Australian marines?

'You were carrying messages, weren't you? You spied on your father and you passed on information he got from the Japanese.'

I had seen enough to know these were Mirza's most private papers. It was where he stored information on people to keep them in order. Only he couldn't control his daughters in that way because anything that reflected badly on them would have reflected even worse on their father.

I held on to the dried mimosa branch. It was almost a foot long with many side stalks, all huddled close to the centre now. I would have to be very careful and keep them in order ...

Caught up in the branch, I had forgotten to pay attention to Nasima. Now she jumped me, throwing a piece of cloth over my head and arms from behind, then grabbing me and pinning my forearms to my body. She used her weight to pull us both to the floor. I was surprised by how strong she was.

She twisted my left wrist till I let go of the branch. I tried to kick her, but I was disoriented by the cloth over my head. When

I managed to pull it off, I saw she had put it back into the globe and was standing in front of it, holding the small dagger with a jewelled handle. It was the weapon she had brandished to defend me against Hideki Tagawa. Now she was pointing it at me.

'You remind me of our father. Once he got his teeth into a puzzle, he wouldn't give up. He didn't care about the consequences for other people. Well, there's more at stake than your precious pride. Leave the house now or I will kill you.'

'You don't understand how important this is!'

'I do, and I will let you see it – but not yet. I have to go through it first.'

'Why? What are you trying to hide?'

'Nothing,' Nasima insisted. 'But I have to go through everything first.'

Maybe she read my apprehension. 'I'm not going to do anything except look at it. Please don't tell anybody about it until I see what's here. If there's anything about my family—'

I could understand that, though I didn't like it.

She was determined. If Nasima decided to kill me, I couldn't stop her.

'Get out,' Nasima said. 'Now.'

I looked at the globe behind her. On its wheeled frame I could have pushed it out of the house. But with a madwoman waving a weapon at me I might get slashed or, worse, the last branch message might be damaged. There was no way I could safely get to the mimosa branch I had found inside the globe. I couldn't risk anything that might damage the last message. Suddenly there was so much that I understood.

And there were other papers I wanted to look through. Stacks of papers tied into bundles and tucked into brown folders. And the appointment book that recorded the names of Mirza's last visitors on the day he died.

'Give me the appointment book,' I bargained, 'and the mimosa branch. That's all I want. I don't care what he might have written about your sister or your family.'

If I left the house without them, she could destroy everything and I would have nothing but my word to prove what I had seen.

'Get out!'

I didn't want to report her, but I was afraid she would destroy the last message branch as soon as I'd left.

'Just let me see it,' I pleaded. 'You don't know how to read it. I do.'

Nasima propelled me towards the door to the veranda. My foot caught on the metal door runner and she pushed me out, overbalancing me so I fell. She slid the doors shut and locked them, then pulled the curtain across the glass.

Outside the gate the single bored Japanese sentry was on duty. Fleetingly it occurred to me to ask him to come into the house and make Nasima give me what I needed. I could protest that she was blocking me from papers his senior officers had authorised me to look through. But there was no telling whose side he would take. Working for Colonel Fujiwara might give me some licence but it was possible that the lower ranks wouldn't care or might even hold it against me. And I didn't know where the sentry's loyalties lay. Had he been appointed by Hideki Tagawa to watch the house?

For now, I knew I should not trust Hideki Tagawa. Why had he not admitted to his appointment with Mirza Ali Hasnain on the last day of his life?

Perhaps because he had killed the man.

I had thought Hideki Tagawa was the only thing standing between Uncle Chen and death. But now it looked as though he was pushing Uncle Chen towards his end . . . for the crime he himself had committed. And proof of that could be in the globe, proof that Nasima might be destroying right now.

Emily Bennington-Smith

———◆———

E ven in a trishaw, it took me more than half an hour to reach
Shori headquarters. I had the paper that allowed me to travel
through checkpoints but I still had to stop and submit it, bow
and wait while the soldiers studied it and me to make sure I was
not some imposter who had stolen my pass.

When I finally arrived at Colonel Fujiwara's office, the colonel
was not there. In fact, there seemed to be fewer Japanese officers
around than usual.

'Some operation is going on up-country,' Emily Bennington-
Smith told me. 'All hush-hush and top secret. Probably just men
going tiger-shooting.'

The universe was balking me at every turn.

'I've no idea when they'll be back. Why not tell me instead?
Unless you want to try to find Hideki Tagawa. He might know.
That man knows everything.'

I felt a surge of hatred at the name. Of course I wouldn't tell
him what I had found. He would destroy the appointment book
and records faster than Nasima could.

It's a good thing that subservience covers all feeling.

'Thank you,' I said. That must have been how olden-days slaves and concubines in China had felt. And how coolies and amahs in Singapore had felt. And how everyone on the island who was not Japanese felt now. Except Emily Bennington-Smith.

It would have been much harder to hide my feelings from her if we had been equals.

I could see Emily disliked me even though she tried to be polite. It was also possible that I had developed a complex that caused me to imagine that everyone who was nice to me was out to get me.

Before the war, a mad old woman had lived in a shack behind the temple. She used to shout at people, accusing them of sneaking into her house and stealing her food, even when we were bringing her food from our families. Maybe I was becoming mad like her.

That was why I found Shen Shen's open distrust refreshing.

I wondered what had happened to the mad old woman. Maybe after the war I would be sharing her spot behind the temple.

Following Emily Bennington-Smith to her office, I saw familiar faces waiting in the corridor: Corporal Wong Kan Seng's mother and grandmother.

'They come every week to beg the colonel for news of him. There's nothing he can tell them. I think he should just arrest them but he won't.'

Was there too much Asian tradition in Colonel Fujiwara for that? He might have been able to order their execution but he could not arrest them in his home.

I had worked with Corporal Wong at the Detective Shack, and greeted the two old women with gladness and sadness. I had seen them selling kueh outside the market to survive, but it was not just food they needed. Corporal Wong had been the treasure of his widowed mother and grandmother.

Like the rest of the police force, he had received notice that he was required to report at the Orchard Road headquarters to sign a formal declaration of surrender to the new Japanese rulers. It was only a few days after the Fall of Singapore, and no one knew what to expect.

Corporal Wong's mother and grandmother had begged him not to go. They wanted him to hide or run away instead. But he believed it was his duty to surrender formally. We never learned what had happened to him. His mother went to prison camps and labour camps, shouting his name from the outside. She was not the only one. Every time a truck of chained workers drove past, desperate women shouted names of husbands, sons, brothers, all of the beloved and missing men who were not yet presumed dead.

Many civil servants ordered to report for 'work' in this fashion were never seen again. Many others had disappeared, too.

Some, like Mr Meganck and Harry Palin, had chosen to disappear on their own. I hoped they had made it to safety wherever they were: overland north through the Malayan jungle or south across the sea to Australia. Of all the missing men, Mr Meganck had probably the best chance of surviving in the wild. But there had been no word of any of them.

Not knowing was the worst for families: they couldn't even grieve and move on.

Yet I was glad there was no word of Sergeant Pillay and Sergeant de Souza: there was a chance, at least, that they were alive somewhere, like Le Froy. I would always choose the smallest hope over certainty of the worst. What's the point in moving on if your only reason for living is gone?

'The locals like a bit of excitement. They're just as bloodthirsty,' Miss Emily said. 'You should see the old women like them poking around the dead bodies. Looking for things to steal. They're stupid. Of course the soldiers remove anything of value before killing the owners. Not that these people ever have anything worth taking.'

I knew the women were searching for something more precious than watches or coins. They peered into the faces of the dead, hoping to be disappointed.

But that was all I was doing, wasn't it? I was trying to do something useful as an alternative to being dead.

'When will Colonel Fujiwara be back?'

'I don't know his schedule,' Emily Bennington-Smith said. 'What's so urgent?'

She looked as calmly and completely in charge as ever. And, also as ever, her slight superiority and impatience were there in the way she rapped her knuckles against the wood of the door as she stared at me.

We were alone in her office, although there were guards outside. When Colonel Fujiwara was around, she behaved as subserviently as any well-trained geisha. But when he was not, she was the imperious memsahib.

'I have to talk to someone,' I said. 'This is really important. She may be destroying the evidence right now.'

She shook her head dismissively.

I wished she would let me sit down. I could walk as far as I had to, but it hurt. And now, just standing on my uneven legs made my lower back and hip ache.

'You must take this seriously. Do you want to be blamed for Mirza's murderer getting away?' I demanded. I sounded rude even to myself. But if she wasn't going to offer me a drink and a chance to sit down, as any guest deserved, I wasn't going to behave like a guest.

'I found Mirza's hidden safe and his papers are inside. I was unable to go through them. Nasima Mirza wouldn't let me, and she threw me out. But I saw his appointment book. Does the colonel know that Hideki Tagawa went to see Mirza on the day he died? That he might have killed him? Is Hideki Tagawa with Colonel Fujiwara right now?'

The frown lines on Emily Bennington-Smith's face deepened. I couldn't tell if she didn't like what I was saying or simply didn't believe me.

'I'm not making this up,' I said desperately. 'Don't you see? If Hideki Tagawa had an appointment to see Mirza that day, he must have been the reason why the door in the back wall was unlocked. And after Mirza unlocked it and let him in—'

'Hideki Tagawa could have killed him,' she said. 'What else was in the hidden safe?'

'I don't know!' I almost wailed. 'I couldn't see! And I don't know what she is doing to the papers now!'

My voice rose in desperation and one of the security officers pushed open the door briefly. Miss Emily bowed and smiled, and he moved away.

I lowered my voice. 'I didn't get a chance to see more. Mirza's daughter wouldn't let me. It's her house and her father's things and I know she blames me for her sister's death. If Hideki Tagawa gets there and makes her let him inspect what's in the safe he'll be able to destroy it all before anyone else sees it. That's why you have to let the colonel know without alerting Tagawa. I dare not ask any of the other kempeitai because—'

'Because you don't know who is working for Hideki Tagawa.' She nodded. 'I suppose Nasima Mirza has seen the papers?'

'I don't think she'll get anything out of them. Mirza wrote everything in code. The same code as he kept his notes in. I figured that out earlier. But there was nothing important in any of his previous papers.'

'Why don't you go and sit down in the kitchen?' Miss Emily finally said. 'Have some water. You look hot and tired. I will see if I can find out where he is.'

She settled me in the kitchen with a glass of water. I drank it and decided I wouldn't make any decisions until I had cooled down.

She must have gone out of the front door because I heard an engine rev, and when I went to look out of the front window I saw her getting into one of the official cars. I had expected her to send a messenger to Colonel Fujiwara, but if she was going, I could go with her.

At the very least I could get a ride somewhere closer to home.

I gulped the rest of the water and hurried out of the house. The driver might have been under orders to take her to wherever she wanted to go, but apparently not to stop for anyone else because he almost ran me down without slowing.

I was hot and breathless again. But there seemed no point in heading back into the headquarters building. I started the walk to the tram stop.

Fire at Mirza House

———◆———

Passing the Mirza house on the way home, I felt even more frustrated. I hoped Emily Bennington-Smith would manage to find Colonel Fujiwara before Nasima had destroyed the contents of the globe. Unless the colonel did something fast, there was no guarantee she wouldn't destroy anything she thought detrimental to her family honour.

There was a Japanese guard outside as usual, not at the gate but under the shade of a nearby tree. I bowed to him as I passed. He ignored me.

I got home at the same time as the children, Little Ling among them, were coming in from an afternoon of fishing, frog hunting and fruit picking under Shen Shen's supervision. They were chatty, sweaty, happy and eager to show off their finds. Most of the fruit was unripe, but would be pickled to go with our yams and tapioca. Life goes on.

Formosa Boy was in the backyard, deftly sorting and stacking the firewood he had spread outside to dry on his last visit. Then, I suspect for no reason other than that he had nothing better to do and didn't want to leave, he started gutting and splitting the fish the children had brought back, threading them onto bamboo skewers to smoke. Formosa Boy reminded me of a stray cat in the old days, always hanging around and hoping not to be noticed, pinching whatever it could pick up.

I didn't want to think of what had happened to the stray cats and dogs. People in the city were even eating rats now.

'You'll make someone a good wife when you grow up,' I told him. I had meant it as a joke, but it sounded nasty. Formosa Boy looked surprised. I didn't often talk to him unless he forced the exchange. But his broad, good-natured face showed he hadn't taken offence.

'I hope so also,' he said. 'I hope I live to grow up.'

I hoped so too.

We both heard the cries of alarm at the same time. People on the road outside were shouting, more in excitement than fear. And, turning, we saw smoke rising even as the smell reached us.

'Bomb!' Formosa Boy said, sniffing like a dog. Then, despite all his fears of death and wanting to live to grow up, he charged down the driveway, running towards the fire, which was clearly blazing in the direction of the Mirza house.

I went after him, as fast as I could but much more slowly.

I was worried for Nasima, of course, but also for the papers and everything in that secret safe. I can't deny it. But I honestly would have given up everything in there to have Nasima out alive. Yes, I had been frustrated enough to want to slap her, but too many people were dead.

And I liked her. I wanted to get to know her when we weren't fighting each other, trying to save the same people.

And I worried she had started the fire, burning the papers in the globe. And maybe herself.

I rushed over. It wasn't easy pushing my way through. There were so many people, soldiers and locals, staring at the smoke coming out of the front of the house. Under kempeitai instructions, a few people were scooping up sandy earth in their hands and throwing it towards the flames. But the heat kept them back and they couldn't get close enough to do any good.

It was about as effective as handing each of our boys a pistol with eight bullets and ordering them to defend the island against Japanese infantry mortars and machine guns.

Maybe we Singaporeans had to stop doing what we were told.

I pushed through the gawking onlookers and went round the side of the house to the veranda and windows outside Mirza's office. The thick shrubbery there had kept most people away. I couldn't see any fire but the rooms were thick with smoke, which was pouring out of the windows. The thought of all the books and maps burning was painful, but I was more concerned about Nasima.

'Nasima! Where are you?'

My voice didn't go anywhere. You don't think of fire as loud, but it was. It was as though the thick smoke stifled sound as well as sight. And over it all was the noise of people shouting, wailing and, like me, calling for anyone inside.

I continued to the back of the building where the schoolroom was. Maybe she had been there – maybe she had got out already.

'Nasima!'

The back-door handle was too hot to hold. I was afraid that opening the door would feed the fire within. Maybe she had started the fire and was determined to die in it. Had I been wrong all along? Had Nasima Mirza killed her father? Her sister too?

'Su Lin.' A hand reached out from a bougainvillaea bush and touched my arm.

It was Nasima. Under her headscarf her face was dirt-smeared and she seemed to be in pain, folding her arms across her abdomen under the full burqa she was wearing. But she was alive. In my relief I forgot my previous suspicions and threw my arms around her. 'Nasima, I'm so glad. Are you all right?'

'Su Lin, I must tell you—'

'Ebisu-Chan. You again. Always making trouble. Always getting in the way.' It was Heicho Han. 'You two. Come with me. Now!'

He was extremely tense, muttering hoarsely in Korean and repeatedly stabbing the bayonet of his Arisaka rifle into the ground almost as though he was possessed. I wondered if he was drunk.

He was directing us deeper into the Mirza garden, towards Mirza's old meeting place.

I couldn't tell if he meant to rescue or rape us. Nasima was staring at him, not moving. Heicho Han raised his rifle – and dropped.

Shen Shen had whacked him from behind with a coconut.

She squatted beside him, still holding her coconut bludgeon by its stalk. 'He's not dead. You'd better go before he wakes up.'

'What are you doing here? Why did you do that?'

'Don't talk so much. Take her back to Chen Mansion.'

'Will you come back to my house?'

'Yes, please,' Nasima said. 'What did he call you? Ebisu-Chan?'

It was what Colonel Fujiwara had called me. Did that mean Miss Emily had reached the colonel and he had sent Heicho Han to destroy the evidence?

The Contents of the
Globe Safe

———◆———

'Did you start that fire?' I asked Nasima.

We had made it safely back to Chen Mansion where we ended up in Ah Ma's bedroom, sitting side by side on my mattress on the floor. The only alternative was Ah Ma's bed and we were both too dirty for that. Nasima was trembling and panting heavily, but not as much as I was.

'Of course not! Did you?'

'No! Why would I?'

'You were so angry when I made you leave. You looked like you'd do anything to make sure no one ever saw Father's papers.'

'I didn't want to destroy them! I wanted to read them! But what were you so afraid of me seeing? You chased me away with a knife.'

'I wouldn't really have hurt you,' Nasima said.

Even if she had meant to, unless she knew exactly where to

stick her tiny dagger and I stayed still and let her, I didn't think she could have done me any great harm. But that wasn't the point. The point was where I had gone after leaving her and whom I had told.

'The fire might have been my fault,' I said.

I told Nasima that I had told Emily Bennington-Smith about finding the secret safe in her father's office, then asked, 'What actually happened? Did you see anyone?'

'I was in Father's office when the window was smashed. I think they threw a brick or rock at it. Then what looked like a glass bottle with cloth tied around it landed on the carpet. The cloth was on fire. The bottle smashed and I smelt petrol. It spread over the floor and started to burn. I grabbed the papers, everything from the table in front of me, and ran out. I wanted to take the Koran too – my father always had it on his desk – but I couldn't carry it all. I dropped it.'

'What was in the safe that you didn't want me to see?'

'Our mother's letters,' Nasima said. 'I thought Father might have kept them.'

'Letters from your mother? To you?' I didn't understand.

'Letters from a man who once loved her. He wrote to her, one letter a month, for years. He had fallen in love with her when they were thirteen and fourteen years old. They never met again after she married our father. But he wrote to her once a month until she died. And I hoped Father might have hidden Dawud's letters to me. Or saved a photograph. But he hadn't.'

'I'm sorry.'

'But this is what I really had to save.'

Nasima lifted off her burqa. Beneath it she had knotted a

batik sarong around her neck baby-carrier style. She untied it
and spread the contents on the floor in front of us. 'I can't read
any of it. Can you?'

The pages were in a simple shifted alphabet code. Every letter
shifted five places to the right. For instance, my family name,
'Chen', became 'Hmjs'. It was there because the first batch of
papers contained Mirza's research into my family. That must
have been because I was working at the Detective Shack. Though
it might also have had to do with my grandmother's black-market
businesses.

Then there was a box folder with hole-punched papers, as I
had predicted. This held records of Mirza's accounts and
appointments.

Third, and most important, was the dried mimosa branch.

'This is the branch your father caught you with, isn't it?
He put it into the safe and was making a fake when he was
killed.'

Nasima didn't say anything. She didn't have to. I could see
the events unfolding.

'Your father was plucking at leaflets on the fresh mimosa
branch he had just hacked off when he was stabbed in the back
with his own tree trimmer. My guess is, he was creating a code
with it to demonstrate the system he had discovered. And he
figured out the leaf code thanks to the dried branch he took
from you. That was why Safia blamed you?'

'You found him dead in the garden and you slipped out that
night to deliver what you thought was the last message. Only
you didn't. You delivered the fake message your father created.
Because that was what you found in his hand. Your father had

hidden the real message sprig in his safe.' I held up the dried mimosa branch. 'Did you decipher it?

'I don't know how. Would you, please?'

I spread open the tiny dried leaflets gently, careful not to tear any. As I counted them, I thanked the nature of the mimosa tree. Even in death it held on to its leaves, protective to the last. The same elastic tenacity that allowed its leaflets to open and close also helped them to stay attached in death.

The message was urgent. The Japanese had narrowed down the location of resistance camps up-country and were planning a massive attack on the next moonless night.

'This is the real message. The branch you took from your father was the fake he made to give to the colonel. That one, the one you delivered, said, "No news."'

'You are right. I found my father dead. I trained as a nurse. I knew there was nothing more I could do for him. But I thought I could at least save the last message, so I took the mimosa branch he was holding. Are you sure he wasn't going to betray them? Ever since he caught me he kept asking me who I was passing the branches to, but I wouldn't tell him. He even got Safia to question me and sneak into my room to read my diary but there was nothing for her to find.'

'It might not have been your father who told Safia to go through your things.'

Nasima nodded. 'I know that now. I knew Safia was in love with Heicho Han. I warned her many times not to trust him but she called me old-fashioned and jealous. Then after our father died, he wouldn't have anything to do with her. She was no more use to him. I knew she was trying to win him back.'

'Could Safia have told Heicho Han your father had solved the mimosa code?'

'She wouldn't have known. I didn't know. Father usually told the Japanese sentry he wanted a meeting and they would get the message to the colonel.'

Someone must have intercepted the message at the colonel's end. I thought of Emily Bennington-Smith screening all callers and going through the mail at the Shori headquarters.

'All Safia could have told Heicho Han was that Father had caught me coming back from the mosque one night and got very angry. He locked us both into the house. She thought it was unfair that she was punished for something I had done. He was just trying to keep us safe. To him that meant not being involved with his business, with the British or with the Japanese. He told me he had promised our mother he would protect us and he was going to, whether I liked it or not.

'Knowing Father, he probably said he wanted assurance that nothing would reflect on us. He didn't want it to become public knowledge that he had only cracked the mimosa code thanks to catching me with a branch.'

'If your father's message to Colonel Fujiwara mentioned he wanted to keep his family safe and uninvolved, someone might have thought it had something to do with Heicho Han and Safia.'

'But why would she kill herself?'

I remembered Safia outside the Mirza gates the last time I'd seen her. She had looked determined, not desperate. 'Maybe she didn't.'

Nasima looked at me. I saw hope rising.

'Supposing something I told you that day made Safia think she could win back Heicho Han. She goes to him with the information. Maybe threatens him. He kills her.'

'But what?'

I couldn't think either.

'You mentioned a Buddha statue,' Nasima said slowly.

'A missing statue. Taken from a temple up north, near the Thai border.'

'Safia mentioned a statue once, too. I remember she asked Father how much it was worth, whether it could be ransomed for more than its weight in gold. Father said it wasn't worth trying because it was too recognisable and people were too superstitious.'

'He's right about people being superstitious.' I remembered how upset Formosa Boy had been over talk of statues.

Just then we heard Heicho Han's voice, loud and angry, in the house. I couldn't make out what he was saying but Ah Ma and Shen Shen were countering him, polite but stubborn. Unless he used his gun, I doubted he would get past them.

Formosa Boy sidled into the room. 'My Big Boss is outside looking for me.' I wondered how long he had been lurking in the corridor. I would have suspected anyone else of eavesdropping, but this was Formosa Boy.

'Tagawa?' I was startled.

'Tagawa is my Big Boss's Big Boss,' Formosa Boy said. He slumped onto the floor by the door, sooty as a sack of charcoal. 'I tried to save things from your house,' he told Nasima. 'I put them in the garden near the wall. I must tell you right away. Or if I die first, the curse on me will be worse.' He pulled a

263

grimy-covered book out of his pocket. It was a copy of the Koran. 'I found this outside on the ground.'

Nasima had been stiff and suspicious since Formosa Boy had come in. Now she took the book from him with shaking hands and bowed, touching it to her forehead before pressing it to her chest.

'Yours?'

'My father's. Look.' Nasima handed me a card from the inside cover and I read, 'One day you will ask me, "Which is more important? My life or yours?" I will say mine and you will walk away not knowing that you are my life.' It was a quotation from the work of Khalil Gibran.

'Your father's handwriting?'

'My mother's. I believe this is why my father cut down the branch and created the false "No news" message,' Nasima said. She turned to Formosa Boy, 'Thank you. I owe you more than you can know.'

'Pray for me,' Formosa Boy said. 'I am going to die soon. Maybe today.'

'No one knows when they will die,' Nasima said.

'It will be soon. I've got an important, dangerous mission tonight. After that I will get reward bonus and promotion.'

'That sounds good.' I had to get rid of him without offending him. 'Do you know what caused the fire at Nasima's house? Did the guard there see anything?'

'The sentry on duty said he was called away by a senior officer just before it happened and didn't see anything. But they think he just went to the WC without permission. He is in big trouble. Bigger trouble than me even.'

The poor boy. But I didn't have pity to spare for Japanese soldiers. If someone was waiting for such an opportunity, who knows how long they were there?

'Promotion to Heaven!' Formosa Boy moaned. 'Every time Big Boss promises to promote people, they die.'

'Then don't go!'

'If I don't go, worse. I already miss the last time because of the crocodile eggs. The Buddha curse or the Big Boss. Which one is worse? Tonight I will have to carry dangerous statues through mud and long grass. I will be cursed again. I want to stay here with Chen Zong.' This last was delivered with a slight bow to my grandmother as she came in. 'Has Heicho Han left?'

Ah Ma nodded. 'You should get back to camp before he goes to look for you there.'

'I am going to die. I know it. I am only sad I cannot see you again.' He bowed to Ah Ma. 'Maybe I cannot even see my family again because they are in Heaven. But I am going to Hell because I do terrible things to the Buddha.'

'Then don't do terrible things!' I said.

'I must. Or I will die.'

'But you are going to die anyway, you said. If you don't do terrible things and you die, maybe you won't go to Hell and you can see your family again.'

Was I really sending Formosa Boy to his death with this mishmash of Buddhism, Taoism, ancestor worship and superstition?

'Cannot. I am a soldier. I must follow orders or they will shoot me.'

'Come,' Ah Ma said. 'I will give you something to eat first. You can take it with you.'

Nasima's Message

———◆———

Once Formosa Boy was gone, I returned to the mimosa branch. I had decided copying down the number of leaflets would be safer than carrying the branch. Who knew how many people were aware that the branches held messages?

'Can I borrow that batik sarong? And write on it? I mean, you probably won't get it back, and even if you do, you probably won't want to wear it again. But the pattern is perfect and it might save lives.'

The batik pattern was intricate enough to disguise the numbers I wrote into the printed leaves. There was something poetic about it, but I put that idea aside to think about when I wasn't trying to save the lives of resistance fighters.

'You remind me of my father. He used to work like that. Sitting and scribbling, staring at his notes, as though he was trying to burn secrets out of them.'

'There's something else.' I teased open the last few stalks right at the base of the branch. 'The Aussies claim they sabotaged the Japanese ships but didn't loot them. They targeted the hulls of seven battleships, no civilian transports.'

That seemed not to mean anything to Nasima.

'What are you going to do with that?' she asked.

'That depends on you,' I said. 'The Japanese have narrowed down the locations of resistance camps up-country and are planning to attack on the next moonless night.' I looked at the date again. 'That's tomorrow. We need to get this message through.'

'I can't. I promised.'

'Then tell me who and how. I'll make sure they get the message,' I held up the sarong, 'and understand it.'

'I can't. I promised,' Nasima said again.

'Come on, lah. You remind me of Formosa Boy! "I'm scared to go, I have to go. I'm scared to die, I have to die"!'

Nasima smiled. 'He's quite sweet, isn't he? Like a big little boy who wants to be good and tries to do as he's told.'

'Even when he thinks he's being told to do bad things.'

'Nobody made me do bad things, Su Lin.'

'Tell me.'

'Father caught me with that branch. You're right about that. I didn't know how it was a message, just that it was important to get the branches from outside the back of the mosque to …'

'To whom? Where?'

Nasima shook her head, 'Father was so angry when he found me with the branch that day. He made me swear an oath that I would carry no further messages. And I swore, more because I saw how upset he was than anything else.'

'What happened?'

'Father guessed at once what I was doing. It was only after that that he locked us into the house. He was afraid of what would happen to me if I was caught carrying messages for the PoWs and resistance. Even though it was only a dried tree branch. Safia thought it was so unfair that she was locked up too. I suppose she must have minded more than I knew. I was the one carrying the messages, not my sister. And I didn't spy on my father. I would never do that, even if he was doing anything worth spying on. I didn't understand what the messages were. All I had to do was pick up the branches stuck in a pile of stones at the back of the mosque.'

'Where did they come from?'

'I don't know. I'm guessing from the jungle around the PoW camps. They used to find letters there. Prisoners pushed them through the barbed wire begging anyone who found them to post them or put them in a bottle in the sea. They didn't know that anything thrown into the sea around there washes up here. That's why there have been so many bodies. When the PoWs push the branches through the fence, the kampung children carry them to the back of the mosque and stick them into piles of stones there.'

It was a clever system. Worthy of Le Froy, I thought.

'What did you do with the branches?'

Nasima shook her head. 'I trust you – that's why I'm telling you what I did – but I don't want to get anyone else into trouble.'

'Did anyone else know about your father and you and the branches?'

'Safia might have told Heicho Han about it. She must have been more deeply involved with him than I realised. I forgot how young she was. And how alone. I have strength from my faith in Allah. You have your family and your books. But Safia had nothing and no one. I should have seen that, but I did not. Not in time. She was romantic, like our mother, and strong-minded, like our father, but not as clever. When Father was angry with me, he said he should have let Heicho Han marry me,' Nasima added. 'I think that made Safia angrier than anything else.'

'Heicho Han wanted to marry you? I thought he was Safia's friend.'

'I was his first choice because I was older and he thought I might inherit more. But he also said he was willing to marry us both if the dowry price was good enough.'

'That was generous of him.' Two more women Heicho Han had offered to marry. If I'd been the jealous sort I would have been upset. Instead I was starting to feel a kind of comradeship.

I wondered if Emily Bennington-Smith had fallen for him too. With her office in the Shori headquarters, she was in the perfect position to intercept the runner Mirza sent to Colonel Fujiwara saying he had made an important discovery. In the same way (oh, how stupid I had been there) she had intercepted my message about finding the secret safe at the Mirza house. But whom had she told? Was she one of the women who had fallen for Heicho Han's good looks and Korean charm? Or was she really working with Hideki Tagawa? Was all the antipathy between them just an act?

'Father was so furious with Heicho Han. He didn't let him see it, of course, just went on working with him and paying him. But after he talked about marrying me – or us – Father would not have told Heicho Han anything that would help him. He told me he would rather I died unmarried than that I married such a man. You'd have had to know my father to understand how much that meant.'

'You loved him, didn't you? And respected him.'

'He wasn't good at being conventional. He thought most social conventions were stupid. He lived by his own rules. But he was a good father. And a good man. And that's why he's dead.'

'So don't let it be for nothing.'

'What?'

'Don't let your father have died for nothing. I'm not asking you to break your oath. Just tell me where you took the previous branches.'

'To the prison.'

'Don't they come *from* the prison?'

'I told you, I don't know how it works.'

'Who do you give them to in the prison?'

'I'm not supposed to say!'

'Tell me!'

'Dr Shankar. At the prison clinic. As I have nursing experience, I go there sometimes and help him with the women and children. And if any branches were left behind the mosque when I was going there, I took them with me and left them there.'

I couldn't go to see Dr Shankar with no excuse.

'Can I borrow your knife?'

'Are you going to write numbers on it too?'

I cut myself. Carefully, a short flesh wound.

'Are you mad? What are you doing?' Shen Shen came in and stared at the blood welling up.

'I have to go to the prison hospital to see Dr Shankar about something,' I said. When Shen Shen reached over, I waved her away. I wanted the blood.

'No, no, wait ...'

Shen Shen took the knife and nicked her thumb. It was a small cut but it bled copiously. She smeared the blood all over my blouse and the cloth in which she laid my forearm, carefully exposing the cut, which now looked like the end of a long slice.

'Go. I will keep her safe here.'

'Is Heicho Han still waiting outside?'

'I made him leave.'

We stared at Shen Shen.

'You made him leave?'

'How?'

'Heicho Han is a greedy man,' Shen Shen said. 'He wants to keep his bit of extra protection money and cut of the black market, but he says he cannot get your uncle out because Hideki Tagawa has him in Changi Prison with the British PoWs. I told him to leave you alone, or no more extra money.'

'He doesn't know you hit him on the head with a coconut?'

'In Singapore, with so many coconut palms, of course people get hit on the head with coconuts.'

'Thanks,' I said. 'I thought you hated me.'

'I hate the Japanese more.'

'You know I am half Japanese?'

'I know you talk too much,' Shen Shen said. 'Three hungry pigs are more dangerous than one hungry dog. And we are very hungry.'

She stepped back and studied me. Then she ran her hand

over the mud Formosa Boy had left on the floor and smeared it over my face.

'If anyone stops you, tell them you were trying to open a coconut and the knife slipped.'

'Wait.' Nasima unpinned her headscarf and shook it out. She folded it into a triangle that she draped over my head with the point at my back.

'Open your mouth.'

'What?'

'Move your jaw, so I don't make it too tight.' She pinched the long folds of the scarf gently under my chin and pinned them together with a pearl brooch. Then she crossed the tails of the scarf and pulled them over my shoulders. I felt her pinning the ends at the back of my head, then pulling and draping fabric over the pin. 'Just to keep it extra secure since you're going out. My mother always said it was to keep us safe. May it keep you safe.'

Dr Shankar Sends
a Message

———◆———

With all the excitement of smoke, fire, alarms and people being ordered into a bucket brigade, no one had paid much attention to a local girl scurrying past with an injured arm.

Even in the prison visitors' compound I wasn't stopped. But that might have had less to do with the gory sight I presented than because fewer soldiers were on duty than usual and no patients had been brought over.

It was more difficult to see Dr Shankar alone.

'There is a fire at the Mirza house!' I said in Japanese. That woke up the two sleepy-looking guards. The wind was blowing in from the sea so there was no smell of smoke, but when you looked inland you could see it.

'The rich man's house? The dead rich man's house?'

'Yes, sir.'

One smirked at my arm. I could see him thinking I had sliced myself trying to grab something through a broken window. And

I saw that thought was followed by another: what else might be available for looting?

'We should go and help.' He nudged his partner. 'Lock them in.'

'Wait,' Dr Shankar said in Japanese. 'What if there is a fire here too?'

'Then you will be roast dog instead of dog!'

'There's some activity going on.' Dr Shankar was clearly under stress. 'Have you heard anything?'

Without asking me why I was there, he put on his spectacles and dampened part of a cotton towel before bending over my arm.

'That's not important. I need to get a message up north.'

'You know very well there's no way of communicating with anyone up north. What do you want from me?' Dr Shankar said.

'The last message from the PoW camp was a warning that the Japanese have discovered the rough location of the camp twenty miles outside Perak. They are going to attack on the next moonless night. That's tomorrow. They're sending soldiers up from all around.'

'I don't know what you're talking about.' Dr Shankar wasn't a good liar.

'Yes, you do. If you have any way at all of warning them, you must.'

'If you're making this up - if they offered you some bargain for your uncle's life or Le Froy's life—'

'No, they didn't. I mean, yes, they did. But I'm telling you, not them.' I wanted to shake the man for being stupid. 'Even Mirza wasn't going to tell them. He hid the real message branch - yes,

I've seen it – and he was making up a fake message when he was killed. That's why the message Nasima gave you said, "No news." But you must have known that was fake, because on all the previous messages, the branches would have dried up before they reached you and that one was still fresh.'

'No, no, no. You mustn't get mixed up in such things–'

'Listen before you say no, you stupid man! The branch Nasima found held a fake message her father had made up. I found the real last branch hidden in his safe.'

'If Mirza was figuring out the locations of the resistance camps, it was only to sell the information to the Japanese. That man ...' Dr Shankar shook his head.

'No. He hid the real message. I have the leaflet counts here.' I unwrapped the sarong I had pulled around my waist. 'You have to send them and warn them.'

'What makes you think I can?'

'Please, Uncle Shankar,' it was a long time since I had called him that, 'they're planning to take the camp. It would be better for the resistance fighters to kill themselves than be taken by the Japanese. You have to warn them.'

He looked at me for a long moment. I could tell he was weighing up his dead friend – who might not have been the traitor he thought – against me: I might be trying to betray him right now.

The homemade radio was in the morgue, inside one of the stinking organ bins. We pushed two tables against the door first. It was locked, but not from the inside. The tables would slow down anyone who tried to come in. And the room was so small that needing to reach the back cupboards was a good enough reason for shifting them. Dr Shankar lifted out two trays of what looked like pigs' organs (I knew they didn't come from pigs, but it was easier to think of them so) and a canvas sack. Inside the sack, insulated in newspapers, was the radio.

Dr Shankar bound up my arm nicely after he had sent the message warning of imminent attack.

'Do you really not know where Parshanti is? Just tell me if she's all right. I won't ask any more than that.'

'You may have just saved her life. Parshanti went up-country with Leask and Meganck.'

'Mr Meganck? The McPherson boys' tutor?' Dr Leask had worked with Le Froy and Dr Shankar for years, but I had no idea he and Mr Meganck knew each other.

And I knew Meganck was as much at home in the rainforest as any *Orang Asli*. He was one of the few white men accepted by the aboriginal forest dwellers. Parshanti was in good hands.

'They came to see us the night they took her mother away. My poor wife. Twenty years of exile for marrying me and now she's locked up for being white. We knew then that it was only a matter of time before they came for me. Leask said they were heading for a community going up north to wait it out in the pineapple plantations till the British come back. At the worst, with Meganck, they could survive in the jungle or the highlands. They wanted us to go with them. I wouldn't leave the island without my wife, but I told Parshanti to go.

'Now I am more relieved than ever that she is out of Singapore. I wish you were too. Mirza played a dangerous game. He thought he had enough information to blackmail senior Japanese officials into protecting his family. Because they don't always know what their men are doing. But Mirza didn't know what his own family was doing.'

'You mean until he found out about Nasima bringing you the mimosa branches?'

'He never knew about Safia. Which may have been the one good thing about his death.'

Somehow I knew he was not talking about Safia's suicide – if it had been suicide.

'Safia Mirza was pregnant,' Dr Shankar said. 'And that wasn't the worst of it.'

I stared at him.

'I warned her of the risks of a pregnancy in her condition. Possible birth defects such as blindness, deafness, mental disabilities, born deformities.'

'But why – who – how—'

'Sexually transmitted infections can lie dormant for a long time. And she wasn't the only one.'

'How did you know?'

'It is easily recognisable in the early stages. Genital ulcers, rash and fevers. I will not discuss my patients, but it is too late for Safia, and if breaking my oath preserves you, I will.'

'Poor Safia! Did she say who it was? Can you tell?'

Dr Shankar shook his head. 'The poor child would not. Not till she'd told him first, she said. Syphilis is called the 'Great Imposter' because of its ability to mimic many other conditions in its later stages. It is caused by bacterial infection, not immorality. Difficult to diagnose because the symptoms are so varied. But they commonly include irritability, delusions and grandiosity.'

'So we can't tell if someone has it, apart from the kind of lies they tell us?'

For some reason I thought of Emily and how much she talked, though I doubted she had infected Safia.

'Does Emily Bennington-Smith come to see you?'

'She and the colonel have pharmaceutical needs. When I have barely enough antiseptic, bandages and aspirin, they demand penicillin and morphine—' He cut himself off. 'Sorry, dear girl. Talking doesn't help.'

'It can help to know who can be trusted.'

'True. It's an old man ranting that doesn't help. Emily Bennington-Smith gets medicines from the pharmacy. Likely she sells them. She also gets birth control from me. No one says no to her because if you cross her she makes up stories for Colonel Fujiwara, and the next thing you know you're hanging by the ankles being split in half. She's made it clear she's willing to trade for information. But I don't play that game. I don't know anything because I don't want to know anything.'

'Just one more thing. About Le Froy—'

'I won't discuss him.'

'Just tell me, have you seen him? How is he? Was he tortured like they say?'

Dr Shankar shook his head. 'I won't discuss Le Froy with you.'

'Just tell me. What did they do to him?' Damn Hideki Tagawa!

Dr Shankar wouldn't say another word.

I knew that he would have reassured me if he could. The only reason he wouldn't was because he didn't want to lie to me and couldn't bear to tell me the truth.

'Please, Dr Shankar. You know that Le Froy trusts me—'

Something in his look stopped me there.

'Le Froy instructed you not to tell me anything,' I guessed. I was hurt, but strangely unsurprised. A lot of other things fell into place and made sense.

'Forget Le Froy,' Dr Shankar said. 'Forget Le Froy and the British. They are the past. Over. *Kaput*. Su Lin, I'm only telling you what I would tell my own daughter. You have to get on with your life as it is now. The important thing is survival. And the only way to survive is to forget how things used to be.'

I was glad he had dropped his cold exterior. But I didn't agree with him.

Our memory of the past was the only thing we had to cling to. I was too Asian to be comfortable saying it aloud but I had to try. 'We must remember things were once good, even if they are never good again. Otherwise what's the point?'

I believe he understood. I couldn't begin to imagine what Dr Shankar was living through. He and his wife had been the most romantic couple I had ever known. It must have been torture for him, knowing Mrs Shankar was in prison and Parshanti somewhere up-country with two men.

I could only answer him as I thought his daughter would. 'There is no way to guarantee that any of us will survive. But I'm still glad to be alive.'

He took my hands in his. As I looked around the miserable little room, I accepted all the feeling in his eyes and the clasp of his hands. It was the way people said goodbye now, with no idea when or if either would be alive to meet again.

'I hear you've learned Hideki Tagawa is a second cousin. That could be a useful connection.'

'I hate him. He's a monster. I know he tortured Le Froy for information and cut off his foot to cripple him.'

'I amputated Le Froy's foot.'

I stared at Dr Shankar. 'No.'

'Yes. Gangrene. He stepped on a rusty can. Hideki Tagawa arranged for the operation. He probably saved Le Froy's life.'

'Why didn't he say so?'

'Maybe he thought you wouldn't believe him.'

There was a commotion in the corridor and we scrambled to move the tables before the door was thrown open.

'Has anyone come here?'

'No. Who are you looking for?'

'The triad gangster Chen you told us to keep an eye on, the one who killed the rich man, he's escaped!' The guard was highly excited.

'Uncle Chen? But why would he try to escape?'

Why now, when he was so close to being released?

'Hideki Tagawa may have authorised his release.'

'Nobody can find Tagawa either. Colonel Fujiwara wants them both found and arrested. Chen's guards say he was taken away on Tagawa's orders.'

'Where is Colonel Fujiwara?'

'On a top-secret mission. His orders are to have Tagawa charged with treason for helping Chen escape and maybe also for kidnapping him.'

'For kidnapping Chen?'

'For kidnapping the colonel!'

This didn't make much sense.

The guard dashed off and we heard him banging on other

doors. The escape, from a different part of the prison, could not be blamed on him and he was clearly enjoying the drama.

'You should go now. Quickly, before they wonder why you're here.'

'But Uncle Chen—'

'Wherever he is, he's not here. And you won't help him by staying.'

No one questioned me as I hurried out. From what I overheard, the soldiers I passed were far more interested in discussing whether a power coup had just taken place. Was Hideki Tagawa ousting Colonel Fujiwara with support from the imperial family? Or had the colonel finally tired of Hideki Tagawa's interfering and ordered him taken away to be shot?

A day ago it would have made little difference to me. Now, as I walked the long track back to the main road, I wondered why he had saved Le Froy's life. In a way he had saved Uncle Chen's too.

What was he planning? Why had Colonel Fujiwara turned on him? Had Hideki Tagawa killed Mirza?

I had no idea where to start. Heicho Han might know something, but where was he now? If I went to Shori headquarters, Emily Bennington-Smith might know something.

But, given her involvement in the fire (most likely), I couldn't trust anything she said.

Something Formosa Boy had said came back to me. And I had an idea of where his 'important dangerous mission' might be taking place.

There was an abandoned soap factory in our district. It hadn't been used for years, but there were tracks leading to it. Young people had sneaked there for clandestine meetings until the Japanese soldiers had declared it off limits.

It was strange that the *lallang*, tall grass tough enough to draw blood, around the old soap factory had been left standing when the surroundings of all the other buildings the Japanese had commandeered had been razed flat.

The Old Soap Factory

———◆———

'Uncle Chen!' I cried. 'Is he hurt?'

'Doesn't matter if he is or not because he will be killed as the ships' saboteur when he's found. Colonel Fat Face almost tracked him down, so he killed the colonel. Nobody is going to help you now. All their attention is on attacking the resistance camps up north. By the time they come back, they will find you and your uncle dead: you will accidentally have set off the remaining explosives that your uncle stole.'

I hadn't seen tyre tracks outside, but I knew I had guessed the right place when I slid open the door and saw Uncle Chen unconscious on the floor, tied hand and foot in front of stacked crates.

I hadn't expected to find Colonel Fujiwara lying there in the same condition – with Heicho Han and Emily Bennington-Smith standing over them.

Heicho Han seemed pleased to see me. Miss Emily looked as sour as usual.

'I thought you were going to frame Hideki Tagawa,' I said.

Heicho Han flashed a boyish smile. He was so handsome, just as the most poisonous bugs are beautiful.

'That would have been the best plan, yes? But getting big-shot Colonel Fat Belly Fujiwara is good enough. You think he's so important? You think that once he calls you Ebisu you're safe? I'm the one who's running everything. I'm the one in control. I always know what they're going to do before they do it.

'Colonel Fat Belly told me to take the gold tribute. Nobody back in Japan would notice, he said. He wanted more and more. Then Tagawa showed up and Fat Belly called me stupid for taking the Buddha and I know he's going to blame it all on me! I'm not letting him bully me any more. I'm not that stupid!'

'You were always smarter than them,' I said. 'But why take my uncle? He has nothing to do with you. If you let him live, he can tell everyone how clever you are. How you got away with everything.'

'Do you think I'm stupid?' Heicho Han bared his teeth but, clearly, the idea that everyone would know how clever he was appealed to him.

'I know you were smarter than Mirza too.'

'Yeah. That snake thought he was so smart, using me, then ganging up with Colonel Fat Belly to sabotage me.'

'Mirza was using you?' I opened my eyes wide. 'I thought you were using him!'

I saw he liked that too. It was my only hope, I thought. To flatter him, to keep him thinking I believed all the stories he told about himself. That I was impressed by him.

And it was easier than I imagined it might be.

'He was ordering me around, calling me stupid, shouting at me with no respect.' He blinked rapidly, remembering. 'He told me to stay away from his daughters.'

'But his daughters liked you.'

'That pig Mirza turned his back on me.' Heicho Han shook, remembering the insult. 'When he needed me, he would bow and respect me. Then when I was not useful, he wouldn't even let me inside his house. He made me stay outside, like a dog.'

I could almost see Mirza, his mind on the decoding and recoding of mimosa leaves, turning his back on Heicho Han after making clear he was unwelcome, although Heicho Han might just have been unexpected, given that Mirza was preparing to meet Colonel Fujiwara.

But if I'd said so Heicho Han wouldn't have listened. He was too caught up in all the wrongs done to him.

'Mirza was going to betray you,' Emily Bennington-Smith said. 'His message said he had important information that one of his daughters had accidentally come across. I knew what that was about, of course. His slut daughters had had their hands all over you and he was going to use that to bring you down. All the colonel needed was an excuse.'

Her jealousy was so strong I could almost smell it through the thick, scented powder that couldn't conceal the ugly rash on her neck. I suddenly knew who had infected both her and Safia.

Emily kicked at the unconscious colonel with a sharp-toed shoe. That might not have been a good idea because he moaned and stirred. 'As though he's so upright himself. No way! The fat toad thinks he's so sexy. I drugged him with his own sleeping powders and gave the order to have Tagawa arrested for stealing the treasure he's been hunting for.' Her laugh was ugly. 'I had to move everything myself and you owe me. The retarded Private Tsai you said would help never came.'

I guessed she was referring to Formosa Boy. 'What did you do to Private Tsai?' Why hadn't I paid more attention to his fears?

'Nothing. He made himself sick eating shit again.'

'I can explain that it was all a mistake,' I said. 'If the missing tribute was on the cargo boat,' I saw from his expression I was right, 'and nobody got to it in time to save it, they should be dragging the seabed, not trying to find out who was on duty that night.'

'Nobody asked you!' Emily Bennington-Smith said. 'Don't think anybody cares what you think. You're a half-breed. The Japanese despise you as much as they despise the Chinese. Don't believe that rat Tagawa when he's pretending to be nice to you. You should hear what he says about you when you aren't around! At least I'm a white woman. Pure white. They respect that!' She watched me with eagerly bulging eyes. She was like a rabid dog trying to decide where to attack next.

Delusional thinking and grandiosity, I thought. Don't show fear or weakness, I told myself. I shrugged as though she was no big deal, which got her more worked up.

'Your mother was a Japanese prostitute. Her family, your family tried to hide it, but now it's out, everybody will know. You can't go around acting high and mighty any more.'

The glee in her voice showed the strain of weeks of being nice to me and months of sucking up to Colonel Fujiwara. Maybe I should have tried to understand and sympathise but, oh, how I loathed the woman.

'You knew Colonel Fujiwara would not go to Mirza himself, but would send for Hideki Tagawa, so there was time for Heicho Han to get there first.' I turned to him. 'What I don't understand is why you didn't kill Tagawa too.'

Heicho Han giggled. 'Did you know that Rat Face Tagawa came to Mirza's garden while I was making sure Mirza was dead? When the door started opening, I hid in the bushes and watched him. If he'd seen me I would have shot him. He stood and stared at Mirza lying there. I thought he was going to puke. But he bowed to the body! Like he was inside a temple! What a fool! When he was gone I laughed and laughed.'

'But you were working with Colonel Fujiwara and Mr Mirza for some time? What went wrong?'

'I got fed up with them. They were a pair of thieves, both of them. So high and mighty and righteous. And all the time they were stealing. Hideki Tagawa is the one who came and stirred up trouble looking for the gold they had taken. Where do you think it came from in the first place? Hideki Tagawa is stealing it from people. Your people, my people, stealing from everybody. He says it is to build the new Japanese Empire. Stealing from all of us to make Japan great again, a world power. Colonel Fat Belly got scared because he used Mirza to turn what he stole into money.'

The pieces were starting to fall into place for me.

'They were so afraid of people finding out. It was all a big secret. They let it be known that they hated each other. But every time we wanted to shake down Mirza, the colonel said, no, leave him alone. Leave his daughters alone. Don't touch his house. Make sure that nobody else disturbs them. Of course people were starting to guess that something was going on. But I was the only one who knew.'

'Did Colonel Fujiwara suspect you? Why didn't you kill him instead of Mirza? Why drag him into this now?'

'I'm not afraid of Fujiwara. He has no reason to suspect me. He is a fool. He has no idea what I am. I eat his best food. I drink his best wine. I know all his plans. I don't know why this stupid woman dragged him out here!'

'Who are you calling stupid, you yellow scum? I saw how nervous he was. I knew he was planning to serve you up to Tagawa on a plate! If it's your word against his, who would believe you? Especially with all this here!' Emily Bennington-Smith gestured at the crates around us. 'I had to take care of the men you used to move the stuff. You never even thought about them, did you? Those idiots would have blabbed it all over the island if I hadn't put them down.'

The two dead soldiers, I thought. Formosa Boy said they had moved cargo into the service vehicle. He had stayed behind to fight the fires while the others drove away. They had not trusted him, he thought, even though he was the strongest for lifting things. And those boxes had been heavy.

Formosa Boy's greed and lack of curiosity might have saved his life.

'Stay where you are. Don't move.'

He was breathing hard, and I realised it was not just the excitement of the kill.

'Take off your clothes,' he said to me. 'You're not worth looking at, but I will do you a favour. You will not die without knowing a man.'

'Leave her alone!' shrieked Emily Bennington-Smith. 'Have you no decency at all?'

She was not protecting me. She was jealous. And offended. Women were as stupid as men, I thought. Possibly even more so.

She dashed forward, her fingernails red claws reaching for his arm. Where had she managed to find nail varnish, I wondered, as he fended her off almost casually with his pistol arm. She clawed at his face, leaving two streaks of red – blood, not polish – welling on Heicho Han's perfect complexion.

And I saw one splotch of red and then another bloom on the front of Emily Bennington-Smith's shirt when Heicho Han shot her.

He looked as shocked as she did. But when she fell he threw back his head and laughed.

'Now you!'

I didn't wait to see whether he would raise his gun or drop his trousers. When he turned to me I braced myself against the wall and, with my weaker leg, aimed a kick at the man's greatest treasure. He went down, making a sound that started as a screech and ended as a moan. I saw Uncle Chen stir, and prayed he would stay down and quiet until I could untie him. And I threw myself on Heicho Han, pushing his gun aside. I had to disarm him and keep him away from Uncle Chen.

If Dr Shankar's warning hadn't already primed me, this would ruin any girl's dream of romance.

He fought, his fingers grabbing at me, still weak but recovering. I jabbed with my bony elbows, looking for the pressure points in his neck, but he was moving too much, swearing and kicking wildly.

I had wasted my time reading Jane Austen and taking first-aid classes. Why hadn't the missionary ladies taught us how to paralyse a man? In self-defence, of course.

But I had other resources. I bit deep into flesh and muscle and he howled. I knew he must have more than his gun on him, and as I was digging the fingers of one hand into his eyes, I was searching the folds of his uniform for a weapon.

But I had lost the element of surprise and he was stronger than I was.

'Hello?'

I froze at the sound of the voice and Heicho Han managed to heave me off him.

Saved by the Devil

◆

'Boss?' It was Formosa Boy. 'Sorry, Boss. I had stomach-ache. I had to stop to empty myself.'

He stared stupidly at the gun, now back in Heicho Han's hand, then at Emily Bennington-Smith, bloody on the ground, and the two men bound hand and foot. Finally his eyes came to me. 'You shouldn't be here,' Formosa Boy muttered, in rapid Hokkien. 'Your grandmother is worried. She asked me to find you.'

His words were drowned out by Col Fujiwara waking and swearing groggily.

'About time you got here, fool!' Heicho Han didn't look at him. 'Where are the others? I'll have you all beaten. The truck is behind the kitchen. Start loading these crates. These men should be waking up soon. One by one, loosen their feet so they can walk, but don't untie their hands. Take them down to the river and shoot them. Then drag the woman down and put her in the river too. What are you waiting for, idiot?'

'Boss?' Formosa Boy half turned and I saw Hideki Tagawa in the doorway behind him.

Heicho Han turned his gun on Formosa Boy. 'You traitor!'

'Don't blame the boy. I was following Miss Chen. And when I saw Private Tsai outside I knew I was in the right place.'

I didn't know if things had just got better or worse for me, but I knew I was mad. 'Why are you following me?'

'You are your mother's daughter,' Hideki Tagawa said. 'Your mother also rebelled. All her life, to the end of her life, she was a rebel.'

'This is even better,' Heicho Han said. He held his gun to the side of Colonel Fujiwara's head. 'Drop your gun or be responsible for the death of your commanding officer.'

'Have you gone mad?' Colonel Fujiwara coughed as he strained at his bonds. 'I will have you shot!'

'Too late, old man!' Heicho Han ground the gun into his temple. He was enjoying this. 'Nobody is listening to you any more. This is the end of you.'

He had forgotten me. Or he had never thought me a threat, even while I was fighting him. Well, I hadn't stopped fighting yet. I threw myself across Colonel Fujiwara, grabbing Heicho Han's weapon arm as my weight knocked him sideways.

Formosa Boy ran forward to help me pin him down.

'When the prison guards told me you took Chen out of prison on my orders,' Hideki Tagawa said, 'I had a watch team put on your men, who have been detained.'

Heicho Han snarled. But Hideki Tagawa had not come unarmed. He held his bolt-action service rifle on Heicho Han while I untied Colonel Fujiwara and Uncle Chen.

Colonel Fujiwara sat down shakily on a wooden stool. A little behind him, Hideki Tagawa stood with his arms folded. I knew the colonel wouldn't have turned his back on a man he did not trust.

I was allowed to stay by Uncle Chen, sitting with our backs to the wall. Our hands gripped tightly, we whispered low while keeping our eyes on the Japanese men.

'Little Ling? Ma?'

'Safe. Shen Shen also. You?'

'I'm all right. Thank you.'

'You were at the port on the night of the attack,' Colonel Fujiwara said. 'You saw your chance after the sabotage of the warships. You looted and sabotaged the small cargo ship carrying the Golden Lily tribute. You were the only one who knew it was there!'

'Sir, I only knew it was there because I put it there following your instructions,' Heicho Han sneered. He still seemed to think he had Colonel Fujiwara in his power. 'Sir, after we saw the explosions, we wanted to keep your cargo in a safe place. That is all. I was protecting it. On your orders, sir.'

'Did you drug and restrain Colonel Fujiwara on his orders too?' Hideki Tagawa wondered.

'That was the *gaijin* woman's doing.' He jerked his head at Miss Emily's body. 'When I learned what she had done, I incapacitated her.'

'And removing my prisoner Chen with forged authorisation?'

'Did your slut tell you that? Lies! You see? More lies! The Chen girl tricked me. I learned her uncle was going to try to escape from the prison tonight and I came to stop him.'

The sneer was still on his face, but he looked a little less confident. 'She is trying to fool you, like she fooled me. Who are you going to believe? Loyal men wearing the uniform of your emperor or some cheap slut?'

Heicho Han knew he was speaking for his life and he gave it his all. I've recorded the points of his speech as I remember them, but it's not verbatim. His Japanese was as awkward as his English. Such things shouldn't make a difference but, unfortunately, they do.

'She killed my men too. She poisoned them after seducing them into giving her information. She knew they would back up my side of the story.'

That was when he went too far. If Heicho Han had stuck to killing locals, he might have got away with it. But this time two of the dead men had been Japanese soldiers. Plus he had threatened a colonel. Double plus, he had been caught with the missing Golden Lily treasure – I assumed that was what was in the crates.

'All this,' Hideki Tagawa gestured at the crates, 'was to be transported to Japan, intended to serve the war effort.'

'That was not my doing. I was following Colonel Fuji's instructions. He is the one stealing from the Japanese war effort. I am only a small man following orders.'

He used the same diminutive for Colonel Fujiwara as Emily Bennington-Smith had. I should have noticed that sooner. Her ignorance as a Westerner and her relationship with the colonel allowed her certain liberties. But coming from Heicho Han, 'Colonel Fuji' sounded, even to my ears, like insubordination.

At least it was better than 'Colonel Fat Belly'.

Hideki Tagawa continued serenely, 'Then when the port was attacked, you saw your chance and bombed the cargo ship, although the loot was not yet on board. You and three of your men transported the treasures to this old soap factory. The men were told it was top secret and they had to keep it safe.'

'Heicho Han told me and my friends we were going to catch fish,' Formosa Boy said.

Usually 'catch fish' meant a little unofficial breaking and entering.

'Two of the men came back and asked you about that operation, didn't they? Even after you transferred them to other divisions. Is that why they ended up dead? When the announcement was made,' Hideki Tagawa went on, 'offering money to anyone who could provide information on what happened that night, they wanted you to pay them more money for their silence, didn't they? You came back here and discovered the boxes had been tampered with. That was when you decided to kill them.'

'I transferred them out because they were careless and unreliable. Useless as soldiers. I wouldn't know what happened to them after.'

'Only Private Tsai Chih-Wei remained in your division.'

Our Formosa Boy.

'No doubt you thought you had covered your tracks well enough. Private Tsai, did you ever look in the crates Heicho Han made you store here?'

'I thought there might be tinned food inside,' Formosa Boy said. 'You know, like American tinned milk or meat. Maybe even chocolate. But there's nothing like that. Only blocks of stuff. Heavy blocks wrapped in sackcloth. And a Buddha statue. I didn't want the Buddha statue to see me stealing so I closed it back up.'

The heavy blocks were gold ingots. The gold Buddha statue,

not yet melted down to make more of the same, must have been picked up later.

'This is treason,' Colonel Fujiwara said. He made a gesture and the men who had arrived on Hideki Tagawa's summons moved swiftly towards Heicho Han.

'Hideki Tagawa is behind it all! This is all his idea!' Heicho Han shouted. 'He planned to use the attack on the resistance camp as a distraction to cover Le Froy's escape. He is obsessed with helping Le Froy escape. To block him, we took out another prisoner and brought him here as arranged. How else would you all know to come here to set a trap? Hideki Tagawa tricked you just like he tricked us.'

'Hideki Tagawa did not tell us you were coming here,' Colonel Fujiwara said. 'Emily Bennington-Smith told us.' He didn't look at her body. Neither did Heicho Han.

Heicho Han stood frozen, his mouth open, for at least five seconds. It wasn't from shock. You could almost see the wheels turning inside his head as he worked this new piece of information into his story. 'That woman was a liar.'

Despite all he had been through, I saw Colonel Fujiwara wince more than once at Heicho Han's pronunciation. Much as he had winced at Emily Bennington-Smith's mistakes.

'Miss Emily had been betraying you for months!' Heicho Han shouted. 'Out of concern for your feelings and reputation, no one said anything. She was passing your private and official information to Hideki Tagawa and other officials planning to rise against you. Hideki Tagawa seduced the woman and made her betray you. He instructed her to blame everything on me because he knew I was loyal to you. Can you believe the word of a dirty English whore over the testimony of a loyal soldier of the Empire?'

'This is treason. Such disloyalty must be punished,' Colonel Fujiwara said.

'You killed his whole family back in Korea,' I heard myself say. Part of me – the part to which Ah Ma, Le Froy and others had tried to teach survival skills – was screaming, 'Shut up! Shut up! Shut up!' inside my head, but my mouth kept talking. I had grown up without parents, but I could imagine how it must feel for a child to watch his parents killed.

'He had to watch his parents being shot. He is guilty of sabotage and theft, but you cannot accuse him of disloyalty after what you did to his family.'

'His family is doing fine back in Korea,' Hideki Tagawa said. 'Han Byung-Woo, his father, works as a mechanic with the agricultural department, as he has done for years. His mother cooks in the officers' club. Han Jin Woo signed up for the army to get away from woman troubles. He made one woman pregnant, and when she wanted him to marry her, it was discovered that he was seeing three women at the same time. Far from being victimised, he tried to get his brother arrested so that he himself could take over their father's business …'

I had been right about Heicho Han having another gun. He pulled a hand pistol out of his pocket and shot Colonel Fujiwara.

And I saved the man's life.

The old first-aid lessons weren't totally useless after all. Evaluate their airways and make sure he is breathing. Then: 'Cover the wound with cloth [Formosa Boy's shirt], press down hard with both hands, and keep pressing.'

We kept him alive till medical help came.

'Are you all right?' Hideki Tagawa asked me, after Heicho Han was taken away. They took Uncle Chen back as well, but I was too worn out to protest. I was even grateful when Hideki Tagawa drove me home.

'I thought you were going up north.'

'It might have been a set-up or someone sent word up north and warned them. We got reports that the resistance camp was abandoned and rigged with explosives. The attack was called off.'

Later I learned Heicho Han had been blamed for warning the rebels up north too. This didn't make any sense, given Heicho Han had been counting on the attack as a distraction.

But sometimes you need a convenient scapegoat.

Final Image

———◆———

The next morning two unfamiliar, fully armed kempeitai appeared at Chen Mansion to collect me and bring me in to Shori headquarters where I was handed a note, signed with Colonel Fujiwara's official seal:

'Your good service is acknowledged. You will be rewarded.'

He made no reference to his injury or what I had done. I might have returned a wallet he'd dropped on the street. So I thought the reward would be something like an extra ration of powdery rice.

But two days later Uncle Chen came home. He was horribly thin, his nose was crooked and he walked with a limp, but he was alive. Shen Shen screamed when she saw him outside flanked by two men in uniform. She ran round the side of the house so recklessly that her wooden clogs went flying in different directions, but she raced on barefoot over the gravel chips till she threw her arms around him, still shrieking.

Startled, Little Ling began to cry. I pressed her to me, turning her face away. Had the kempeitai brought Uncle Chen home to make him watch them rape and murder his wife and daughter?

But they didn't stop Shen Shen, and I saw Uncle Chen wasn't tied up.

'Miss Chen?' One of the uniformed men handed me a note. 'From Colonel Fujiwara.'

The colonel wrote that he was sending what was due to me. The word he used was hōshū, meaning reward.

I had done what I'd set out to do.

Uncle Chen told me Hideki Tagawa had said he would pick me up at nine the next morning.

When the time came I was ready.

'Thank you. I really mean it,' I said to him.

'Heicho Han won the hearts of many women. Emily Bennington-Smith and Safia Mirza were only two of many. He flirted with you too, didn't he? Why didn't it work?'

'He tried. But I know I'm not beautiful so I wasn't taken in. Where are we going?'

'You were immune because your attention is already focused. You have tasted the real thing. And that protects you from being seduced by the false.'

Was he talking about himself? I hoped not.

'You are part of an old samurai family. Even if the blood means nothing to you, you are in line to inherit some of your grandmother's jewellery.'

'That's nice. Is that where we're going now? To look at jewellery?'

'No.'

At the prison Hideki Tagawa told the guard to unlock the door and leave. 'I will be back for you in thirty minutes.'

'You're not staying?' I said stupidly, as though he was dropping me off at a tea party.

'I doubt he will talk to you in my presence.'

He?

A man sat on one of the two chairs in the tiny room. I could smell him – the stink of bad health and stale sweat – before my eyes got used to the dim light. One of his legs ended in a bandaged stump.

'Why did you bring her here?' The voice was angry but his eyes darted all over me, rapidly grabbing details to be processed later. I knew, because I was doing the same. He was much thinner and his hair had gone grey, but his eyes were still bright. 'Get out! Go away!'

I barely registered the door closing behind me.

'I'm glad you're alive,' I said. I sat down on the other chair.

'I don't trust that bastard.'

'Didn't he save your life?'

'Why do you think I don't trust him?'

I laughed.

'It's good to see you, Su Lin. Why did he bring you here?'

'Maybe as a kind of reward.'

'What for?'

'I kind of saved Colonel Fujiwara's life.'

'Why?' It was his turn to laugh.

'It seemed like the right thing to do at the time.'

'Then it probably was. Jumping out of rough water does not save the fish.'

'Nothing can save the fish that is already in the bucket waiting to be killed.'

'We're not in the bucket yet,' Le Froy said. 'I don't trust Hideki Tagawa, but we have something in common.'

'You're smart and you think the same way,' I agreed. 'And you're both impatient too.'

'I was referring to our concern for you. There are bonds other than nationalities. We choose what we want to see as our bonds with others.'

Suddenly it no longer mattered whether or not he had suspected me of being a Japanese spy.

'You shut me out.' I hated that my voice was trembling but once I started I couldn't stop. 'Nobody would tell me anything. I wasn't even sure you were alive until I heard your foot got cut off – and nobody would tell me about that. You told them to shut me out, didn't you?'

'Hideki Tagawa hinted they were watching for connections between us. So, yes, I tried to make sure there were none.'

'He *hinted*? Are you sure it wasn't a threat?'

'It was a warning.'

'You, him, my grandmother, why does everybody keep things from me – things *about* me – supposedly for my own good? Why not just tell me I was being watched?'

I stopped because he was smiling at me. Laughing, in fact.

'One day you'll look back and realise how lucky you were. When all the information starts pouring in.'

'We'll have to survive this before we can look back.'

'We'll survive.'

We got a whole metal tin of milk powder, marked 'National Dried Full Cream Milk', the equivalent of seven pints, for Little Ling.

The other metal tin, marked 'Joyful Biscuits', contained two pressed gold bars.

We had survived for now. But the war was still on.

Cracking the Code

	1	2	3	4	5
1	A	B	C	D	E
2	F	G	H	I	J
3	K	L	M	N	O
4	P	Q	R	S	T
5	U	V	W	X	Y

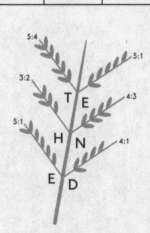

Acknowledgements

———◆———

Thanks go, first and always, to my agent Priya Doraswamy of Lotus Lane Literary, without whom all my books would exist only in my head. Massive thanks go also to the wonderful people at Little, Brown/Constable Crime, especially Editorial Director Krystyna Green, Editorial Manager Amanda Keats, Eleanor Russell, Sarah Murphy, Hannah Wann and John Fairweather. Grateful thanks too, to designer Andy Bridge and copy-editor Hazel Orme who makes me look like a better writer than I am. Many thanks, too, to Simon McArt and Beth Wright, for getting copies of *The Mimosa Tree Mystery* onto bookshelves.

And thank you for reading this book!

Please visit my Facebook page if you'd like to share any comments or feedback.

Book Club Questions

———◆———

What is *The Mimosa Tree Mystery* about? Part murder mystery, partly a look at official racism, family love and jealousies in Occupied Singapore, an equatorial island then covered with lush unspoiled rainforest. But most of all it looks at how life is best lived with a touch of humour, one day at a time.

1. *The Mimosa Tree Mystery* shows the harshness of life under Japanese Occupation. But the Japanese claimed they came to liberate Singapore from 'Western Oppression' (i.e. the British Empire). How much difference do you think being ruled by Asian foreigners vs Western foreigners made to locals?

2. Su Lin learned to speak English from the British Mission workers and to speak Japanese from the Japanese hairdresser she was apprenticed to. Do you think her language skills give her the advantage? Or (like some of her relatives) do you think speaking a foreign language brainwashes you into seeing things a foreign way?

3. Would you feel different about Mirza's death if he had been trying to betray his daughter rather than save her? Does betraying a family member seem worse to you than betraying your country?

4. Su Lin gets involved in the murder investigation when a hooded informer randomly picks her uncle as one of the killers. What do you think of the claim that it's better for the Japanese to kill one person (even if not the guilty party) than go on torturing and killing dozens more in an attempt to find the culprit?

5. Heicho Han and Hideki Tagawa are both part of the Occupying Japanese force. Yet they are both outsiders. Heicho Han has aspirations to rise high and Hideki Tagawa is from an old samurai family fallen on hard times. Do you think ending up in Singapore is good or bad for them?

6. How would you feel if, like Su Lin, you discovered your parents weren't who you always believed – if you carried the blood and DNA of your enemies and present oppressors in your body? If you were her (and didn't know how the war was going to end!) would you exploit your noble Japanese lineage?

7. Why do you think Col Fujiwara allows Hideki Tagawa to take Su Lin under his protection?

8. Operation Jaywick (an actual incident) didn't do lasting damage to the Japanese naval force and resulted in the 'Double Tenth

Massacre' of locals. Yet local morale soared once it got out that the Australians were behind the harbour bombings. Do you think the boost to morale was worth the torture and lives lost?

9. After years of spying on Chief Inspector Le Froy, Hideki Tagawa has come to respect his abilities. In different circumstances, could the two men have been friends?

10. If you were Su Lin, would you have stepped up to try to save your uncle's life, or stayed safe and unnoticed? Does this also apply in how you approach challenges in your daily life?